ASSUMED

BY
MHR GEER

ISBN: 979-8-9871159-2-3

For Sam

Chapter 1

A constant stream of jubilant holiday-goers jostled my suitcase as I paced the arrivals gate, but Sandy's mobile went to voice mail a fourth time. I hung up without leaving another message and strolled past the baggage carousel. Again.

"Where are you, Sandy?" I muttered under my breath.

A man in a white Panama hat vacated a bench, and I collapsed onto the cold metal and hugged the handle of my suitcase. The other passengers exchanged greetings and gathered their baggage, and the automatic door slid open with a swoosh to receive them. Every time the door opened, humid air blasted my face.

The man in the white hat reappeared but saw me and turned away, presumably to find a bench without a slouching, scowling American. I raised my shoulders from a slump and crossed my legs.

"What now, Anne?" I asked myself, tapping the screen of my phone and resisting the urge to check the time.

A young boy, about five years old, wandered over and climbed onto the bench next to me. We exchanged nervous smiles. Couples and families regrouped near the door, and I watched their faces, expecting someone to claim the boy, but the door opened and closed, over and over, and he remained.

I was just about to ask where the boy's parents were when a tall woman entered and rushed toward us, shouting in French. Her profile was dark against the bright sunlight outside, and her long hair swirled in the vortex of the doorway. The boy pressed against me, and I almost wrapped my arm around him, but the door closed, and she smoothed her hair back into place.

She pulled the boy from the bench, gripping his arms with long, slender fingers. I couldn't understand her words, but her reprimand was clear. Her green eyes flashed with fear and anger. She blamed me for his disappearance. I shrugged, trying to remember how to apologize in French. *Je suis desole?* But I was unsure of the words, so I didn't say anything, and she didn't wait for my explanation.

He left with her, his little hand firmly inside hers, and when the door opened and whipped her hair back into the air, the boy turned back to me with a smile. I waved.

And then I was alone again.

I jumped when my phone buzzed.

Sorry, Sandy texted. *Can't make it. Take a taxi to 16 Rue de l'Aile Perdue.*

I stared at the text and considered purchasing a ticket for a return flight, but my phone buzzed again with a second text.

Please, Anne.

I squared my shoulders and pulled on my sunglasses. Then I walked through the whoosh of the doorway and into the sunlight.

The taxi line had already thinned; it took only a few minutes before a lively man ushered me into the back of a bright green sedan. The driver offered a brusque "Welcome to Saint Martin," and turned up her radio. Taxi code for no talking. Fine with me.

We sped through narrow streets, dangerously close to sunburned tourists wandering street markets. Stalls spilled out from under a rainbow of awnings, hawking loud shirts and oversized beach towels. The air was thick with cardamom and curry, mixed with the yeasty smell of a patisserie. My stomach rumbled. In my rush to make the early morning flight, I'd skipped breakfast.

We left town and traveled up and down winding roads that cut into the hillsides. The villas grew larger and farther apart and then disappeared into thick foliage behind security gates. I caught occasional glimpses of dirt lanes and even fewer paved driveways. When the driver pulled off the road, I leaned out the window to watch the tops of towering palm trees lining a long gravel driveway. We stopped on a cobbled motor court in front of a massive house.

I stared up at the imposing facade from within the safety of the taxi before I bravely stepped into the blazing sun. I thought there must be some mistake, but before I could say anything, the taxi drove away. Why had Sandy sent me to a dismal mansion and not to one of the dazzling resorts I'd passed?

Beyond the house, the sea stretched to the horizon. Sunlight reflected off the water, awakening childhood fantasies of pirate ships and mermaid tails. But the hot sun quickly melted the daydream, and I retreated into the shadow of the mansion.

Up close, the house was shabby and weather-beaten. Peeling gray paint revealed a history of more colorful choices. The porch railing leaned at a precarious angle, and as I cautiously climbed the rotting steps, the wood complained but held, and I reached the front door and knocked. The sound echoed within the house, but only silence followed. I knocked again, louder, and waited. Nothing.

"Now what?" I asked the house.

The house ignored me, but a piece of paper stuck between two floorboards fluttered in the ocean breeze. I stepped over and picked it up. She'd left a note—an inconsiderate welcome, even for Sandy. I exhaled loudly and unfolded the scrap of paper.

Go around the side. Guest house at the back. Key is under the mat.

"Guest house?"

I pulled my phone out of my pocket to check for texts from Sandy and noticed her text.

Please, Anne.

"I hope the guest house is nicer than this place," I mumbled. "No offense."

I backed away and suffered temporary blindness as I fumbled to pull my sunglasses from their perch atop my head. My free hand provided enough shade to find a gravel path that curved out of sight around the house. My suitcase wheels were useless on the gravel, and I left a wide scar in my wake. I hefted the bag, huffing, sweating, and cursing Sandy, but when I reached the back patio, I dropped my suitcase and stared.

Laid out before me was a two-page spread from Travel & Leisure magazine—azure pool, white umbrellas, and red-roofed porticoes. And the backdrop was a glittering sea.

I glanced around, half expecting a waiter to take my cocktail order, but no one appeared, so I plucked the gravel from my suitcase wheels and dragged it past the pool and along a lower terrace of empty chaise lounge chairs. Something about the placement of the chairs in a deliberate arc caught my attention, and I stared until I figured it out. The shadows. Seven chairs, set apart from each other, and every other chair was in full recline. As the sun moved across the sky, someone could achieve perfect sun exposure by changing chairs at regular intervals. A vain person lived in the mansion.

I watched the house over my shoulder, but it remained silent and reproachful. A wide staircase split in half from an upper floor and curved down both sides of a cavernous, covered patio, like a yawning giant with huge, pale arms.

I suppressed a shiver and resumed my search.

Beyond the terraces, the cobblestone path meandered through a manicured lawn, and the guest house appeared brilliant white from behind the trees. The key lay under the mat, just as Sandy's note had promised, and I let myself in.

"Hello?" I hollered, but when nobody answered, I discarded my bag in the entryway and walked through to a sliding glass door overlooking a smaller patio with another pool, this one small, kidney-shaped and shallow—a lighter shade of aquamarine than its mother pool. I couldn't see neighbors, and if there were any, they couldn't see me. Not that it mattered. I wasn't exactly the sun-bathing-in-my-birthday-suit-type.

The sliding glass door opened with an easy whoosh, and I stepped onto the patio, sank into a lounge chair under the shade, and wiped the sweat from my forehead with the back of my hand.

Only twenty-one hours had passed since Sandy had summoned me.

"Anne, I'm in trouble," she'd said over the phone. "Can you come to Saint Martin? Tomorrow?"

I'd declined. "I can't leave work, Sandy."

But twelve minutes after we'd ended the call, my boss, Mr. Sampson, had called me into his office and accused me of wire fraud—not *exactly*, he'd merely asked a few mildly probing questions, but I'd overreacted and requested immediate vacation time. After thirteen years at the company without incident, I'd begun to notice things— quiet rumors, closed-door meetings—and Sandy's invitation had provided a convenient excuse to distance myself from whatever was coming. I'd jumped on the first flight out of Miami.

Under the shade, the ocean breeze cooled my irritation. I stretched back in the lounge chair and kicked off my shoes. There were worse places to be invited on a vague rescue mission. On the far side of the pool, a vine-wrapped arbor towered on four narrow columns that framed a panoramic view of the sea. Tangerine trumpet blossoms hung overhead, their perfume mild in the midday sun, and the soft lapping of waves sounded from somewhere below a stone wall.

I'd only known Sandy for fourteen months, but when I met her, buying honey at my local farmer's market, she'd filled a void. Of course, there were other people in my life. Co-workers, the regulars at the community pool, and people I knew from high school, but Sandy was the only person who barged into my house at odd hours with a bottle of anything. She wore me down, deaf to my protestations and declined invitations, and forced herself into my life. I never asked her why. Perhaps my quiet, solitary life balanced her gregarious noise, but I'd gotten used to her. She was my best friend—my only friend, really, and she'd asked for help, so I was here.

But she hadn't explained what she needed.

My stomach growled again, and I rose to explore the house. I found three bedrooms and three bathrooms with soft, bleached-white linens. I threw open the windows to let in the breeze and parked my bag in the bedroom with the second-best view before I went to the kitchen.

The fridge was empty. I willed it to produce something, an egg or a shiny green apple, but the cold bulb flickered, and nothing appeared. I pulled my phone from my pocket and texted Sandy.

I'm at the guest house, but I'm hungry. When will you be here?

I wanted to add more questions like *Why am I here,* but food was the priority.

While I waited for her response, I walked back to the patio and leaned over the stone wall. Steps descended to a narrow strip of rocky beach. I followed them, but halfway down, my phone buzzed.

Sorry. Got hung up running errands. There's a market only a few miles down the road. Use your phone, map it. There's a bike on the side of the house.

Ugh. Biking. I changed into shorts, pulled my hair into a ponytail, and emptied my backpack onto the bed, but I hesitated in the doorway.

When will you be back? I texted.

Her answer arrived immediately this time: *Not for a while. Eat without me.*

My stomach grumbled again, and I sighed and went to find the bike.

Two bikes leaned against the side of the house. I chose a baby blue beach cruiser and tested it on the grassy area in front of the house. It worked well enough, so I walked it up the terraced patio and ignored the judgmental glare of the gray house as I climbed onto the seat.

#

I mapped a route, choosing the shortest path. The road rose and fell gradually at first, and my legs acclimated to pedaling. When I hit the first steep, uphill climb, I was overconfident—there were no gears. I sped up on the downhill part and pedaled furiously, but the hill was too steep. The bike slowed to a painful crawl. I slid off and walked. My calves burned from the effort, but I pushed on, wheezing, one foot in front of the next, leaning on the handlebars for support. Sweat ran in rivers down my back.

My reward for reaching the peak was the view. A wide valley stretched below. Sections of the road appeared intermittently between the trees, and it seemed a mostly downhill ride from where I stood. Red-roofed villas dotted the hillside, and a long line of resorts filled the coastline of a large bay where several boats were moored, the silver masts a sharp contrast against the cobalt sea.

I climbed back on the bike and coasted. The wind dried the sweat from my hair and cooled my back. Around a corner, the grade again grew too steep, and I braked hard, hoping I could slow the bike enough to hop off, but the brakes squeaked loudly, refusing to cooperate, and the bike continued to gain speed.

When I reached a straight, downhill stretch of road, I knew I was in real trouble. There was nowhere to ditch the bike. One side of the road was a rock wall; the other side plunged over a cliff.

I gripped the handles, holding the bike on a straight course, but the road was poorly maintained, and I had to swerve to miss a pothole. The wide tires afforded some stability, and for a fleeting moment, I thought I'd be okay.

But then I hit a minefield of gravel.

The tires lost traction, and I screamed as I lost control. The front tire hit something, and then I was in the air, weightless for a long moment before I landed on the road and skidded to a stop.

My head throbbed. I lay on my back in the middle of the narrow road. I raised my arms, one at a time, testing them. My right shoulder screamed with searing pain. I struggled to raise my head and realized I was laying backward on the incline. My left arm seemed undamaged; I used it to push up until I sat at an awkward forty-five-degree angle to see my legs. My toes wiggled; my legs were bleeding, but they worked. No broken bones.

I shifted my legs to the right, trying to rotate and use the incline to stand up, but I heard the rumbling of a car engine and pushed hard with my left arm, managing only to shift my legs a few inches to the right. I couldn't move fast enough; I was a turtle on its back. Brakes screeched, and I pulled my head into my shoulders and squeezed my eyes shut, preparing for impact.

Chapter 2

I opened my eyes to the grill of a pickup truck that had stopped inches from my face. A door creaked open, and a man shouted, "Are you insane? Why are you sitting in the middle of the road?" Footsteps crunched the gravel as he approached.

"You're bleeding," he said. "You can't stay here. We need to get off this road before someone hits the back of my truck and sends both of us over the cliff."

He lifted me easily. A wide-brimmed hat cast a shadow across his face, and I wrinkled my nose at the smell of diesel mixed with coconut oil and sawdust. He carried me around to the passenger side of the truck, pinned my body against the side to open the door, and set me gently on the bench seat.

"Stay there. I'll get your bike," he said.

About fifty feet ahead, the bike lay across the road. He jogged to it, carried it back, and I heard it drop into the truck bed. Then he was in the driver's seat, and we were traveling downhill.

"Wait," I croaked. Something was wrong with my voice. I cleared my throat and tried again. "Wait," a little louder this time.

"Oh, yeah. You lost your shoe. I picked it up." He tossed one of my flip-flops onto the seat next to me.

"I don't know you."

He laughed, and I blinked as the sound jarred my throbbing head. "Look, lady. I'm not leaving you bleeding on the side of the road. Where were you headed?"

"The market," I answered.

He reached into a small cooler between us and pulled out a bottle of water. "Here, drink this. It'll help your throat. I'll drop you at the market."

I nodded and cringed—the movement made me dizzy. I struggled to twist the cap from the bottle of water, and he snatched it back and opened it.

"Why did you try to ride down that hill? You're not even wearing a helmet. There's a trail that follows the beach. It's longer, but there aren't any big hills. Are you new here?"

"I just got here," I said. I accepted the opened bottle and sipped the cold water. "Thanks."

"Well, next time you need to go to the market, just take a taxi, okay? You're lucky I didn't run over you."

"Thanks for not running me over," I said.

He grinned. "Is there someone you want to call? Tell someone you had an accident?"

"No, I'm here alone," I admitted. And immediately regretted it. Why was I telling a strange man I was traveling alone? And I wasn't really alone. Sandy was here. Somewhere.

"When we get down the hill, I'll clean that arm and have a better look at it. Make sure you don't need a hospital." He gave me another sideways glance and then added, "I have a first aid kit in the back."

My shoulder hurt, but it felt like road rash—not something that required an E.R. visit. "Just drop me at the market. I'm sorry to bother you, and I appreciate the ride, but I really just want to shop and head back."

He took his hands off the wheel and held them up defensively. "Sorry, lady. Just trying to help."

He stayed quiet until he pulled the truck into a parking spot and pointed out a storefront. "That's the market. Go shop. I'll look at your bike. See how much damage was done."

"I'm fine," I said and opened the door and hopped down to the pavement, but my right ankle buckled, and I collapsed. My arms wobbled, and I bit my lip against the trembling.

"Yeah, you seem fine," he called out from inside the truck. Then I heard a loud sigh, and his door opened and slammed shut. "You're still bleeding. You can't walk into a store like that." He lifted me again, but this time he carried me to the back of the truck and set me on the tailgate. "Will you let me look at it?"

I nodded, and he dragged a large plastic box across the truck bed. It looked like a fishing tackle box, but he flipped it open to reveal an impressive array of first aid supplies. He handed me the water bottle again.

"You're in shock, lady. Drink this."

I wanted to argue, to push him away, but I couldn't. Any strength I had left was used up fighting back angry tears. I wasn't angry at him. I was angry at Sandy for not being there when I got off the plane, and I was mad at the bike for crashing.

"Stop calling me lady! And I'm not in shock," I shouted. "I can take care of myself."

He gave me a surprised look, and I wouldn't have blamed him for pushing me off his tailgate and driving away, but instead, his voice was calm and kind. "Look, I'm just trying to help. You're hurt and maybe a little scared, yeah?"

He took off his hat, tossing it into the truck bed, and I saw his face for the first time. He was younger than I'd thought. Maybe thirty, around my age. His hair was dirty-blonde and probably curly, but it was plastered against his head in wet strands. He ran a dirty hand through it, shaking it loose. It hung almost to his eyes, and he kept pushing it back—something he did often based on the dirty smudges across his forehead.

He looked like so many guys I knew from home— guys who worked in construction so they could align their work schedules with the surf report. He wore the uniform: work pants, boots, sweat-stained tank top. I'd seen a shirt on the front seat; it probably had his name embroidered on the left pocket.

He grinned. He had nice teeth, straight and bright white against his bronzed skin. "You need to clean up that arm before you go into the market, right?"

His kind words softened my anger. He had a point.

"Yeah, okay," I agreed.

He pulled on latex gloves and gingerly lifted my arm, holding it to the side, over the pavement. He doused it with a water bottle, and the cold water stung. I grimaced but didn't complain, and one side of his mouth turned up in a subtle smirk.

"It's deep, but it's so mangled, I'm not sure what they would stitch. It's going to scar."

I shrugged and winced.

He used alcohol wipes to clean the scratches. I couldn't see the damage. It extended from just above my elbow and wrapped around my shoulder blade. As he worked, I squeezed my thigh with my left hand to avoid crying out.

"This will need a good cleaning when you get home. You've still got some road in that scrape. You'll need to get that out: so it doesn't get infected. But I think you're okay. No need for the hospital. Nothing's broken. But I'm happy to take you if you want."

I shook my head.

"Figured you'd say that. I'll wrap it up to control the bleeding while you shop." He taped a large white pad across my shoulder and wrapped my upper arm in gauze, securing it with more tape. Then he cleaned the scratches on my legs. They were superficial. "You're lucky. Just some wicked bruises. I'd pick up painkillers if I were you. When the shock wears off, you're going to hurt in places you never knew existed."

He grinned again.

"Thanks," I mumbled. "I think I can walk now."

He chuckled. "You're pig-headed, aren't you?"

I preferred to call it being self-reliant. All my adult life, I'd been the only person I could count on, and I wasn't going to start leaning on anyone just because I had a few bruises.

He stepped back, and I hopped off the tailgate. I remained on my feet this time. I took a few steps, and my legs worked. My head was beginning to clear.

"The bike," I said.

He went to the passenger side of the truck and brought back a shirt. "Put this on. It'll cover up the worst of it. Go shop, lady," he said. "I'll make sure your bike still works, and then you can cycle back home if you want to."

I didn't want to wear his shirt, but mine was dirty and torn, so I gave in and pulled on the shirt. Across the pocket, embroidered in red thread, was his name: Luke. I rolled my eyes and walked into the market.

The first aisle held first aid supplies. I selected boxes of gauze and sterile tape and dropped them into a shopping basket. At the end of the aisle, a display of lotions reminded me I'd forgotten to pack sunscreen. I found one with an SPF of 50 and a mild scent and added that to the basket before moving on to the food section.

All my favorite comfort foods joined the first aid supplies: bow tie pasta, marinara sauce, a baguette, a small herb chevre, and chocolate chip cookies.

I stood at the meat counter, trying to decipher the options. Nothing looked familiar. A man approached the counter and glanced at me, waiting for me to order. When I didn't, he spoke to the woman behind the counter.

"What's fresh?" He had a clipped British accent that made me feel dull—not due to my head injury, but boring. He sounded so refined. I waited eagerly for him to speak again. "Blue crab, possibly?"

His deep voice complemented his bulk. He wasn't too tall—just under six feet, perhaps, but his shoulders were broad and solid. He wore pressed khaki shorts and a white linen shirt, mostly unbuttoned, as if too urbane to be bothered with trivialities such as buttons. A tattoo crossed one side of his chest; the black ink was almost hidden on his dark skin.

The woman behind the counter pointed to a pile of white-fleshed fish. "No blue crab. Codfish. And prawns."

"Prawns," the dark stranger next to me said. "A half kilo, please." He turned to me and said, "Codfish. As if."

He smiled, pleased with his disdain for codfish, and I returned the smile as if accepting his invitation into an exclusive club of codfish haters. My head began to spin again. He was wonderful. Cultured and snobby.

"Yes, prawns for me as well, I think," I said. Did I suddenly sound British?

"Take these," he offered me the package and turned back to the woman. "Same again, please."

I stood there smiling like an idiot. He gave me a polite nod and walked away. I wandered into the produce section, glancing over my shoulder occasionally, hoping that he'd join me as I selected salad greens. We could scoff at the iceberg and call the arugula arrogant, but he didn't appear. I paid for my items, packed them into my bag, and walked back to the truck. Luke was leaning against it, arms folded.

"That took long enough," he complained.

"You didn't have to wait. I told you I'm fine."

He sighed. "Look, I'm not going to just ditch you here. Obviously, you have to get back up that hill. I'll drive you home, make sure you get inside safely, and then you'll never see me again, okay?"

"Thank you," I agreed. I would have preferred a ride with the prawn man, but he was too refined to drive a pickup truck, and I needed to get the bike back to the guest house.

"I'm Luke, by the way," he said.

"I know. That's what it says on your shirt," I said, but I added, "I'm Anne."

"Hey, that's my best bowling shirt!"

My eyebrows knit together as I tried not to roll my eyes again. Bowling completed the trifecta. Construction worker, pickup truck, and bowling league. I removed his shirt and handed it back to him.

"Thanks. Sorry about the blood."

He grinned. "Blood stains'll make me look like a bad-ass bowler."

"I doubt it," I said under my breath, but I smiled back at him.

He drove silently, drumming the steering wheel and humming along with a reggae song on the radio. When he pulled down the huge drive and saw the gray mansion, he whistled.

"Nice house."

"I'm staying out back in the guest house," I told him.

He insisted on walking me to the door, and he lifted the bike from the bed of his truck.

"It's okay, by the way," he told me, his boots crushing the gravel underfoot. "The bike, I mean. Needs oiling. The handlebars were bent, but I fixed them."

"It's not my bike." Jeez, Anne. "I mean, thanks," I added. "Sorry, I'm not usually so rude."

"You're typically more friendly after a bike accident?" He grinned again. He did have a nice smile. "Promise me you'll call a taxi next time?"

He was quiet as we passed the pool, and I directed him along the path to the guest house.

"You shouldn't be alone," he said. "You may have hit your head."

I stood in the doorway, unsure about his intentions. Was he suggesting that he should keep me company until Sandy arrived?

I didn't want to be alone in the strange house, but inviting a stranger in without knowing when Sandy would return was unwise. Especially an attractive man with a coy smile. I knew that smile. He was a Chad—a lesson I'd already learned the hard way.

"I'll be fine," I told him. "My friend will be here soon."

He nodded. "Don't forget what I said about that scrape. Make sure you clean it." He backed away with a quick wave.

"Thanks," I said one more time before I closed the door.

The house was quiet, and I didn't bother to call out for Sandy while I unloaded groceries onto the kitchen counter.

I cleaned the prawns and dropped them into a bowl with olive oil, crushed garlic, and some black pepper I found in the cupboard. There were too many for me to eat—seven large prawns, but I sautéed them all. The scent of frying garlic made my mouth water, and as soon as the prawns pinked up, I slid them onto a plate. While they cooled, I made a small salad with greens, scallions, and chopped mango and ate on the patio to enjoy my private ocean view. The first bite of prawn snapped with a juicy burst of sweet-saltiness, and I greedily ate all seven.

After I ate, I cleaned my arm. The bathroom mirror showed the damage as I unwrapped the bandages. The skin looked like I'd been attacked by a cheese grater. In the shower, I dislodged bits of gravel and dirt. Most of it would heal easily; I'd only scratched the top layer of skin, but the fleshy part just above my armpit felt like I'd exposed raw nerves. The water pressure was almost unbearable, but I endured a rinsing, watching the blood-stained water circle the drain, hoping it was enough to get it clean.

After I dressed, I descended the patio steps to explore the private beach. I tiptoed cautiously over damp rocks and flipped off my shoes to feel the wet sand underfoot. The guest house was situated at the end of a peninsula, and a thick outcropping of palm trees blocked the view in both directions. I chose left, picking my way around jagged rocks. The water was crystal clear; the rocks were easy to avoid. As I walked, the cliff face grew above me, and after only a hundred yards, the sand disappeared into an unscalable wall of rock that jutted several feet into the water. A dead end.

I turned and walked in the other direction, rounding the point where I'd started, passing my discarded shoes.

"Ahoy there!" A voice called out from above.

"Hello?" I answered, searching for the source.

I recognized his shirt. He was barefoot now and smiling as if we were old friends.

Chapter 3

"Hello!"

I was so surprised to see him on my beach; all I could say was, "You're the prawn man."

He laughed—not at me, it was an inclusive laugh, as if we shared our own private joke, and he joined me on the narrow strip of sand.

"What a lovely surprise to find we're neighbors!"

I smiled and searched for something to say, but my only thought was of the prawns. "They were lovely, by the way."

His head tilted to one side with a questioning look.

"The prawns," I explained. "They were lovely."

He laughed again, and I flushed and stared at my feet.

"Mind if I walk with you for a bit?" he asked.

He didn't wait for an answer. I doubted anybody ever declined his company.

"What brings you to the island?" he asked.

"I came here to meet a friend. I'm on vacation, I guess." Not quite a lie.

"You guess," he chuckled. "Oh, aren't you the most refreshing woman." Yes, I was, wasn't I? Refreshingly awkward. "Have you been to the island before?"

"No, actually," I answered. "I live near Miami, but somehow I never made it here. Too busy, I guess."

"There you go, guessing again." Another chuckle. "Welcome to the island." He glanced back in the direction of the guest house and asked. "Where's your friend? Back at the house?"

I hesitated. Admitting I was alone seemed unwise. But he didn't seem to notice my discomfort.

"Have you made any plans for your stay?" he asked.

"Not really. It was a last-minute thing," I admitted.

"How wonderfully impulsive of you. I must plan these things months in advance."

I wasn't impulsive, but I didn't bother to correct him.

While we walked, he did most of the talking. He'd flown in a few days ago after several stifling weeks in Europe, and he was here to unwind. He rattled on about his flight and the adjustment to the heat. His lengthy explanation of the weather was unnecessary, considering I was experiencing it alongside him, but his self-deprecating descriptions were entertaining and very British. His voice was deep and lyrical—like a bassoon. He could have been reading from a technical manual, and I would have listened, enthralled.

"I'm boring you," he said.

"Not at all," I answered. "I'm enjoying your accent."

He laughed and said, "You're the one with an accent. You sound very Southern."

"Is that a bad thing?"

"Just the opposite. Your drawl makes me feel like we're in some epic Southern drama."

My smile deepened, and I watched our feet, bare toes squelching with each release of the wet sand. The lapping waves, embarrassed by the intimacy of our footsteps, attempted to erase the trail, but faint depressions remained, his wider and deeper than the ones made by my slender feet. A few times, his hand lightly brushed against mine, and my arm erupted in electric pleasure.

I searched for something interesting to say, an anecdote that would delight him, but my mind was blank aside from the closeness of his hand and the way his open shirt fluttered to reveal dark, curly hair and his tattoo—spiraling lines that disappeared into his sleeve. We walked quietly until the beach ended in a wall of rock, and we turned together and watched the sea.

A lone catamaran rocked in the gentle waves; its hull clean-white against the turquoise sea. I let my mind wander and imagined myself on the boat, anchored for a siesta, relaxing on a deck chair next to him. A silly daydream. I looked up at him, hoping he couldn't read my thoughts, and found him studying me. I blushed again and looked away.

Despite my embarrassment, I wanted to remain in the daydream. On the catamaran, I was confident, carefree Anne. But the surf stole the sand from beneath my feet. I stumbled, and he caught me easily.

"Let's get you back on solid ground," he said. His hand lingered at the small of my back, and I considered tripping on purpose just to be held again.

We walked back slowly, not talking. The intensity of my attraction to him was difficult to understand. All my past relationships were drizzly afternoon showers compared to the electrical storm I felt walking next to him. What had sparked it? Was it mutual?

I slipped my hands into my pockets and tightened my arm tight against my body. I needed to avoid contact.

He was a stranger, and my situation on the island was uncertain. But I remembered his kindness at the meat counter and thought of his easy laugh, his steady hand on my back. I relaxed. He was just a tourist. He was just being friendly.

When we neared the end of the peninsula, he spoke. "I was thinking about taking a drive. Maybe catch some late afternoon sun. Would you care to join me?"

I took a slow breath before I answered. "Sure," I drawled casually. As cool as a Southern belle. "Sounds nice," I said. Nice? I couldn't do better than nice?

"I assume you're staying in the guest house?" I nodded. "I'll pick you up in the driveway in about... fifteen minutes?"

My heart skipped a beat. I couldn't. I was here for Sandy. But Sandy's problem couldn't be much of an emergency if she wasn't even here, and the Anne in my daydream would have agreed. I wanted to be like that Anne.

I answered, "Okay."

We reached the steps to his house, and he said, "Thanks for the walk. See you in a few, Anne."

I smiled as he spoke my name. I barely registered the sand under my feet as I rounded the point and danced up the steps to the guest house.

I selected a loose-fitting, long sleeve tunic to keep my arm hidden from the sun and borrowed a wide-brimmed hat from the closet. I brushed my hair, wishing it did something more than hang limply to my shoulders, and applied a touch of mascara and clear lip gloss. I didn't wear makeup often, but mascara accentuated my blue eyes. I didn't need lipstick. My lips were my best feature, full and rosy pink. More than once, I'd been asked what shade of lipstick I was wearing, only to answer that they were naturally that color. My plump lips were at odds with the rest of me—thin and flat-chested.

I dropped a bottle of water and sunscreen into my bag with my book and a beach towel from the bathroom cupboard.

I didn't know his name. But he knew mine. How? Had I told him at the meat counter? Maybe I'd been shell-shocked enough to forget that we'd introduced ourselves. I didn't know much about him—just that he was dark and beautiful and well-traveled. Normally, I wouldn't hop into the car of a strange man so quickly. Perhaps the head injury had affected my cautious personality, but Luke had said I shouldn't be alone after a potential head injury. Going for a ride with a dark stranger was a good decision, medically speaking.

I locked the door to the guest house and pulled out my phone to text Sandy.

Headed to the beach for a bit. Be back soon.

I paused by the door and waited for an answer, but my phone stayed quiet, and I walked up to the big house.

He arrived in a red convertible—wonderfully cliché. He jogged around to open the door for me, and as I sat, he handed me a coffee cup.

"Latte?"

"Thanks," I said. "How did you have time to get coffee?" But he didn't seem to hear my question. "I'm sorry. If you told me your name, I've forgotten," I said.

"Lucien. Lucien Smith." He put the car in gear. "Ready?"

As he drove, he talked about the history of the island. He pointed out landmarks and historical sites, the best restaurants, and the only place to buy croissants. He wasn't in a hurry; he slowed to a crawl near crowds of tourists and detoured to show off the best vistas. I reclined in the seat, sun on my face, sea breeze in my hair. He could have driven us off a cliff, and I would have gone smiling.

At the top of a hill, he stopped the car on the side of the road and opened his door. "I want to show you the view," he called out on his way around the front of the car. My hip had stiffened during the drive, and I winced as he helped me out of the seat. "Okay?" he asked.

"Yeah, everything is sore."

"I saw the bruises earlier. Did you at least win the fight?"

"No," I smiled. "It was a bike accident. The road won."

We walked along a narrow ridge. Saint Martin was a small island; the ocean was visible on both sides. A lonely view, as if the rest of the world was an endless ocean.

"This is where I come to be alone," he said. "Except now because you're here."

He was sharing his special place with me. Maybe the attraction *was* mutual. But who was I kidding? He was just being neighborly.

"Beautiful, isn't it?" he said. "When I'm home, I miss this—the serenity and solitude that I feel here. But when I'm here, I feel homesick and miss my family. Doesn't make any sense, does it?"

I shrugged. "I don't have anyone at home to miss."

"No family?"

I shook my head and held my breath, expecting the inevitable questions. But he remained quiet, staring at the waves below.

After a few minutes, he finally spoke. "Shall we head back down? Visit the beach? I brought a picnic."

We returned to the car, and he drove to the bottom of the hill and pulled off the road.

"It's not far. Can you walk a bit?"

"Of course," I said.

Lucien pulled beach chairs from the trunk and led me down a dirt path through a forest of purple cannas and birds of paradise. We stepped through a break in the foliage to find a wide, white sand beach. I followed him across the sand. He stopped mid-way between the water and the tree line and eased me into a chair.

"I'll get the picnic," he said and jogged back to the car.

I pulled my book from my bag, but Lucien returned quickly and set up an umbrella, and laid out a blanket. On his final trip from the car, he brought back a wicker picnic basket.

He'd only just invited me—there hadn't been enough time to prepare a picnic. Had he planned to be alone, or was I taking someone's place? If so, what had happened to her?

"Is this your favorite beach?" I asked.

"It's not as crowded with tourists."

"Except us."

He winked at me. "Our little secret."

My book remained in my lap while I watched children splash in the waves. Their parents dozed nearby on blankets, baking in the sun. Under Lucien's umbrella, the heat was tolerable. A constant breeze rustled palm fronds, and the sound harmonized with the crashing waves in an inescapable lullaby. I dozed. When I woke, we waded into the water to cool down, and then Lucien unpacked fancy cheeses and fruit. After he ate, he stretched out on the blanket and closed his eyes, and I checked my phone. No messages from Sandy.

When the sun fell behind the trees, Lucien made trips to the car, insisting that I stay in my chair until he was finished, and I watched the happy families gather their belongings and trudge wearily across the sand after their perfect day of sun. I thought about my own family and wondered if they had worn weary smiles on their last day at the beach. Had they also enjoyed a perfect day in the sun?

"Ready?" Lucien asked.

I nodded and stood. He took the chair in one hand and offered me his other arm, and we trudged across the sand. The path through the trees was dark. The wide canna leaves leaned in the breeze, grazing my legs as we passed. I flinched, and Lucien's grip tightened until we reached the road. I slid back into the car, and he sped away.

"Anne, darling, you need rest to heal those bruises. I'd like to spend tomorrow with you if you aren't already bored by me."

"I'd like that," I said.

"If you're up for it, we could take the ferry. I'll arrange another picnic."

"Sounds wonderful," I said.

He remembered to stop at the market, and I was more clear-headed, selecting a couple of chicken breasts and requesting another package of prawns. I smiled at the display of codfish.

He walked me all way to the guest house, and I faced him in the doorway.

"I'll arrive promptly at eight with breakfast."

"Thanks." I smiled and watched him jog back up the path. When he was out of sight, I stepped into the house.

"Sandy?" I called out, "Where are you?" but there was no answer.

I texted her the same question, *Where are you?* and collapsed on the chaise by the pool. I felt guilty about going on the beach trip with Lucien, but she'd summoned me here without any explanation, and then she hadn't even shown up.

My arm hurt. I'd kept the wound wrapped all afternoon to prevent sunburn, but I decided to unwrap it and clean it once more in the shower. The gauze stuck in places, and I had to tear the fabric away, making it bleed again. The water pressure was still unbearable, but I rubbed the crusted discharge and rinsed the salt water from my legs. I gently toweled and re-bandaged my arm.

I made a late dinner of sliced mango with bread and cheese and ate alone on the patio, watching the dark sea through the framework of the arbor. Then I went to bed. My phone screen glowed in the bedroom, displaying my repeated texts to Sandy—five identical lines asking, *Where are you*, but the phone stayed silent.

CHAPTER 4

My phone buzzed while I was still in bed. A text from Sandy.

Anna Banana. Change of plans. Rented us an Airbnb. Don't tell anyone. Just go now.

I stared at my phone, hoping for more, and a second text arrived with an address.

Anna Banana was our club code to be used in emergencies. Like a suspected spiked drink or an escape from a creepy guy. She'd never used it for an emergency. There hadn't been one. The only time she ever used it was when she'd been cornered by a guy in a too-tight lavender polo, but she hadn't been in danger, just bored of his golf stories. I'd used it once to get out of a conversation about shrubbery with my neighbor—the only time I'd been desperate enough to use the ridiculous rhyme.

Her number went directly to voicemail, and I dropped the phone and rolled over. Searing pain erupted in my arm, and I sat up, groaning as sore muscles in my back and hip complained. My arm was hot to the touch, and the dressing had leaked pale, yellow discharge onto the sheets.

I swung my legs over the side of the bed and tiptoed into the bathroom. I undressed, inspecting my hip. A purple bruise began at my back and wrapped around my hip. Ugly and painful, but it would fade. My arm was the issue. I peeled away the dressing. The skin around the wound was angry red. A hot shower melted some of the stiffness in my back, but I couldn't endure the water on my arm. I bit my lip and tried a second time, but my eyes welled up with tears, and I squeezed them shut, panting until the pain subsided.

I stepped out of the shower, toweled off, and redressed the wound.

My suitcase was packed when I heard a whistle from the patio. Lucien.

I walked out to meet him, and he handed me a coffee and a small bag. Breakfast, as promised. He wore another white linen shirt, unbuttoned and untucked, over crisp, turquoise shorts.

"Morning! How are you feeling? Any better?"

"Yes, much," I lied.

"Anne, darling, I must leave the island for a few days. I have to cancel our plans."

"I understand," I said, relieved that I wasn't the one canceling. "Thanks for the coffee."

"I'll pop 'round when I get back to town. Get some rest, Anne. See you soon."

He tipped his hat and disappeared. I heard his shoes shuffle down the stone steps. I wanted to call after him, to tell him where I was going, but Sandy's cryptic text echoed in my head. *Don't tell anyone.* Odd words. I'd been here less than a day. She knew I shied away from meeting new people. She couldn't have known I'd made friends on the island. I dialed her phone again. Still no answer.

I sat at the patio table and tore off a piece of croissant. What was her point? Was she trying to scare me, or was this an elaborate set-up? She was always trying to pull me out of my routine. There was a chance her invitation to the island was just another ploy. We'd both abused the Anna Banana code, using it for non-emergencies. Was she using it now as a way to poke fun about tricking me into an unwanted vacation? Or was there a real threat?

Buttery flakes spilled onto the table as I finished the croissant. In the distance, calm waves approached in a constant, unhurried rhythm. I struggled to feel any urgency. The guest house was serene. Strange that such an isolated place felt less lonely than my own home. But I'd already had two visitors. At home, weeks would pass between Sandy's visits, and in between, I was alone.

I stayed until I'd finished the coffee, and then I wiped down the table. I packed my groceries and made one final pass through the house to make sure I hadn't forgotten anything. I locked the front door, tucked the key under the mat, and walked past the gray house to wait for a taxi.

#

Sandy's Airbnb rental was an anonymous one-bedroom condo. Two days ago, the small patio would have been glorious, but the view was marred by noisy crowds on the beach, and my mood had soured after leaving the guest house.

I unloaded my groceries into the fridge, but cooking felt like an unnecessary chore. On the drive over, I'd spotted several restaurants nearby, and I considered take-out for dinner in front of the television. A depressing thought. Vacation in the condo seemed a lot like my typical day at home.

For the first time since I'd arrived on the island, I thought about work. I pulled out my laptop and checked my email, but there was nothing from the office. That seemed odd. I didn't have an inflated sense of my importance; my daily tasks were essential, and it was surprising that no one had questions about how to accomplish them. Perhaps Mr. Sampson had realized I needed time away, and he had asked them not to reach out to me.

Or perhaps he actually was investigating me for wire fraud—not that I was guilty of anything. But something had been brewing in the office for months.

Two days ago, Mr. Sampson's request for a face-to-face meeting had seemed a nuisance. He knew I always left the office at precisely four-forty-five to make it to my five o'clock swim, and the clock read four-forty. Anything that warranted an in-person meeting probably couldn't be handled in five minutes.

I'd ignored his gesture to sit and remained in the doorway. Standing made my intentions clear: stick to the point. I didn't concern myself with personal matters during the business day. My co-workers wasted so much time sharing stories of their children's latest pursuits. Piano recitals. Sporting events. I liked children. I wanted to have children myself someday, but I was sure I wouldn't need to validate my parental ability by sharing their every trivial success and failure.

Mr. Sampson held a thin stack of papers, but I stood too far away to read the print.

"Anne, do you know anything about a series of foreign wire transfers?"

It was an odd question considering my job was to authorize all outgoing wires for the entire company. I stood straighter, taking a half-step back with my right foot, shifting my weight like a prize fighter, and answered with a defensive tone.

"You're going to have to be more specific, Mr. Sampson. I send foreign wires all the time."

"Yes, yes, Anne," he said. He set down the pages and lifted both hands, palms facing me as if to show off his kid gloves. "Do you remember a series of funds sent to a new account in Switzerland to a company called DG, Inc?"

I did remember, but I answered carefully. "Yes. The paperwork from purchasing was all in order." I didn't offer details—like the fact that something about the account felt off, and when I questioned Terry, the kid from purchasing, he looked like he was about to cry. He was a new hire, a fresh-faced kid with a degree and zero experience. Years ago, I'd been in the same place—without a degree, and Mr. Sampson had seen my potential and given me a chance.

I'd told Terry I would wire the funds anyway and made him promise to track down the missing details on the account. When he requested additional wire transfers for the same company, I went to his office to tell him I needed the information first. He surprised me by shouting.

"Just send the funds, Anne!"

He'd calmed down and promised the information was forthcoming, and I'd sent the funds. Several months passed. I continued sending funds. Despite my frequent reminders, he never followed through, and I hadn't yet decided if he was inept or just lazy. Dishonesty hadn't crossed my mind until I was standing in Mr. Sampson's office.

My heart thumped as I tried to recall specific details on the account. Mr. Sampson stared at the papers on his desk for a long moment.

"Something doesn't add up. Are you sure you followed the wire protocols?"

"It feels like you're trying to accuse me of something," I said.

"No, no. I'm just trying to establish facts at this point."

I bristled. Over my thirteen-year tenure at the company, I'd been promoted twice when two employees left the department, and I assumed their roles. The extra work was supposed to be temporary, but replacements never materialized, and I just worked more hours. I never complained, but the resentment from years of being taken for granted had built into a powder keg. My sudden uncertainty about the integrity of the wires lit a fuse.

"If anything was wrong, you'll need to speak with Terry Stoller. It's his account." My voice was high-pitched, strained. His bushy eyebrows lifted in surprise. "Also, my friend just called, and she needs my help. I need to use my vacation time, and I'm not sure how long I'll be away. Starting tomorrow."

He didn't answer right away. His surprise softened into something else—something that weighted his sallow cheeks into a deep frown. It looked like pity.

"I'll be at my desk," I snapped and escaped his office.

I stayed for over an hour, making notes on my ongoing projects and sending emails to co-workers asking them to cover my essential tasks. Just before I left, Mr. Sampson approached my desk and asked in a quiet voice, "Anne, are you okay?"

His question sparked fresh anger. Other employees took personal days, and there was never any assumption that anything was wrong. "I'm fine!" I almost shouted. "I just need time off to help a friend. I do have friends, you know. I have a whole life outside of this office. Go talk to Terry about those wires. He requested them. I just did my job. I didn't do anything wrong."

I left the office with a shakiness that didn't wear off for hours. On the way home, I realized I'd lied. I didn't have a life outside the office.

At home, I called Sandy and delivered the news.

"I'm coming to Saint Martin."

She squealed as if she'd asked me to go on a girl's weekend instead of a rescue mission. "Thank you! I honestly wasn't sure you'd come."

"Mr. Sampson accused me of stealing funds," I told her. He hadn't actually accused me, but I was still angry about his insinuations. I'd broken protocol for Terry, and I wasn't sure what kind of fallout I'd face when I returned to the office.

"What?" she shouted. "Why?"

"It's no big deal," I said, not wanting to explain. "I'll figure it out when I get back. What's going on? Do you need money or something?"

"I'll explain when you get here. I'll get you a ticket for the first flight in the morning. Go pack," she told me.

"Tell me. How can I help if I don't know what the problem is?"

"I promise I'll explain. I'll meet you at the airport tomorrow."

I mixed a special gin and tonic—the way my mother used to make them. Dry gin, soda water, and lime juice.

Her cocktail probably had a better name, but she'd always called it a g-and-t. I once ordered a gin and tonic at a restaurant and almost spat out the sticky-sweet cocktail. From then on, I made my own special version at home, just like she used to.

The drink cooled my temper. Mr. Sampson's questions made some kind of sense. I *was* the only person at the company to suspect. It was my job to send all wires—large sums, and I had little supervision. I was the only person with all the passwords and bank codes.

I could hardly have explained to Mr. Sampson that if I'd stolen funds from the company, he wouldn't have noticed. It would've taken me time to siphon off funds in six-figure amounts each month. Not too much time. That was the trick—steal it slowly enough that nobody noticed but fast enough to leave before you got caught. Five months. Six tops. Two quarterly reports of lowered profits would have invited too many questions. But an average of six hundred thousand over five months was a decent amount of money. I could retire on that. Most people could.

After a second drink, I regretted my defensive reaction. Mr. Sampson was a kind man, and he'd always treated me with respect. I dialed his phone, but it went to voicemail. "Hi, it's Anne," I began after the tone. "I'm sorry for shouting. You took me by surprise. And I'm worried about my friend. I'll stay in touch and let you know when I'll be back. Email me if you need anything. I have my laptop with me. Bye."

I poured a third g-and-t while I packed. I usually stop at one. I never had a third cocktail, but I needed all three to build courage for the trip. I'd regretted all three drinks the next morning as I rushed to make the flight with a hangover.

Remembering the g-and-t's made me thirsty, and I closed my laptop. My imagination concocted images of my co-workers combing through my files to search for evidence of wire fraud. I knew leaving abruptly made me look guilty. Someone who had stolen three million dollars would have done exactly that—run away. And I'd immediately gotten on a plane and left the country.

Jeez, Anne.

I stowed my laptop and paced the small living room. Still nothing from Sandy. How was I supposed to help her if she wasn't around? I slipped my phone into my pocket and grabbed the hat I'd borrowed from the guest house. I needed a cocktail. It wasn't quite lunchtime, but this was a tropical paradise, and I was sure it wouldn't be hard to find one.

CHAPTER 5

After a short walk along the beach, I found a cafe and took a seat outside at a table overlooking the sand. At home, I'd order a boring white wine, but I wanted something that felt like a vacation, something cold and outside my comfort zone. A rum punch.

The beach was crowded. Unlike the day before, it wasn't relaxing. I couldn't hear the ocean over the screams of the children on the playground, and the sand was overrun with bright umbrellas and beach towels. Yesterday, with Lucien, I'd been a part of the scene. Today, I watched as a lonely outsider.

My rum punch disappeared quickly, but my mood didn't improve. I ordered a second drink, and a burger to go along with it. Being drunk at midday felt too far outside my comfort zone.

"Anne?"

I looked around, searching for a familiar face. A man approached me, smiling. He was wearing only shorts and a bandana as a headband. Was there another Anne in the cafe? I looked over my shoulder, but then he laughed, and I recognized him.

"Luke," I said. "You told me I'd never have to see you again."

"True. But it's a really small island, so that may have been a short-sighted promise. Plus, I thought you were staying on the opposite side of the island. What are you doing all the way over here?"

"I have no idea. My friend just told me to move. Into a condo over there." I pointed to the building.

"Cool. I live just over there." He pointed to a tall building of condos on the far side of the restaurant. Can I join you? Just played volleyball, and I'm starving."

Before I could decline, he grabbed the railing and swung his legs over in one fluid movement.

"Can you eat here without a shirt on?" I asked.

He snorted. "Look around. They do things differently here on the island." He signaled to the waiter. "How are you feeling, by the way?" he asked.

"I'm fine," I lied.

"And your arm?"

I couldn't answer because I was captivated by the bits of sand that clung to him, on his chest, across his shoulders, down his arms. As he moved, the sand came unstuck and cascaded down his torso. He brushed it away absently.

An awkward silence settled until he said, "Look, I'm sorry I was so rude yesterday. I had a really bad day, and I kinda took it out on you. You scared me—in the middle of the road like that. I could've killed you."

"I'm really glad you didn't."

"Me too," he grinned.

He wasn't bad looking when he smiled. Especially shirtless. He smelled better today—like sunscreen. He pulled the bandana from his head and used it to mop his face.

"I wasn't very nice either," I admitted. "I'd just found out my friend ditched me. I was tired, hungover, and hungry."

"Wicked combo."

"Exactly," I agreed.

The waiter arrived and took his order: a beer and a burger.

"You're American," I said. "But you live here?"

"I was born here, actually, but my mom is from California. I was raised there mostly. I spent summers here with my dad's family. I moved here full-time about ten years ago."

"It's beautiful here."

The conversation stalled again, and I sipped my drink.

"Where's your friend?" he asked.

I shrugged. "I haven't seen her yet."

"Whoa. Is she always flaky like that?"

"Sometimes," I said. But Sandy wasn't flaky. If she said she was coming over, she'd be there. It wasn't like her to cancel at the last minute. None of this was like her. Concern grew within me, and I checked my phone again. No new texts. Something was wrong with Sandy, but I didn't know what to do about it.

Unaware of my thoughts, Luke kept the conversation going. "First day here, your friend ditched you, you crashed your bike, and I almost ran you over."

"Pretty much."

"Can I buy you a beer to apologize?"

"Thanks, but I've had two of these already." My second rum punch was almost gone.

"I'll buy your lunch then. It's the least I can do," he said.

"Shouldn't I be the one thanking you? For the first aid and the ride?"

"Okay, you buy next time then."

Smooth move, Luke. Well played.

"When I'm done, can I take a look at your arm? You're bleeding again." I turned my arm over. A pink stain bloomed just above my elbow. "I can re-wrap it for you."

"I'm okay," I said but changed my mind. "Actually, that would be great. I'm not very good at it."

When he finished eating, we walked back to his condo. His place was tidy, and I hid my surprise. While he retrieved his first aid supplies from his truck, I wandered around his living room, glancing at the photos. There were many with a tall, blonde woman I assumed was his mother because he had her smile. On the patio, two surfboards were propped against the railing—those didn't surprise me, but his kitchen did. Expensive-looking knives lined the wall behind the stove, and a checkerboard-patterned cutting board sat on the white granite countertop, chaffed by frequent use. The stainless-steel stove top gleamed from a recent cleaning.

I sat at the kitchen table, and he dropped his first aid tackle box next to me. He undid the poorly wrapped bandage and made a tsk-tsking sound.

"Doesn't look great. I'm going to clean it and apply anti-bacterial ointment, but I want to see it tomorrow. If it's not improving, you'll need to see a doctor."

"Are you sure?" I asked.

"Yeah. You don't need medical training to see how red and swollen this is. Do you feel like you have a fever?"

"It's so hot here. How would I know?"

"Right. Well, I'm going to clean this out. It might hurt."

He draped my elbow over a large bowl. I took a deep breath and turned away from him. It didn't hurt at first as he rinsed it with warm water, but then he started poking at it with sharp tweezers, and I flinched at each stab. I wished for another rum punch to dull the pain.

"Try to hold still. I'm being as gentle as I can. There's still some gravel in here."

At the next sharp pain, I pulled away from him, and he wrapped his left arm around my shoulder, pulling my body against his to hold me still.

"Ouch!" I cried out as the tweezers dug deeper.

"Almost done." He held me tighter, and I rested my head on his arm, closed my eyes, and tried to ignore the pain. But the pain was searing, and I gasped.

"Sorry," he said softly, and he swiveled me to face him. "I think I got all of it. You okay?" he asked. But then he saw my tears, and the tweezers dropped onto the table. Both his arms went around me, pulling me into him, and I cried into his shoulder.

"It's okay," he said softly. "It's all over." He stroked my hair.

It wasn't just the pain in my arm. The rum punch had loosened me, heightening my concern for Sandy, the uncertainty of why I was even in Saint Martin. And it was his tenderness, the ache of being so close to a man after so many years without intimacy. I sniffed loudly, and he pulled away just enough to reach beneath my chin and tilt my head to meet his gaze.

"You okay?" he asked again.

I nodded and smiled. We sat that way for a long minute, his eyes on mine. Then he leaned forward in slow motion. I held my breath as he drew closer, and my lips parted just as his mouth covered mine.

When he finally pulled away, he looked embarrassed.

"Sorry," he mumbled.

"It's okay," I told him.

He busied himself with my arm, pouring warm water that ran into the bowl, pink with fresh blood. When he was satisfied, he dried it gently, applied ointment, and wrapped it with clean gauze. He worked silently. I could still feel his hands on me—in my hair, on my back. It was only one kiss, but it left me dazed.

He offered me a glass of water and took a seat across the table from me like he was afraid to be too close. I sat quietly, waiting for him to put his thoughts into words.

"I shouldn't have done that," he said, staring at his hands. "You were just so…vulnerable."

"It's okay," I repeated. "I should probably go."

"Yeah, okay. I'll change that bandage tomorrow morning. Keep it covered. Don't get it wet, okay?"

"Thanks for taking care of it. And for lunch," I said.

"Sure," he said. "I'll walk you home."

He was quiet at first, and I wondered if he regretted the kiss. Maybe he had a girlfriend, and his reaction had been guilt.

"You have plans for tomorrow?" he asked.

"Not yet," I answered. "Hoping my friend shows up." I paused, "If I think something happened to her…" but I didn't know how to finish the question.

"Oh," he stopped walking. "Is that what you think? That something is wrong with her? When was the last time you heard from her?"

I sighed. *Don't tell anyone*, she'd said. Only a few hours had passed, and I was already telling someone.

"I'm probably overreacting," I said. "But what would you do? Here on the island. Who would you call?"

"The Police."

We walked a little farther. Was I ready to call the Police? I'd heard from her this morning. Would they think I was overreacting?

"Wait. You said she told you to move. That was today?"

I nodded.

"But she never showed up."

"Maybe she has. I've been gone for a while."

"Let's go look," he said.

Something in his voice made me hopeful, and I opened the door and called out, "Sandy? Are you here?"

Luke waited in the doorway, and I wandered through the small condo. No Sandy. I returned to the door and shook my head.

"Do you want me to take you to the Police station?"

"No. Not yet. I'll give her a few more hours."

"I'll be home all day. You know where to find me if you change your mind. Is it okay if I stop by in the morning to change your bandage?"

"Yeah, thanks," I said.

He stepped backward, nodding. "Okay. See you then."

The rest of the afternoon, I stayed inside with the air conditioning blasting and the patio door closed to shut out the beach crowds and the hot wind. I tried to read, but I couldn't concentrate. I kept checking my phone. There were no new emails, no new texts. Sandy never called. I looked up the phone number for the Police and set a deadline. Four hours. But when four hours passed, and I didn't hear from Sandy, I hesitated to make the call, and I set a new deadline.

My arm throbbed. I collapsed on the sofa and turned on the television, searching for a distraction. My lips burned with the memory of Luke's kiss. Meeting Lucien had flipped a switch inside me, igniting something I hadn't felt in years. I returned to my daydream of Lucien on the catamaran and imagined him kissing me, and I slept.

#

A loud knock woke me, and I rubbed my eyes and checked my watch. Just after seven a.m.

"Sandy?" I called out.

I opened the door to find a uniformed police officer and a man in a pressed suit and a tie.

"Anne Wilson?" the man in the suit asked.

"Yes," I answered and cleared my throat. "Yes, I'm Anne."

"We'd like you to come with us to the station. We have a few questions for you."

"About what?" I asked.

"We'd prefer to have that conversation at the station."

Something *was* wrong with Sandy. Why had I hesitated to make the call?

"I just woke up," I said. "Can I have two minutes? To brush my teeth?"

The man in the suit nodded, and I opened the door wider to let them step inside.

"I'll be right back," I called out and hurried to the bathroom. I ran a brush through my hair, cleaned my teeth, and smoothed my wrinkled clothes.

I returned to the living room and pushed my phone into my pocket. The uniformed officer led me to a police car and helped me into the back seat. As we pulled away, I thought I heard someone calling my name, but when I turned to look, the street was deserted.

#

They didn't ask me anything on the car ride, and I didn't offer any answers. My head felt sluggish. I needed coffee. We'd driven a few miles before I considered another possible reason for their visit—the wires. But I dismissed that idea. Sandy was missing. This *had* to be about Sandy.

The police station was a small building at the top of a wide staircase. Inside, the man in the suit disappeared, and the officer led me into a small room with no windows and a useless ceiling fan. Despite the early hour, the room was stifling, and I was glad when the officer left the door open. I took it as a positive sign. I sat on a folding chair and waited.

After about ten minutes, the man in the suit entered the room and sat across from me. He moved gracefully, at ease in his small frame. His hair suited him—close-cropped, graying slightly at the temples.

"Can you describe the nature of your relationship with Gilda Jorgensen?"

"Who?" I asked. My confusion must have been obvious because he removed a plastic bag from a large manila envelope and pushed it across the table. I recognized the contents—a phone case with a mural of doves in nauseating pinks and purples. Sandy's phone.

"That's Sandy's phone," I said.

"This phone belonged to Gilda Jorgensen."

"No, not Gilda," I told him. "Sandy. Sandy Brown."

He nodded, "Sandy Brown was her alias. When did you last see her?" he asked.

"Alias?" I echoed. "Um, last weekend, I guess."

"You haven't seen her since arriving on the island?"

I shook my head. "No."

"Have you spoken to her?"

I paused. He'd used the past tense. All the moisture inside my mouth disappeared, and my voice was hoarse when I answered.

"No, she only texted me. The last text was yesterday to tell me that I had to leave the house where we were staying—I was staying, I mean. Yesterday, I moved to the condo where you found me. She said she was in trouble. That's why I came here, but she never showed up, so I don't know what was wrong."

He nodded as if confirming what he already knew.

"You were in the condo all day yesterday?" he asked.

"Yes, well, no. I went out for lunch. I spent the rest of the afternoon there. I slept there."

"Can anyone confirm that you were there all night?" he asked.

Luke? No, I'd left his place early. I shook my head. "I was alone all night. Can I ask what this is about? Is Sandy—I mean Gilda, is she alright?"

"Gilda Jorgensen was found dead this morning. Her mother is flying here for formal identification, but I would appreciate your assistance in the interim. She was badly beaten, and she spent some time in the water, so physical identification might be difficult. Did your friend have any birthmarks or tattoos?"

The room got smaller and began to spin.

"Sandy's dead?" I whispered.

He nodded. And waited.

"Yes, she had a tattoo—a dove across her right shoulder."

He reached into the manila folder, removed a photograph, and slid it across the table. It showed a woman's back; her skin was pale against the shiny metal of the sterile table beneath her. Wet strands of blonde hair had been pushed aside to reveal a tattoo: a dove, frozen in flight across her shoulder blade.

"Yes, that's her tattoo," I said in a flat voice that I didn't recognize.

I reached out to the table for support even though I was seated and raised my hand to my forehead. I was sweating. My skin was clammy. My hand trembled.

"Sandy's dead?" I asked again.

He nodded. "We are treating her death as a murder."

The man in the suit must have delivered similar news before. He reacted quickly, coming out of his seat, grabbing a trash can, and pushing me sideways, all in one graceful movement. I hung over the trash can for a second, marveling at his reflexes, and then I threw up.

The interview ended after that. I was told I couldn't leave the island without permission. The man in the suit, Detective Inspector Moreau, according to the card he gave me, took my contact information and told me he'd be in touch.

I walked out of the station, and the heat was a comfort, a warm blanket around my chilled shoulders.

Luke stood out front, leaning against the grill of his truck, arms folded, and I almost collapsed with relief to see a familiar face.

CHAPTER 6

Luke began asking questions before I made it to the bottom of the steps. "Anne, are you okay? What's going on? They wouldn't tell me why you're here."

"Why are you here?" I asked.

"I followed you. I was on my way to check on you when I saw you leaving in the back of a police car."

"Can you take me home?" I asked. "I mean, to my condo."

"Yeah, of course."

We climbed into his truck, and he pulled the car onto the road, glancing at me with a worried look.

"What's going on?" he asked.

Voicing the truth would make it a reality. I hesitated.

"Anne?"

With my head in my hands, I answered, "My friend, the one I came here to help, she's dead."

Out of the corner of my eye, I saw his head whip toward me, but I stared at my legs. "Whoa. What happened to her?"

"I don't know. I didn't ask. I was so upset I threw up. Do you have any water?"

He opened the cooler between us. "No, but I can

stop and get some. Just water? What about a coffee?”

"Sandy isn't Sandy. Her real name is Gilda. That must be a mistake.” I was telling myself as much as I was explaining it to him. I needed to repeat what I'd heard to digest it and try to make sense of it, but he assumed I was talking to him.

"What kind of name is Gilda?” he asked.

I ignored him. Her name wasn't the issue. “On the way over, I thought maybe it wasn't about Sandy at all. That they wanted to talk about what happened at work.”

"What do you mean? What happened at work?”

He pulled into a parking spot outside a coffee shop and turned off the engine, but he didn't get out. He turned toward me, expecting the story.

"They think I stole three million dollars,” I said. A hysterical laugh escaped from my throat, and I took a long breath. “Well, no one has actually accused me yet. I'm overreacting. But I wanted it to be that—the money. Not about Sandy.” My voice trailed off.

"I'm not following. You think your friend had something to do with the money?”

"No, the two things aren't connected. They can't be. I just meant…I don't know. I wish it was anything other than Sandy. My head's having trouble processing it. And I'm really thirsty.”

"Yeah, I'll be right back. Want a coffee?”

"Just water, please. Maybe a muffin? I'm a little queasy.”

I leaned my head out the window and watched him jog inside the coffee shop. My forehead was still sweating.

Sandy was dead.

Luke returned with a cold bottle of water and a little paper sack with a blueberry muffin. I tossed the paper sack on the seat next to me and sipped the water. Luke started the truck, but before he pulled out onto the street, he said, "I have to run a quick errand before I head home. Won't take long. You mind?"

I shook my head. Luke glanced at me as he drove one-handed, his other arm draped across the open window frame. The air cooled my damp face. I leaned my head against the headrest and closed my eyes. I was drowsy, drifting to sleep, when the truck bounced, jolting my eyes open. We were climbing a hill, and I recognized the view—the hill where I'd crashed the bike. I shivered and rubbed my elbow. My arm throbbed. Luke slowed, and I caught a glimpse of the wide bay before it was lost behind the trees.

"Why are we going this way? Isn't this the way back to the guest house?"

"Yeah, but we're not headed there. I have to drop off supplies at a job site. I was supposed to be there earlier, but I was waiting for you."

"Sorry."

"No, I didn't mean that. I'm glad I waited. I'll just drop these off, and then I'll get you home."

Halfway down the hill, he turned onto a dirt road that I didn't remember seeing on my bike ride. He parked behind a line of trucks at the end of a narrow driveway. On one side, I glimpsed the sea through thick brush. On the other side, a dark metal roof rose above the tree line.

"Where are we?" I asked.

"I'll only be a sec," he called out as he climbed out of the truck and closed the door. But then his head appeared in the open window. "Look, I know you're in shock right now. You just had bad news. Maybe you could use a distraction? Want a tour?"

"Sure," I said. I didn't think a distraction was going to help, but I was curious.

"C'mon," he beckoned.

We had to walk past the line of trucks before I could see the rest of the house. There were only two exterior walls—the back and left side. The other two sides were open aside from steel columns set at regular intervals around the perimeter of the concrete slab. The interior of the house was interrupted by the wooden framework of walls.

"Watch your step," Luke said, pulling me onto the concrete through an opening that seemed like a front door, but there was no step and no door.

"It's missing walls," I said.

He laughed. "Last thing to go in. All windows. You'll understand when you see the view. This is the entryway, of course. Living room and dining room through there." He pointed, but it was hard to imagine rooms when the walls were see-through. We walked through a series of archways that split the house in half. "Here's the kitchen."

The kitchen was easier to imagine as a finished product. The framework of an island spanned the middle of the large space. The rest of the room was empty. But my focus was drawn outward. From the kitchen, the view was no longer interrupted by wood framing.

"Wow," I breathed.

"Exactly," Luke said. "Come see the rest."

We wandered through a series of smaller bedrooms. I followed him, turning sideways and passing through the walls like ghosts. The tour ended in the master bedroom. The master bath and walk-in closet were at the far back corner—the only rooms with solid walls. A workman paused when we entered the closet. The rest of the house was breezy, but the closet was a sauna without windows for ventilation. A spotlight set on a tripod felt like a space heater.

I mopped my forehead again and wandered through the master bedroom and outside—a strange distinction without a doorway to pass through. The concrete patio had a gaping hole I assumed would become a swimming pool.

Luke joined me at the edge of the concrete. Below us, golden sandstone formations cascaded down to the water's edge. One large boulder protruded like the thumb on a giant hitchhiker's fist.

"Eventually, a series of steps will lead to the water. They just finished the scaffolding. Not much of a beach down there, but very private. There are no neighbors up here. Just through those trees is the road you biked on, and the big house where you were staying is over there." The roof of the gray house was unmistakable. A huge, dark scar across the bright greenery below. The guest house was hidden in the trees at the tip of the peninsula, but the long pool was visible, the water a lighter shade than the sea below.

The height made me dizzy. I took a step back from the edge and turned around. After staring into the sunlight, the house was a dark cave. But then the ground became unstable, and I reached out for Luke as I began to fall.

He caught me with one arm and eased me onto the concrete. "You're burning up."

"Yeah, it's hot here," I said.

"No, you have a fever. Your arm must be infected. I need to get you to the hospital."

"But—" was all I could manage.

"You're so stubborn. Why are you always arguing with me? For once, just say, hey, thanks, Luke. Thanks for not running me over, Luke. Thanks for cleaning my arm, Luke. Thanks for saving me from sepsis, Luke."

He picked me up and carried me back to the truck. Another man jogged alongside him, opening the door so Luke could toss me inside. It was becoming a habit, his tossing me onto the seat like a sack of potatoes. He stood outside my window, talking to the other man, but I didn't hear them because everything went dark.

#

I woke to the bright whiteness of the hospital. I was groggy, and it took me a few minutes to register what the doctor was telling me. I had sepsis from the infection in my arm, and they were treating me with IV antibiotics. My arm throbbed with fresh pain, and he explained he'd surgically removed the infected tissue and stitched up my arm. He said I was lucky, but I disagreed. I felt awful.

When the nurse left the room, I lay staring at the sterile wall, with only memories of Sandy to keep me company.

Sandy was gone. I knew I'd recover eventually. That was the benefit of having experienced loss—I knew what to expect. Many years ago, a well-intentioned neighbor handed me a pamphlet outlining the stages of grief. I'd expected the glossy, tri-fold cardstock to hold a secret— a way forward, a method to shake free of the pain and emerge smiling like the woman on the front of the pamphlet. Instead, it told me what I already knew: grief made me angry.

I wasn't angry yet. Only sad—a selfish sadness as I imagined myself sipping a g-and-t in my living room or meandering through the farmer's market each Sunday. Those moments were now devoid of laughter because I'd be alone again.

How could she be dead? She was full of life—more than anyone I'd ever known. I bet she fought back, giving her attacker a taste of her haughty attitude. I smiled sadly, wiping away warm tears, imagining her peering at me over the top of her oversized sunglasses. "Don't be so pedestrian, Anne," she'd say.

She worked for a pharmaceutical company, and she traveled constantly—always complaining about a sub-par hotel or the paltry meal served on a flight. I enjoyed her stories. Her life was glamorous compared to mine. The day I'd met her, she told me she'd just gotten off a red-eye from Paris, and I'd exaggerated my importance as a lowly accounting clerk and bragged about sending millions of dollars in daily wire transfers.

"Not *really* millions," she'd drawled.

I hadn't answered right away. I'd run my hand across the lemon-yellow squash of the vegetable stand where we'd stopped. Every Sunday, I bought two green zucchini, but that day, ten minutes after meeting Sandy, I wanted something different. I wanted crookneck squash. And I wanted Sandy to like me.

"Well, not millions every day," I said. "But some days, sure. And definitely millions every week."

"Cool," she'd answered. "Wanna split a watermelon?"

I'd laughed. "How would that work?"

"First, we buy the watermelon, and then we cut it in half."

Her answer was so like her: straightforward on the surface, complex underneath. Splitting a watermelon isn't straightforward. Once cut, it's drippy and sticky and needs to be covered and contained. And that's how our friendship started: She bought a watermelon, and I figured out how to split it.

And now, in her death, I'd discovered how complex she'd really been. All the time I'd spent with her, she'd lied. She was someone else—Gilda Jorgensen.

The medication made me drowsy, and I dozed, but my brain kept working while I slept. I woke with a disturbing memory and found Luke by my bedside.

"I need to talk to the Detective Inspector," I told him. "When can I get out of here?"

"Hang on, what's the rush?"

"I remembered something," I said.

"I'll ask the doctor, but you probably aren't getting out anytime soon."

The doctor ordered more blood tests. I tried to remain patient, but it was dark before the doctor returned with news.

"We caught it early, and it responded quickly to the medication. We can switch you to an oral antibiotic, and you can go home tomorrow. But you must rest. Return immediately if you have any fever or nausea. Do you understand?"

"Yes," I agreed.

I spent a restless night. Every twenty minutes, the blood pressure cuff on my left arm filled with air until both my arms hurt. Luke slept in a chair next to me, and despite the considerable discrepancy between his height and the size of the chair, he snored softly.

When the sun was up and the morning shift change was completed, Luke brought coffee and a fresh blueberry muffin.

"Feeling better?" he asked.

"Yeah, but I need to get out of here. I remembered something. Can you take me back to the police station?"

#

Luke dropped me at the front of the police station and scribbled his cell on a scrap of paper. I shoved it in my pocket and climbed the steps.

"I'm heading to the job site for a bit. Call me when you're done," he called out behind me.

Inside, I asked to speak with the detective inspector and was shown to a different room than the one I'd thrown up in. He arrived promptly, wearing a different suit—light gray paired with a dark blue tie. He appeared as crisp as he had the day before. I folded my arms. I hadn't showered or brushed my teeth. If he noticed the needle marks on my arms, he didn't react.

"I remembered something," I began.

He relaxed back into his seat and crossed his legs.

"The name Gilda Jorgensen, I've heard it before. I didn't remember right away. I was sick. I don't just mean because I threw up yesterday. I had to go to the hospital after I left here, and when I was laying there in the hospital bed, I remembered."

I stopped to catch my breath.

"There's no hurry," he said. "Slow down. Start at the beginning."

"I'm not really sure where the beginning is, and I don't know if there is a connection between these two things, but it feels like too much of a coincidence."

"Go on."

"First, the name Gilda Jorgensen. I've heard it before. It's been months—six months, maybe, but it sticks out, you know? It's not a common name. At least not where I'm from."

I stopped for another big breath.

"Gilda Jorgensen worked for a company that I wired a lot of money to. It was part of my job. And I think it was millions, but I can't tell you the exact number. I remember speaking to Gilda Jorgensen to confirm banking details for the wire transfers."

I paused. I felt clammy again, but not due to the infection. I'd been awake most of the night trying to decide whether or not to share the next part. He watched me patiently as if he knew I needed time to find the courage.

"Just before I came here, my boss asked me about the same fund transfers. Sandy, I mean Gilda, had just asked me to come here. She told me that she was in trouble, but she didn't tell me how or why. I flew in the next morning. I haven't seen her since I got here—I told you that already."

He remained quiet, waiting for me to finish, but I couldn't continue. My head struggled to connect the pieces. Sandy was my friend. But Sandy was also Gilda, and Gilda might have stolen three million dollars from my company.

"Can I ask what happened to her? How she died, I mean?"

"She was beaten and strangled."

I covered my mouth with both hands. The detective inspector glanced at the trash can in the corner, but I shook my head.

"Do you know who did it?" I heard myself ask, but I didn't really want to know.

"I cannot share details with you. I appreciate the information, and please contact us if you think of anything else."

I nodded. My imagination was painting gruesome images of Sandy, and I needed to leave the small room. I hurried from the interview room, but a familiar accent caught my attention.

Lucien.

He sat inside a glass-walled office, talking to a uniformed woman. The woman's jacket had bars of multi-colored decorations, and the wall behind her was filled with pictures and official-looking documents. Her dark hair was pulled into a neat bun at the top of her head, accentuating her severe cheekbones.

My confused stare caught the woman's attention. Lucien turned, and our eyes met. He and the woman stood and shook hands, and he hurried across the room.

"Anne," he called.

The woman watched him for a moment before she sat and turned her attention to her desk. Lucien took my elbow and steered me down the corridor and out of the police station. I collapsed on the top step.

"Darling Anne. I've been so worried about you. I'm sorry to hear about your friend." He sat next to me.

"Why are you here?"

"They called me yesterday and asked me to come in. I returned on the ferry this morning. They had questions for me about your friend, Gilda. I confirmed you were staying next door."

"I can't stay there any longer," I said. "I had to move out."

He patted my good shoulder. "Nonsense, you must stay. I'll arrange it. You need a comfortable place to rest, Anne. You've just lost a friend."

"I thought you were going to be gone for a few days."

"Where have you been staying? Let's get your things and return you to your sanctuary."

My sanctuary? Home was my sanctuary, but I was tired and sore. Home was a three-hour plane ride away. I pictured the kidney-shaped pool and the shady patio. I wanted to fall asleep listening to the waves gently lapping my private beach.

"Are you sure it's okay?" I asked him.

His only answer was to pull me up and take my arm as we descended the steps. I directed him to the condo to pick up my belongings, and he waited in the car while I packed. As we drove away, I texted Luke.

I found a ride back. Thanks for taking care of me.

Lucien pulled the car into the long driveway and parked by the gray house. I stared up at the imposing facade and wondered who owned it and how Sandy had known them. *Gilda,* I corrected myself. Not Sandy.

Lucien carried my bag with one hand and took my arm with the other. He guided me along the gravel path. I turned the key in the lock and opened the door. The guest house was bright and airy. Welcoming. I stepped inside, and Lucien followed me.

CHAPTER 7

I walked straight through the house and collapsed on a chaise on the patio. Lucien dropped my bag and followed me outside.

"We need to keep you busy. What shall we do?" Lucien asked.

"Lucien, do you have a regular job?"

"Not really."

"I'm supposed to rest because of my arm," I told him. "I just got out of the hospital."

"When were you in the hospital?" he asked.

"Last night."

"You're feeling better now?"

I nodded. "Tired." I paused. "Overwhelmed."

"Let's keep you out of trouble. I have an idea. Best place for you today. The casino. It's indoors and air-conditioned. What do you think?"

"The casino?"

"Perfect, right?"

"At this hour in the morning?"

"No, of course not. Relax here for a bit. I have to run some errands. I'll be back in a while, we'll grab lunch, and then we'll go to the casino."

I didn't have any other ideas, and I didn't want to sit in the guest house stewing about Sandy. I agreed, and he promised to return in an hour.

I unpacked again—into the same bedroom I'd used before. As I was about to step into the shower, a text arrived from Luke.

Where did you go?

I raised my hand to my lips, remembering his long kiss. But Luke was a dead end, a mistake I only wanted to make once. And I'd made that mistake several years ago. With Chad.

Chad was also tall and tan, with a mop of curly hair. One coy smile and I was his. I couldn't decide if I wanted to run my hands through his unruly hair or trim it, tame it into something I could control. He moved in, and we played house for a few happy months before he started working less and surfing more. Construction jobs became scarce and then stopped altogether. I paid the bills, but there was never anything left over. We fought, we made up, and then we repeated the cycle over and over until one day, he just stopped coming home.

A year later, I saw him in a grocery store with a baby and a baby mama. His hair was short and neat. She'd tamed him and dressed him in a white button-down shirt, and I wondered what caused the change. Was it the failed contraception, the responsibility of a new, tiny human, or had he simply loved her more?

He didn't see me in the grocery store because his world was the two of them, and I didn't mind. I was happy for him. If I'd been face to face with her, I probably would have thanked her because I was better off alone.

Luke was a good guy, but he was a Chad. Another dead-end. The dangerous kind that could draw me in with a quick smile. I needed to keep him at arm's length.

Resting, I texted back, and my phone remained quiet.

\#

Lucien returned in an hour. He drove fast—like he was trying to outrun something. I gripped the door handle as he whipped the car around curves. My hair swirled wildly in the hot ocean breeze, blocking my view. When he finally slowed the car and pulled to a stop, he rested his hand on mine, and my heart, already beating too fast, almost burst. We were at the vista point where he'd taken me before.

"I made reservations, but we're early. Figured we could pass the time here."

He came around to my side and took my hand as I stepped from the car, and he didn't let go. We followed the narrow path. I was unsteady, still slightly queasy, and Lucien's strong grip was a comfort.

"Something you said made me curious. You told me that you have no family. What happens at holidays?"

It was a common question, and I answered it with my standard response, "Some people are alone on holidays."

"You don't have grandparents or cousins?"

I shook my head. "I have an aunt. She tried to stay close, but seeing me made her sad. She still invites me occasionally, but I don't think she's disappointed when I decline. My only living grandparent is my grandfather, and he's in a care facility in Georgia because he has dementia. I never see him. I never really knew him."

I assumed he was feeling what everyone feels when they imagine me sitting alone on Christmas morning: pity. But he stayed silent, and I wondered if he understood. Maybe he'd lost someone too.

Once I got used to it, being alone on the holidays wasn't that bad. I made all of my own choices: what to do, what to eat. But last Christmas was different. I had Sandy. She wanted to travel over the holiday, but I convinced her to stay with me. We picked out a tree and decorated it, and I forced her to sing carols while we drank too much spiked cider. She spent the night, and in the morning, I made bacon and cinnamon rolls, and we ate until we were sick. She told me it was the best Christmas she'd ever had. But we only had the one, and now I was alone again.

"What happened to your family?" he asked.

"They were killed in a car accident. My parents and my younger brother and sister."

He let go of my hand and wrapped his arm around me, and I endured the pity to feel him next to me. I leaned into him and told him the rest of the story because I knew he would ask anyway.

"I wasn't in the car. I was seventeen, old enough to stay home by myself. No one could predict it would become a permanent arrangement."

I was grateful for his silence. I rested my head on his shoulder, and we watched the rippled sea. Endless waves approached from distant places.

There was a time when I wished I'd been in the car that day. I could have enjoyed that final day at the beach. If I'd set aside my selfish teenage attitude, I could have splashed in the waves and built sandcastles with my brother and sister. Perhaps my presence would have been enough to alter the course of events. Sometimes, I wished that I'd died alongside them, but I hadn't felt that way in a long time. Life marched along and carried me with it.

#

After lunch, we visited the casino. Most of the tables were empty; a few people sat at slot machines. Lucien gave me a plastic card pre-loaded with a cash value, and he taught me how to use the machines. It wasn't difficult—easier than using my dishwasher. He had a strategy for choosing a game, and he moved around the room at random intervals. I played slowly, watching the chatty dealers and the cocktail waitresses who rarely stood still. Lucien checked on me occasionally, but for the most part, he was out of sight.

When I became bored with playing, I went to find him. It was a small casino, but he was nowhere to be seen. I selected a machine with a good vantage point of the room and pretended to play while I waited and watched. Thirty minutes passed, but there was still no sign of him.

I tried not to panic, but I couldn't think of an explanation for his disappearance. I wandered the entire floor once again. Searching took more effort since the tables were busier. Still, he didn't appear. I couldn't call or text him because I didn't have his number. I checked my phone anyway and found another text from Luke, but I ignored it. I thought about calling a taxi and returning to the house, but if Lucien showed up, he wouldn't know I'd gone, so I settled on waiting.

I was anxious and distracted by every movement around me. I barely noticed the machine's display as I continued pressing buttons, and another thirty minutes passed. I was scanning the room again, studying each face, when I recognized a man by the roulette table. Terry, the guy from the purchasing department. I blinked, trying to clear my vision, and assumed my brain was playing tricks, but when he reached up to adjust his glasses, I knew it was Terry.

Why was Terry on the island? It couldn't be a coincidence. He was the other person involved in the questionable wire transfers—he'd been the one that ordered them. He and Sandy-Gilda were connected. No, I was overreacting. It had to be a coincidence. A daily, non-stop flight connected Saint Martin and Miami. It was a popular vacation destination. But an uneasiness settled in my stomach.

A tap on the shoulder startled me.

"Anne," Lucien said.

I let out the breath I'd been holding. "I couldn't find you."

"I ducked into a poker room and lost track of time," he said. "Ready to go?"

On the way to the exit, I looked over my shoulder for Terry, but he'd disappeared. I wondered if he'd seen me.

Lucien was quiet on the way back to the guest house. He pulled into the driveway and reached over to squeeze my hand.

"Did you have a good day?" he asked.

"Yes," I answered. "Thanks."

"I'm afraid I'm engaged for the rest of the evening. You'll be alright on your own?"

I nodded. Of course, I would.

"I'll bring breakfast in the morning, and we can discuss what to do tomorrow."

I let myself out of the car and walked back to the guest house.

The pool mocked me, sparkling with the late afternoon sun. I couldn't swim because of my arm, but I longed to float, weightless. I compromised and sat on the second step, submerged to my chest, resting my arm on a towel by the pool's edge.

Why was Terry here? What was the connection between him and Sandy? *Gilda*, I reminded myself. And how did I fit into it?

The pool step was uncomfortable after twenty minutes, so I toweled off and pulled on the only swim cover-up I'd packed. I'd never worn it. It was a bit risqué—a black, open crocheted pattern that didn't actually cover up anything, but there wasn't anyone to see me. I made a salad for dinner and poured myself a glass of wine. I was sitting down to eat on the patio when there was a knock on the door.

"Luke!" I exclaimed from the doorway.

"You weren't answering my texts, so I came to find you. I just wanted to know that you're okay. Can I come in?" he asked.

"Of course," I answered.

I led him into the kitchen and felt subconscious about my cover-up as he stared.

"You shouldn't swim," he scolded.

"I didn't. I sat on the step, and now I'm having dinner. Can I get you something?"

"No, thanks. Go ahead and eat. Why did you leave?" When I didn't answer, he continued, "Did I do something wrong?" he asked.

"No, of course not," I answered.

"Why then?"

"Because I couldn't stay at the condo."

"Why here? Do you feel safe here?"

"As safe I would anywhere, I guess. Whatever danger Sandy faced is over now. She's dead."

"Are you okay?"

"Of course, I'm not okay. Sandy was murdered, Luke. Beaten and strangled." I shuddered as I said the words. My imagination threatened new images, but I kept them at bay by talking. "I had to go back to meet with the detective inspector because I wanted him to know there might be a connection between the money I was accused of stealing and Gilda. And today, I saw someone else from the company where I worked. He must be involved. I mean, Sandy was the person I wired funds to, but I didn't know it at the time. I thought she was my friend, but…"

I gulped my wine, and he watched me, waiting for me to finish.

"I thought she liked me. It's obvious that she was just using me to get to the money. The thing I don't get is…if they have the money, why am I here? What does any of this have to do with me?"

"Are they setting you up to take the fall? You said they accused you of stealing money at work, right?"

"Yes, but it doesn't make any sense. Sandy invited me here. She *wanted* me to come. If she was setting me up, wouldn't she want me to stay home? I can't take the fall from here."

"Someone else must be involved," he said.

"Why?"

"Because she's dead, Anne," he said. "Someone killed her."

We were both quiet as the weight of his words settled around us like a heavy fog.

"Anne, come stay with me. I want you close so I can keep an eye on you. You shouldn't be here alone. You might be in danger."

"I'm fine here. I like it." I paused. "And I've imposed on you enough already."

He smiled at that. "Yes, you certainly have, but I don't mind. I *want* to take care of you."

My next words sounded angrier than I intended. "I don't need anyone to take care of me, Luke. Certainly not you."

"I didn't mean it that way, Anne. Jesus, you're stubborn. I respect that you're used to taking care of yourself, but sometimes it's okay to let someone help you—that's all I meant."

I didn't answer.

"Look, I'm going to go. You have my number, so call if you need me."

I nodded.

"Can I look at your arm again before I go?"

I nodded again and led him to the bathroom, where I kept my first aid supplies. I closed my eyes as he unwrapped the bandage.

"Does it hurt?" he asked.

I flinched but not from the pain. It was the ache my body felt at his touch. My lips still burned with the memory of him.

"It doesn't hurt," I told him.

I watched him in the mirror as he turned my arm left and right, inspecting the stitches. He probed my arm gently with his fingertips. His forearm brushed against my bare skin, and I bit my lip.

"Any tenderness?" he asked.

Our eyes met in the mirror, and I knew he felt it too—the heat between us. He looked away and focused on wrapping my arm in clean gauze. I steadied myself against the bathroom counter until he was done. Then, I walked him to the front door. I wanted him to leave. But part of me wanted something else.

"I'm sorry about your friend," he said softly.

He paused in the doorway, and I swallowed loudly.

"Call me if you need anything." He spoke slowly. Neither of us reached to open the front door.

"Thanks, Luke," I said.

My voice broke as I said his name, and with it his resolve. He leaned toward me and took my face in his hands, pulling me into him, and I kissed him back. He pressed me against the wall, kissing my lips and my neck. At my shoulder, he lingered, his lips brushing my skin lightly, catching his breath.

"Anne," he whispered.

As his hands moved downwards, his fingers caught in the crocheted holes of my cover-up. He pulled at the fabric frantically, stretching it taut across my body, and it finally gave way and fell to the floor. He hesitated for a moment, staring, chest heaving. Then he lifted me and carried me into the bedroom.

CHAPTER 8

I woke with the sunrise. Luke had left hours before, whispering a hasty goodbye in the darkness, but his kiss became part of my dream, and I slept on. The sheets were wrapped around my legs, and I fought to free myself. A breeze through the open window lifted the tiny hairs along my back, and I quivered with the memory of Luke's hands along my spine. His scent lingered on me, in my hair. I pulled a tight bun at the top of my head and dressed.

Letting him into my bed was a momentary weakness. He'd stirred my emotions, forcing me to feel something, and then he'd been there in the wake of the storm that followed. He'd hesitated a few times, studying me, silently asking permission, and I'd pulled him back to me. He was a considerate lover, instinctively understanding when to slow down or stop. I'd needed him with an urgency I hadn't experienced in several years.

But in the morning light, I remembered Chad. Luke was so much like him—gorgeous, kind. They even had the same goofy smile. I'd loved Chad—the only time I'd ever felt that way about a man. But Chad needed too much. He expected me to open up and share myself. He wanted to *understand* me. At first, I liked sharing small things—how fascinated I'd been by my brother's tiny, chubby hands, the way my mother wore her hair, and the annoying way my sister followed me everywhere. But it wasn't enough. He pushed, and I shut him out.

Luke reminded me of Chad. It had to be a one-time thing.

I needed a distraction. I couldn't swim, so I sat on the patio, opened my laptop, and scanned my email. Still nothing from work. It was a strange feeling not to go to the office after thirteen years at the same company—almost half my lifetime. In all that time, I'd only taken occasional sick days. Two years ago, I took a week off when Mr. Sampson demanded that I use some of my vacation time, but I returned to such a backlog that he never suggested it again.

Were they handling everything without me? I considered emailing someone in the office to discretely ask what was happening, but I hesitated. What if they asked me about the wires? I didn't have any answers.

I logged out of my work account and opened my personal emails. My credit card payment was due tomorrow, but payment was already scheduled. Delete. I received a coupon from a restaurant near my house, but I didn't know if I'd return before it expired. Delete. Spam. Delete.

My thoughts returned to Sandy. Why was she killed? For the money? That made sense; three million dollars was enough of a reason to kill. Perhaps Luke was right, and she had a partner—someone other than Terry. Or was it Terry? But it was hard to picture Terry as a killer. He was a nervous kid. He must have been manipulated into helping Sandy.

Someone else had to be involved. Someone killed Sandy because they didn't want to share the money. But who? Would the police figure it out?

I deleted more spam, but the next email caught my eye. *HoneyWyld,* the subject line read—the name of the farmer's market stand where I'd met Sandy.

Anne, if you're reading this, it means something has gone wrong, it began.

The return email read *sandeebrownee@gmail.com.* It was sent two hours ago. How did a dead person send emails?

I think they're onto me.

Lucien's voice startled me. "Morning, darling Anne," he called out. I snapped my laptop shut.

"I hope you're not working," he called out. "You're supposed to be on vacation." He sat and slid a coffee cup across the table toward me. "Are you feeling alright?" He asked. "You're ghostly pale." I couldn't answer. "Anne," he said, sensing my panic. "What's wrong?"

"She emailed me." The words slipped out.

"What?" he looked momentarily shaken, but he recovered quickly. "Who? Your friend?"

I nodded. "Sandy, I mean Gilda, whatever. She emailed me," I repeated.

"When?" he asked.

I opened the laptop to double-check the time, but I'd seen it correctly the first time. "Today. A few hours ago."

"What did she say?"

"That's what you want to know? Not *how* she sent it? She's dead, Lucien. She can't send emails anymore."

"What did she say, Anne?" He was more insistent now.

"I haven't finished reading it yet."

I paused to take a sip of coffee, and my hand trembled, but I had to keep reading.

Be careful, Anne. Don't trust anyone. Find the money. Take it and run. Make a new life for yourself. You were a great friend. I'm sorry for ruining your life. I hope you can forgive me someday. Love, Sandy.

My eyes teared up. From fear or grief or a combination, I wasn't sure. Lucien turned the laptop so he could read the screen.

"What's this at the end?" he asked.

I wiped my tears and looked. There was more—a postscript.

P.S. Find HoneyWyld.

"I don't know," I said. "That's how we met. Buying honey at a farmer's market. But I don't know what she means. HoneyWyld is local to Miami, and I can't go home."

"Feels like she's trying to tell you something. What does she mean find the money, Anne?" he asked.

"I don't know. Maybe the money she stole from where I worked? Maybe she wanted to give me a chance to find it and return it? But I don't want to find it. I don't want to be a part of this."

"But if you did find it, you could clear your name and return to your life. I could help you, Anne."

I re-read the email. *Find the money, Anne. Make a new life for yourself.*

"If you find the money, would you do as she says? Take it and run?" he asked.

He hadn't asked, would you run away with me, but it felt implied. Or was that just my overactive imagination? I pushed my chair away from the table.

"Anne?"

He wanted an answer, and his insistence made me angry.

"I don't know, Lucien! You're probably right. I should find the money, return it, and go back to my life, but I can't help thinking that if I start chasing the money, I'm deeper into this than I ever wanted to be. If I start actively poking my nose in it, then whoever killed her is surely going to find me and…"

"I won't let anything happen to you, Anne."

He caught my arm as I walked past, and I didn't pull away. His dark eyes bored through me, searching for answers I didn't have.

"Why do you care? You don't even know me. Why do you want to help?"

He grinned. "I told you. I'm a sucker for a good Southern drama. And I don't have anything better to do today."

"I need to think," I said.

#

I needed a swim. Swimming was my daily escape. It calmed me. I enjoyed the weightlessness and the repetitive motion as I pulled myself through the water. Under the water, sound was muffled like a cocoon. But I couldn't submerge my arm, so I settled for a walk along the beach. Lucien joined me, but he stayed quiet.

Find the money, Anne. Make a new life for yourself.

I repeated Sandy's words in my head. *A new life.* It wasn't the first time she'd mentioned it. "What would you do if you didn't have to work, Anne?" she'd ask.

"But I do have to work," I'd answer, and then she'd roll her eyes and toss a throw pillow at me.

If Sandy stole money, had she invited me here to share it? Is that what she'd been asking all along? There were so many questions, but the biggest one was: did I want to find the money? Lucien was right. If I did figure it out, I could go home. I'd get my life back. But what did I really have to go back to? A lonely house? A dull, dead-end job that I liked because it was safe? With money, I'd have other choices. With *stolen* money. The only option was to find it and give it back.

I glanced at Lucien, and he smiled back at me. He buzzed with excitement about the search for the money, and that meant if I agreed to the search, we'd spend more time together.

"Okay," I said. "Let's find HoneyWyld."

We returned to the guest house and ran a Google search for HoneyWyld. The closest result was a hair salon called Honey & Wilda.

"Fancy a haircut?" he asked.

"No, but I could use a shampoo. It's difficult to wash my hair one-armed."

"Fantastic!" He exclaimed. "Let's go check it out. Meet you in the driveway in five minutes."

The island was quiet; it was too early for the tourists. Lucien parked in front of the salon, but when I stepped out of the car he remained seated.

"I'll wait here," he said.

The salon was deserted except for the owner, Wilda. Her short stature made her long braids seem like an unnecessary weight, but they swayed easily as she moved. She had friendly, amber eyes and a thick French accent. She agreed to shampoo my hair and suggested a deep conditioning treatment.

"Your hair is…broken," she said, frowning as she ran her fingers through my brittle strands. I smiled. I spent a lot of time in a pool, and my hair suffered. Lucien's convertible rides weren't doing it any favors either.

She tipped my head into a large shampoo bowl and worked up a lavender-scented lather. I closed my eyes as her strong hands massaged my scalp.

"How did you find me?" she asked.

"My friend Sandy told me to come here."

"You're Anne?" she asked. Her hands continued massaging, unfazed by the mention of Sandy.

"Yes, I'm Anne," I confirmed, surprised.

She rinsed my hair. "She spoke of you," she said, applying conditioner that smelled of coconut and reminded me of Luke. "She said you'd come."

I wondered if Wilda knew Sandy was dead. I didn't want to be the one to deliver such news, so I sat quietly, my head in the bowl, my hair wet with the conditioning treatment.

"I remember the first time she came into my shop. My name reminded her of you. The time you met."

"Yes," I said, smiling at the memory. "At a market stall. I was buying honey, and she stopped to taste it. She spilled honey on my arm, and when she tried to wipe it off, it got on her hands. She kept trying to wipe the honey with a paper towel, but little bits of paper stuck to her…and me. We had to find a restroom to wash up. She always said we've been stuck together ever since."

But not anymore.

"She probably told you that story already," I said.

Wilda nodded. "Her version is different." I wondered how Sandy's version differed, but I didn't ask.

She set a timer and wandered away. I stared at the ceiling and wondered why Wilda and I knew Sandy as Sandy and not Gilda.

Wilda was the HoneyWyld Sandy wanted me to find, but I didn't know what to ask. Why did she want me to come here?

A timer sounded with a bright *ding*, and Wilda returned and rinsed my hair. Then she led me to her chair and blow-dried my hair, pulling on it forcefully with a brush. I watched her in the mirror. How did you ask a complete stranger if a mutual acquaintance had left three million dollars for you?

"You need a trim," she said. No judgment, just a statement of fact.

I shrugged. "Next time, maybe."

The mirror showed a different version of myself than I remembered. The sun had burned highlights into my normally dull, brown hair, and freckles had sprouted across my nose from the time I'd spent in the sun. I removed my wallet from my bag, but Wilda shook her head. "No, Anne. A friend of Sandy's is a friend of mine."

"Thanks," I said.

I moved to leave, and she looked at me expectantly. "Something happened to her?"

I nodded and swallowed the lump that formed in my throat. Her face was stoic, but her eyes betrayed sadness. She didn't ask for details, and I didn't share.

"This is a strange question, but did she leave something for me?"

She reached behind the counter and brought out an envelope.

"Sandy gave this to me a few days ago. For you. She was worried about something, and she asked me to hold it for you. Be safe, Anne." She hugged me. "*A bientot.*"

"Thank you," I said, hoping she understood my thanks encompassed the shampooing, whatever I'd find in the envelope, and her kindness to our mutual friend.

I returned to the car to find Lucien on his phone. When he saw me, he ended the call abruptly. "Well?" he asked.

I held up the envelope triumphantly.

"What's in it?"

"I haven't looked yet, but before I go anywhere in that car, I need a scarf or a hat. The wind is killing my hair. I'm going to pop into that shop across the street and find something."

"And make me wait," he said.

"Yes," I grinned. "You must wait."

He flopped across the seat dramatically, and I laughed. I'd lied—not completely, I did need a scarf, but I also wanted to open the envelope on my own. Sandy told me not to trust anyone, and that included Lucien. I wanted to know what was in the envelope before I decided to share it. I crossed the street and entered the shop—a clothing boutique with mannequins in flowery, pastel dresses. Not my style, but I only needed a scarf.

"*Bonjour!*" called a woman from the back of the shop.

"Hello," I answered.

"Can I help you find something?" She approached me, weaving around the racks of clothing.

"A scarf?" I asked.

"Ah, you've just seen Wilda, haven't you? Your hair is lovely." She gestured for me to follow her to the back, and she pointed out a table with silk scarves. They looked luxurious and pricey, and I ran my hand along the smoothness of the silk display, admiring the vibrant colors. I carefully slid one from the pile that reminded me of wispy clouds in a summer sky.

"Ah, that's lovely. Matches your eyes." The woman said.

I loosely wrapped it around my hair. "I'm riding in a convertible," I explained.

"*Oui*," she said. "And what else? A new dress?"

I didn't need a new dress, but I had a very limited wardrobe because I'd packed poorly. Also, I owned nothing that matched my hair.

She read my silence as a yes. "Something in blue as well, I think." She disappeared around a display, and I could hear her muttering softly in French. "*Et voila!*" she called out and returned with a pale blue dress, a wrap-around style with tiny white flowers and a flounce at the bottom edge. Without asking, she herded me into a dressing room.

I changed into the dress and was surprised that I liked it. The soft blue accentuated my new tan. Additional dresses flew over the top of the door, but I ignored them and sat on a tiny stool in the corner to open the envelope.

Chapter 9

Play the game, Anne. Trust Wilda. She holds the key.

I stared at the mostly white page. *Play the game, Anne.* What was she trying to tell me? What was the game? Is that what she thought she was doing? This was a game to her?

The saleswoman's voice interrupted my barrage of questions. "How is everything working for you?" She assumed I was still trying on dresses.

"I like the first one," I called out. "Can I wear it out?"

"Yes, but, of course," she answered.

She circled me several times at the counter, removing the tag, smoothing wrinkles, and I paid for the dress and the scarf and left the shop with my discarded clothes in a shopping bag.

Trust Wilda. She holds the key.

What did that mean?

Lucien was slumped in the seat, eyes closed under the shade of his hat. I tiptoed past him and returned to Wilda's salon, glancing back at the car to ensure he remained hidden underneath his hat.

A man sat in her chair. I heard the snip-snip of her scissors for a moment, and then she called out, "I'll be right over." She bent to his ear and spoke quietly and then approached me, wiping her hands on a towel. She motioned for me to follow with a subtle jerk of her head and led me into an office in the back. She stood behind a desk and stared at me.

"Her note said that you hold the key."

She smiled and nodded and retrieved something from her desk drawer.

"Sandy told me to save this for your second visit and said I wasn't supposed to give it to you unless you used the word key. I didn't understand why. It wasn't like her to be so mysterious. Strange, *oui?*"

"Thank you," I said as she handed me a keyring with a single key, a wooden charm embossed with my name, and a piece of thick paper that read: *The bank across from the snail.*

"Do you know what that means?" I asked.

She shrugged. "No. I have to get back to my client. Come see me again, Anne," she said. "I'll trim your hair." She gave me a quick hug.

Before I stepped outside, I dropped the keyring into my shopping bag, covering it with my T-shirt, and then I returned to Lucien.

"Thanks for waiting," I told him as I slipped back into the car.

"The suspense is killing me," he said.

"Really? You couldn't be that anxious. You were napping."

I handed him the piece of paper and watched his reaction, but his expression never changed. "Do you know what it means?" he asked.

"No idea," I said, and I wasn't lying. I didn't know what Sandy was trying to tell me. But I didn't tell him about the key.

"You haven't said anything about my dress," I said.

"You look lovely," he answered. With his accent, the word lovely became something more—a caress. I felt his eyes on me, and then he ran the back of his hand lightly down my arm, and I trembled. "Lunch?" he asked.

I bit my bottom lip and nodded.

#

Lucien pestered me all afternoon.

"What does it mean, Anne? Play the game? Did you play a game together?"

"No idea," I kept repeating. I wasn't lying. The only game I could remember was a mini-golf session late at night after too many mojitos. She'd won, of course. If I was drunk enough to agree to play mini-golf, I was too drunk to play well.

"I don't know, Lucien. There must be something else. Something I'm missing."

"She must have thought it would trigger a memory. Think, Anne."

But there was nothing to remember. It wasn't something we'd talked about. Eventually, he gave up and suggested a swim, and we walked down to the tiny beach by the guest house. I kicked a few rocks away to clear a sandy spot big enough for a blanket, and I sat and watched him wade into the water.

By the snail. I pictured a giant bronze snail statue, hot to the touch in the midday sun. Even if such a ridiculous statue existed, how would I find it? I could ask Lucien to drive me around searching for a giant snail, but on this small island, it would probably be faster to visit every bank. And I didn't want to tell Lucien about the key. Not yet.

I hated snails. Each year, the slimy pests launched a nightly assault on my butter lettuce, easily crossing every barrier I constructed: coffee grounds, eggshells. I'd tried everything, and nothing saved my lettuce from the voracious snails. I doubted Sandy was talking about garden snails, though, because she didn't garden. She barely cooked. The only time she ever mentioned snails was after she'd returned from a weekend in Québec.

"Anne, have you ever eaten snails?" she asked.

"Of course not," I answered with a sneer. "Disgusting."

"They're actually quite delicately flavored," she said. "They just taste like garlic and butter."

"I could eat garlic bread and get the same result," I answered dryly.

"Sure, but you'd miss out on the escargot experience." She'd pronounced escargot with a dramatic flair, "Es-car-go. It's French for snail, you know?"

I'd rolled my eyes. "Yeah, Sandy. Everybody knows that."

The snails were forgotten as Lucien emerged from the sea. Water ran off him—rivers and tributaries negotiating the geography of his muscle tone. He stretched out on the blanket next to me, and I lay next to him, propped on my left side. He didn't seem to mind me staring.

"I'm going to take a nap," he announced. "And then I'll make you dinner."

I settled into the curve of his arm and closed my eyes. Sleep was impossible. I could *feel* him. I lay still against the warmth of his skin and let my imagination wander into the places I wasn't brave enough to go.

#

It was the first evening he'd stayed late. Long after the sun had set, we remained on the patio at the guest house. His silence was mostly comfortable, but my anticipation of intimacy grew with the darkness. I stood at the railing, watching the moon rise. Its reflection danced across the water, infecting me with its lightness, and I held tight to the railing.

The night was filled with the intoxicating perfume of the trumpet vine and just enough breeze to gently nudge the flounce at the hem of my dress. It tickled the backs of my knees, and when I almost couldn't stand it any longer, I heard the soft scraping of the chair legs as he rose and approached me from behind.

"It's late, Anne darling." He spoke quietly into my hair. "Let's get you to bed."

I turned to him, and he was compelled—by the moonlight and the soft lapping of the sea, to kiss me. His lips were full, his mouth different than Luke's, open and strong.

"Come with me," he said, pulling me along into the house. He slowed in the hallway. There were too many doors, and I pointed to my bedroom.

"Anne," he said. "You need rest."

"Later," I said.

He kissed me again, but he held back and pulled away with a long sigh.

"Rest, darling."

And he left me with only the doorway for support. I collapsed into my bed and smelled Luke among the tangled sheets.

#

In the morning, I was in the kitchen examining the key from Wilda when I heard Lucien's steps on the patio. I opened the nearest kitchen drawer and dropped the key inside.

"I assume there are really great French restaurants here?" I asked, joining him outside. "Since half of the island is French."

"Of course. You like French food?"

I'd never been to a French restaurant. "Maybe. Do you know of any?"

"Are you just trying to distract me from asking about your friend's cryptic note?"

I smiled. "You got me."

"It won't work. Your friend hid money on this island, and we're going on a treasure hunt."

"So, it's just about the money for you?"

He pulled me into an embrace. "Not at all."

"Now, *you're* trying to distract me."

"You're quite hard to resist," he said.

"You resisted well enough last night."

He stiffened as if I'd hurt his feelings. "Anne, I'm a gentleman. I won't take advantage of you."

"Even if I want you to?"

I hoped my words came across as playful and coy, but I tried and failed to read his expression. He tightened his grip around my waist and whispered, "Anne, I missed the signals. Give me another chance?"

I couldn't answer because my heart was in my throat. He kissed me until we were both breathless, and then he began to work his way down my neck slowly, but I was impatient. My hands were in his hair, pressing him, urging him along. He fought me, relishing my frustration. With a finger, he slid the strap of my tank top from my shoulder, and I let out a soft moan as he reached the top of my breast.

A loud knock at the door interrupted him. Lucien chuckled softly as he pulled away to answer the door. I followed him into the living room, pulling the strap of my tank top back into place and silently cursed whoever interrupted us.

A uniformed policeman strode into the room, followed by Detective Inspector Moreau. "Anne Wilson, you are being detained for questioning regarding the death of Arthur Sampson, and we are executing a search of your house."

Lucien told me to stay silent.

"I'll find you a solicitor," he called out.

The officer held my arm and marched me up the terraces, past the long pool, along the gravel path, and pushed me into a waiting police car. I stared out the window as we drove, the scenery passing by unseen.

Mr. Sampson? My boss?

At the station, I was placed in an interview room. Not accompanied or invited but placed —like an object and left alone with my questions for over an hour. Why Mr. Sampson? He was a nice man, soft-spoken and compassionate. Our last exchange had been an unfortunate one.

When the door finally opened, I felt relieved. It was hard to be alone with my questions.

"When was the last time you saw Arthur Sampson?" the detective inspector asked.

"Thursday. At my office in Florida."

He nodded. "And where were you Thursday night?"

"At home. Alone. What happened to Mr. Sampson?" I asked.

"I am not at liberty to discuss the details. The Miami police department contacted us and requested an interview with you."

"I didn't kill him. I liked him."

His face didn't register any response. "You argued with him on Thursday?"

"We didn't argue. He asked me questions, and I answered them. Then I asked for time off to come here. I came here because Sandy was in trouble."

He pursed his lips, thinking. "Have you ever been to Saint Martin before?"

I shook my head. "No."

"Can you explain why you transferred funds into a Saint Martin bank account three months ago?"

I had no idea what he was talking about. "No." The detective inspector watched me, reading my reaction. "I'm sorry. Can you repeat that? You found an account under my name? Here on the island?"

He nodded. "Three months ago, you opened an account at Banques des Antilles. The account was funded with a single wire transfer originating from a Swiss bank under the name Sandy Brown. The amount of that wire was three million US dollars."

He had a methodical way of speaking, pausing often. I was grateful for the pauses as it took time to process his words.

"The account that was opened—that wasn't me. I wasn't here then."

"The account was opened online. Not in person."

Oh.

"I have no idea what you're talking about."

I shifted in my seat and waited for his next question. "You were friends with Gilda Jorgensen."

"I knew her as Sandy."

"How long had you known her?"

"A year. I already told you this. Yes, I was friends with Sandy, and I was the one that told you about the missing funds, remember? And I told you that I remembered the name Gilda Jorgensen, but I swear I thought all the wires I sent were legitimate. There are records to show the orders."

"Yes, the company confirmed there were no irregularities in the wires you made."

He sat quietly for a few more minutes while I thought about the implications of his words. No irregularities? "But if there were no irregularities, then why was Mr. Sampson killed?"

"That's what we are trying to determine. Today, we executed a search of your house. At this time, I am not arresting you, but you will surrender your passport. You will make yourself available for future questions regarding both cases."

"Of course," I said. "I want to help in any way I can."

He nodded, but he didn't look like he believed me.

"So, I can go?" I asked.

"Is there anything else? Anything you haven't already told me?"

I shook my head. Because there *was* more—Terry and the email from Sandy, but I didn't understand the connection to Mr. Sampson's death, and both things made me seem more involved than I was. And I didn't want to answer any more questions without a lawyer.

Chapter 10

Lucien was waiting for me out front.

"I found an attorney and made an appointment for you in two hours. I can drop you at the appointment, but you'll have to find your own way back. I have a prior engagement. I'll be back later, and you can fill me in."

He handed me a slip of paper with the name Francois Laurent and two phone numbers. I took the paper but didn't say anything. I wasn't used to people doing things for me. Selecting an attorney was an important decision. He should have asked my opinion.

"The second number is mine. Call me if anything goes wrong." He squeezed my hand. "But it won't," he continued. "You'll be fine."

I didn't feel fine. I felt so many other things: fear, anger, and confusion. Why had Sandy moved the money into an account in my name three months ago?

We returned to the gray house. Lucien parked in the motor court, and I scowled back at the gray house until he opened my door.

"Don't worry," he said.

He walked me to the guest house and followed me inside. The patio table held our breakfast dishes, but the rest of the house was a shambles. Couch cushions lay on the floor, kitchen cupboards were ajar, and the bed linens were askew.

"Anne, this…" he gestured to the room.

"I'll move out."

He nodded. "That's probably a good idea."

"I'll clean it up." I began to cry.

"No, no, darling. Don't cry. I can't handle that. Come on, there now," he patted my back. "You're just hungry and tired. Clean your face, we'll find you some lunch, and you'll be right as rain. Yes? I'll be back in a few moments."

He left by the back steps, and I went to the bedroom to splash cool water on my face. My bloodshot eyes stared back from the mirror. I wouldn't be alright. I needed a place to stay. And even a few nights in a hotel would put a huge dent in my savings.

Find the money, Anne.

I remembered the key and ran to the kitchen and yanked the drawer open. The key lay nestled between a bottle opener and a spatula, hidden in plain sight.

I dropped it into my pocket. All I needed now was a snail.

#

The attorney was a fidgety man with a pencil-thin mustache and too much hair gel. When he wasn't doodling in the margins of his legal pad, he chewed on a ballpoint pen. He began the conversation with a few general questions and then asked me to tell him what happened in the interview room at the police station. Once I began the story, I couldn't find my way out of it, and I rambled for several minutes.

While I spoke, he nodded often. He occasionally interrupted with a, "*oui, bien sur,*" as if my story sounded reasonable.

"What should I do now?" I asked.

His face contorted as if someone had dipped the end of his pen in lemon juice. "Nothing. You haven't been arrested, so there is nothing to do but wait for the police to build a case against you. When you are arrested, call me."

I'd wasted an hour.

I returned to the guest house to clean and pack and search for a snail. The search browser remained empty while I thought about what to type. The cursor blinked impatiently, like a tapping toe. I typed *snail* and hit the Enter key. The results included articles about snails—nothing helpful. I changed the search to the French version: *l'escargot.* The top search result was a French restaurant. I entered the address into a map app and searched for banks nearby. Just across the street was a bank.

The bank across from the snail. Was it too easy?

I cleared the browser history and called a taxi.

#

The bank occupied the corner unit on a busy street. I stood out front, weighing my options. There were many reasons to walk away and call the detective inspector, but the email and the key were damning evidence that I was involved. Inside the bank was an opportunity to take control, but the most compelling reason to walk into the bank was to satisfy my curiosity.

I asked the teller for access to the safety deposit box, and she directed me to a desk at the end of the counter. She met me there and asked me to fill out a slip with my name, address, and box number. When she asked for ID, I panicked for a moment. I didn't have a passport, so I handed her my driver's license and held my breath until she replied, "Madame Wilson, everything looks in order. Please wait here for a moment?"

I watched the clock on the wall behind her desk. Two minutes clicked by in long seconds while I imagined the police arriving, arresting me, pushing me to the floor, and handcuffing me. I discreetly dabbed the sweat from my face with my sleeve.

She returned with a pleasant smile. "Will you please follow me?"

She led me into a small room with a table and two chairs, just like the interview room in the police station, but there was a notable difference: on the table sat a metal box. She inserted her key and gestured for me to do the same. The box clicked open, and she nodded. "Please return outside when you are complete."

I smiled at her mistake. If I found three million dollars in the box, would I be complete? Would that be the end of this?

I held my breath and opened the box.

The box held piles of cash. I counted fifteen stacks of US dollars in neatly bundled sets of ten thousand, and underneath the US dollars were Euro notes, another fifteen bundles of ten thousand. The last currency I didn't recognize. It was labeled East Caribbean Bank, and unlike the US and Euro bills, these included various denominations, all held together with a rubber band. Not a substantial amount—pocket money. The combined total was definitely not three million, but more cash than I'd ever held at one time.

There was also an envelope. Inside I found a passport, a single key, similar to the one on the keyring, and a letter from Sandy.

I opened the letter.

Anne. Sorry for the cloak and dagger. I had to make it difficult enough that nobody else could figure it out. And it won't get easier for you. You have to follow the clues. You have everything you need. You have to remember, Anne. Every story. You liked my stories, right? I just hope that you were listening to me.

Each clue leads to the next. There's no jumping ahead. The key in this envelope leads to the next one, and so forth. I won't tell you how many clues there are. I've been doing this for so long now I've forgotten anyway.

I'm sorry, Anne. If you make it to the drop I made about three weeks ago when it all started falling apart, you'll find a letter I wrote when I was drunk. But please don't read it. If you're here now, and I'm not with you, it means I'm gone anyway, and it doesn't really matter any longer.

This is my last drop. Stay safe, Anne. Don't trust anyone, and remember—you have everything you need.

I'd felt so many things about Sandy since arriving on the island. Anger, disappointment, shock. This was the first moment I truly missed her. I *had* enjoyed her stories. They made me laugh and made me dream of something more than my isolated life. Even in her death, she found a way to challenge me.

The passport was mine. It had the same picture as the one the police confiscated. A duplicate. How had she managed that? But it made sense. She would've had to become me to open the safety deposit box. It was in my name. And then she'd dropped it inside the box when she didn't need it anymore. Like a snake shedding its skin.

There was another key. This one had a tag that read, *Worst Paris story of all time.* My next clue.

This was her game.

I stared at the money and considered my options. I could take the money to the police station and turn myself in, but if this box held Sandy's apology, then perhaps the next one would include an explanation. In order to find it, I needed time and a place to stay. I needed the money. But if I took the money, I'd be involved, and whoever killed Sandy would come after me. Perhaps they'd come after me regardless.

I sat at the table, my right hand resting on the pile of cash while the clock on the wall across from me ticked off the seconds. Tick, tick. Only fourteen seconds passed before I placed one bundle of US dollars and the whole stack of Caribbean currency in my purse. I left the passport and pocketed the key. Then I locked the box, walked out of the room, nodded to the woman behind the desk, and left the bank.

I needed a place to stay. And a car.

#

The photographs in the window of the real estate office were variations on a repeating theme: ocean view, lounge chairs, pool. I wanted one.

"I can't afford much," I told the man in the sales office. Barely a man, a college student, maybe.

"And you're looking for something for at least a week?" he asked.

"Yes. I might extend it beyond a week. I don't have any set plans at the moment. Can I even afford something like that?" I pointed to the window.

"We have small villas. Let me see if we have anything available." He typed furiously and then turned the screen toward me. "This is a new listing. Very private, but it's not in a gated community if that matters. Keeps the cost down a little. It has beach access. One bedroom, pool, coffee maker." He flipped through a slide show, but by the third photo, I was in love.

"Do you take cash?" I asked.

"Sure," he said. "We'd need it up front. This place has a weekly rate of five thousand US, plus a security deposit of a thousand."

Gulp. Six thousand. I stared at the photo of the living room on his screen. It wasn't anything special—monochromatic degrees of beige other than the dark brown wicker furniture. But beyond the drab interior was a chartreuse lawn and a cornflower sky.

"I'll take it."

"Great. We also offer an additional daily housekeeping service—"

"No, thanks," I interrupted. "I can clean."

The paperwork was straightforward. I signed a rental agreement and counted out six thousand dollars. In return, I received a single key.

"Any idea where I can get a car?" I asked.

"There's a rental place at the airport," he said. "But a lot of tourists just rent scooters. There's a place to rent them a few blocks away."

I called a taxi. The idea of riding around the island on a scooter with bundles of cash seemed ridiculous. For some reason, the idea of carrying stolen cash was acceptable, but doing it on a scooter wasn't. It was good to know that I was able to draw a line somewhere.

The taxi driver knew of a car rental location closer than the airport, and I negotiated a low weekly rate on a smelly Hyundai Accent with a broken air conditioner. The stench of spoiled milk was tolerable when I rolled down the windows.

I used my phone to navigate to my new villa. It was nestled in a community of larger properties. The view wasn't breathtaking, and the pool was an oversized bathtub, but it was clean, comfortable, and private. I unpacked, unloaded the few groceries I had left into the fridge, and started a load of laundry.

After settling in, I followed a well-worn grassy trail for about four hundred yards. The path wound around a small hill and joined a trail from another villa, and ended at a white beach that stretched as far as I could see. Out in the water, several surfers bobbed in a rolling swell. As the waves approached the beach, they crested, curved, and crashed with enough force to spray sea mist in all directions, and the breeze carried it across the sand.

I crossed the hot sand and walked in the surf, cooling my toes in the water. Spending the money had been impulsive. Even though I was sure the money was stolen, I'd handed it over so easily, my justification inadequate. I did need a place to live while I followed Sandy's clues, but the expensive villa wasn't necessary. I'd *wanted* it.

I could pay it back. It would mean taking out a mortgage—I didn't have that kind of cash in my account. But thoughts of replacing it was just further justification. By pocketing the money and spending it, I'd crossed a line. I'd wanted something nice, something that I hadn't worked for, and maybe I even deserved it, but I knew it was wrong.

A blue bucket bounced in the surf just ahead of me. I skipped through the water to pick it up and carried it to a boy sitting in the sand, digging holes. He was blonde, about seven years old, and I thought of my brother, John.

John's curiosity had been insatiable. I was a teenager, anticipating my impending independence, and couldn't be bothered by his questions. He'd be twenty years old now. In college, probably. Still learning. I rarely allowed myself to wander down the road of what-ifs, but I knew John would've grown into a compassionate and intelligent young man. He'd probably study philosophy in an attempt to answer his favorite question: "Why?"

I smiled at the boy in the sand and wondered if he had an older sister. Years ago, I would have shouted at her across the sand. To tell her to help him build the sandcastle of his dreams because today could be his last day at the beach. But I wasn't angry at his sister for not being there with him any longer. Most seven-year-old boys get to celebrate their eighth birthdays.

I turned and headed back to the villa. I couldn't follow any more of Sandy's clues because the banks closed shortly, but I would start early in the morning. I'd play her game.

CHAPTER 11

I was standing in the kitchen, eyeing the few options for dinner, when my phone rang. I smiled as I saw his name. "Hi, Lucien," I answered the call.

"How did it go with Francois?"

"Fine. I told him the story, and he said we'd have to wait until the police built a case against me. And I found a place to stay."

"Do you have plans for tonight?"

"No," I said.

"I'm wrapping up a meeting at the casino. Can you meet me? Join me for dinner?"

"Sure," I drawled with my heaviest Southern accent. "What time?"

"Seven. I'll reserve a table. See you then."

Perhaps we could pick up where we'd left off before the police interrupted us? Only hours had passed, but it seemed like days. So much had changed in one day. I was sure Lucien would ask about the game. I heard Sandy's voice in my head. *Don't trust anyone.* Lucien wasn't involved; he was just a guy I bumped into at the meat counter, but for now, the keys would stay secret.

My arm was healing now. The redness had faded to a healthy pink, and I decided to swim. I changed into my suit, but before I slipped into the pool, my phone buzzed with a text from Luke.

How are you? He texted.

I'm fine. Things are crazy with the police investigation. I don't want to drag you into it. I texted back.

Nice spin, Anne. There was no way he wanted to be dragged into it.

I'm here if you need me, he answered.

I slipped into the pool. What did that mean? If I needed him for what? For sex? First aid? I'd already used him for both, and I didn't need him. I had a date with Lucien, and tonight fireworks were finally going to go off.

I took a taxi to the casino. I wanted to be able to have a cocktail—or three, but it was really a ruse to get a ride home from Lucien. I spent time on my hair, attempting to recreate Wilda's magic, and wore my new blue dress.

Lucien met me at the casino door.

"Anne, darling," he greeted me with a kiss on each cheek. "Did you stay out of trouble today?"

I took his offered arm before I answered, "I stayed busy."

His reservation was a small table with an ocean view and a bottle of champagne on ice. He had romantic intentions, too.

"I ordered for you. The lobster. We're celebrating."

"How did you know what I wanted? What if I wanted a steak?" I kept my tone playful and swallowed my irritation at his presumption, but he didn't seem to notice. That happened often—his ignorance of my feelings. Was that what I liked about him? He didn't pry. He didn't need to understand me. Made things easier.

"What are we celebrating?" I asked.

"Our treasure hunt, of course. Did you figure out what the note meant yet?"

I shook my head.

"What did you do all day? Run any errands?"

I sipped champagne. "I had to find a place to stay. I visited a real estate office and moved my things."

"And? You didn't, I don't know, do any banking today?"

His tone was teasing, but alarms sounded in my head. Had he been following me? If so, I couldn't deny that I'd visited the bank. He'd know I was lying. But I couldn't share the truth. Not yet. Not now.

"I did, actually," I began. "This is going to sound insane," I paused to take another sip of champagne, stalling. "Oh, tickly bubbles," I giggled. Jeez, Anne. "Remember the detective inspector told me that Sandy had wired the money into an account in my name here on the island?" He nodded. Of course, he remembered. I leaned over the table and lowered my voice. Drawing him into the story. "I had a thought. What if she put the money in a different bank? What if it's here, and I have to visit every bank to find it?"

"And?" He leaned in too. He was hooked.

"So, I went to a bank. Picked one at random and asked if there was an account in my name. I looked like a total idiot. Can you imagine? The teller was nice enough. She really did look, and if she thought it was weird that I'd forgotten where I'd put my money, she hid it well. Maybe that sort of thing does happen. Anyway, it was a dumb idea. There are a lot of banks here, and it's not possible to check them all."

I sat back in my chair, half expecting the room to erupt in applause at my performance.

"I knew it! I knew you couldn't resist chasing it. Your idea…it's interesting," he said. "I doubt there are too many banks. Might take a few days."

"No, it's silly. And simply walking into a bank and asking—that's not a game. She told me to play the game, so she must have meant something else. But I didn't have any other time to think about it. Moving took a while. My new place is nice. Would you like to see it?" Good, Anne. Change the subject.

He nodded absently. "I might make a list of banks tomorrow. See how many there really are. See if it's possible. Might be worth trying anyway."

"No, Lucien. I can think of better ways to spend the day."

I reached across the table and smiled, hoping my eyes twinkled alluringly in the candlelight. He took my hand.

"I was hoping that you wouldn't find it without me, Anne. I want to be part of your adventure."

And then I relaxed. He wasn't spying on me. He *had* missed me.

After dinner, Lucien wanted to spend time in the casino, so he deposited me in front of a slot machine again. I played slowly, passing the time, pushing buttons enough not to draw attention to myself while I scanned the room, but I didn't see Terry. After only ten minutes, Lucien returned.

"That was quick," I said.

"Wasn't feeling it," he answered. "Let's go see your new place." He winked, and butterflies took flight deep within me.

After a brief tour—the villa was small, I suggested a walk, and he agreed. The moon conspired with me by painting the wet sand in sapphire. We walked arm in arm, watching the waves, each one building strength from the receding water, growing until they could no longer sustain their size, ultimately crashing against the beach.

"What did you do today?" I asked.

"Meetings. Nothing interesting."

"What is it that you do, Lucien?"

"This and that. Nothing interesting."

"You said that already," I teased.

"That's how boring it is. And repetitive."

He stopped walking. "I don't want to talk about work, Anne. I don't want to talk at all." He kissed me, and I leaned into him. We lost our footing on the unreliable sand and fell. He chuckled; I giggled like a schoolgirl, nervous and excited.

We remained on our backs in the sand, staring at the glittering sky while the bravest waves licked our bare feet. Then he rolled onto his side and pulled me into an embrace.

"I enjoy being with you," he said.

His kiss was different this time. More tentative, his tongue exploring my mouth. His hand was also curious, moving up my leg, sneaking past the thin barrier of my dress with a quick flick of his wrist. The farther he reached, the slower his hand moved. My anticipation grew like a wave, building into something I could no longer control. When his finger slipped beneath the lacy edge of my panties, I cried out.

He pulled away and laid his head on my chest.

"You're a sensual woman, Anne. Hard to resist, but I can't give myself to you. Not now. Not like this."

The sea quieted on our walk back. Inside the villa, he kissed me once more and grabbed his car keys. "I'll call you tomorrow."

I brushed the sand from my clothes and my hair and poured myself a glass of wine. I couldn't stop smiling. He was stringing me along, each intimate moment a step beyond the last, taking me to the brink without satisfying me. And I loved it. It was respectful—holding back until he was ready to give himself fully. He was invested in us; he was playing the long game.

#

The next morning, I made myself scrambled eggs and brewed my own coffee—not as good as Lucien's brand. I ate outside under an ominous sky, admiring the expanse of yellow-green lawn where tiny purple wildflowers gathered in patches. In the distance, rows of coconut palms thrashed, announcing the coming storm.

I fingered the key I'd concealed in a side pocket of my purse. The tag read: *The worst Paris story of all time.*

There were a couple of Paris stories; it was one of Sandy's favorite places.

"Everyone's so wonderfully rude," she'd described it once. "It's like New York but with better cafes."

She'd returned from a Paris trip only a few weeks ago and collapsed on my couch with a dramatic prattle in French. I'd assumed she was swearing.

"What's wrong?" I asked, playing the dutiful friend.

"I was mugged."

"What?" I exclaimed.

"Paris," she sighed. "This will forever tarnish Paris for me."

"Were you hurt?" I asked.

"No, no. Nothing like that. It was all very gentle-manly. This was Paris, remember? Even the muggings are classy."

I've never been to Paris—or to Europe, for that matter, but it was hard to imagine threatening someone in a classy way. Still, I wanted to hear the story.

"What happened?" I asked.

"I was alone in a dark alley—" I interrupted with a gasp, and she threw me an impatient look. "Sorry, go on."

"I was alone in a dark alley, and this guy approached me. He had his hand in his coat pocket and had something pointed at me. '*Donne moi tes bijoux,*' he said. Gimme your jewelry. I was wearing these amazing emerald earrings. Brilliant cut. They absolutely sparkled. I hadn't had them long."

"What did you do?"

"Well, I wasn't about to hand over emerald earrings to some stranger. So I asked him what he was gonna do about it."

"What if he had a gun?" I asked.

"It's France, silly. Not Detroit. Nobody has guns in France."

"What did you do?" I sat on the edge of the couch. She was clearly unharmed and healthy after the fact, but still, I worried for her in that dark alley.

"I walked away," she said.

"Just like that?" I asked. "How is that being mugged? That's not being mugged, Sandy. I don't know what that was. That was the worst Paris story of all time."

They were my words. So where was the clue? Something about Paris? And jewelry—emeralds? I opened a web browser and typed emerald and Paris. The results included French restaurants, reviews, and a handful of jewelry stores. I narrowed the search by including Saint Martin Island, but none of the results were helpful. I needed something more specific. I added brilliant to the search and got a result.

"*L'emeraude brillante.*" Brilliant emerald—an apartment building. Across the street was a bank. "Very clever, Sandy."

#

Parking added a new variable. I ended up a few blocks away and browsed the shop windows until I passed a cycling shop and quickened my pace, rubbing my arm and cursing the baby blue cruiser. There were no bike rides in my immediate future.

The next storefront was a cellular store with a confusing, cluttered array of electronics, kitchen appliances, and toys—like a miniature department store. Then I passed a hair salon, and I thought of Wilda.

A display of hats in the next window altered my course. I'd left the borrowed hat at the guest house, and I needed a replacement. I looked up at the sky as I entered the store. It could rain at any moment. Inside, I twirled the display and tried on a beige straw hat, floppy, with a bow in the same color. The style was understated and classy and matched my entire wardrobe. A black visor was more practical since I often wear my hair in a messy bun at the top. I couldn't decide between them, so carried both to the register.

I passed a rack of raincoats in bright colors and tried on a cheery yellow one with a stiff collar and a hood. As I paid for both hats and the jacket, I saw the bank entrance across the street and exited the side door carrying a massive shopping bag and wearing the jacket and the visor.

I knew what to expect this time, and I was more relaxed, taking time to remove my jacket, fold it neatly and tuck it into the bag next to the hats while I waited for a teller to assist me. I went through the same process, showing my driver's license, and being led to a smaller room, and then the box was open in front of me, and I was counting stacks of cash again. The box held three hundred thousand in US, and the same amount in Euro. I was over a third of the way to the three million.

The box held another clue, *what I ate in Destin,* a key, and a jewelry box, but no note of explanation from Sandy. I opened the jewelry box to find emerald earrings and laughed—a sharp sound that echoed in the small room. Sandy's story about the mugging in Paris had been fake—a silly, made-up ploy to trigger my memory and send me down a path to find the clue. The earrings were garish, not something I would ever wear. Sandy would have been delighted with her joke. I missed her more than ever.

I dropped the four thousand that remained from the first box and left everything but the next key. I added it to the keyring with the others and secreted it in my purse.

Chapter 12

It was raining when I left the bank. I turned up the collar of my new raincoat and hurried to the car. I drove to a cafe, found a seat inside out of the rain, and ordered a coffee.

What I ate in Destin.

Destin was the trip where she came home with food poisoning, but I didn't remember how she'd gotten sick. I searched the internet for Destin and Saint Martin, but all of the results were located in Destin.

She'd arrived at my house, burning up with a fever, and vomited all over my bathroom. I'd gotten her in the shower, cleaned her up, and helped her dress in a pair of my sweats. She spent the night on the floor of the bathroom, on a makeshift bed of blankets that I changed every time she missed the toilet. I woke when she threw up, held her hair, and rubbed her back gently while she retched. By the morning, I had to endure the heat and humidity to air out my little house. I took a rare sick day from the office, and we slept most of the day. When she woke in the afternoon, she was herself again.

Things were awkward between us for the next few days. I'd seen her at her most vulnerable. I'd shampooed her hair and toweled her feverish body—intimate moments that skewed our friendship. It took time to normalize.

Most of what she said that night was gibberish, mumbled as she clutched her cramping guts and moaned. This memory was different than the last—real, not imagined. Then I remembered there was more. She'd mentioned it again more recently—just before she'd left for the Paris trip, at the farmer's market, our Sunday ritual.

I closed my eyes and pictured her standing at the booth. What was it? Ceviche! We'd passed a stand selling homemade tortilla chips, and they offered bowls of ceviche and guacamole for tasting. As I reached to grab a chip, she'd slapped my hand away.

"That's what I ate in Destin!" she exclaimed. "Ceviche. Absolute poison. Friends don't let friends eat ceviche. We're friends, Anne. Amigas!" she exclaimed with a flourish, and then she repeated it all with enough emphasis that I'd thought she was suffering heat stroke.

Ceviche was a stupid clue on this island. More than half the restaurants probably had ceviche on their menus. Was she making this difficult on purpose? Once I'd figured out the other clues, they made sense, but the searching was exhausting and emotionally draining. It was unfair to dredge up forgotten memories; I preferred to avoid missing her.

I ran a browser search and confirmed my suspicions. Most restaurants in Saint Martin boasted the best ceviche on the island.

The waitress arrived and asked me if I wanted anything else.

"Do you know where to get the best ceviche on the island?" I asked.

She thought for a moment. "I haven't eaten everywhere on the island, but the best ceviche I've had was at a place called La Cochina. It's a great place to get a cocktail, too."

La Cochina. Worth a shot. I ran a search for banks nearby. The closest one was three blocks away. Seemed unlikely that was the answer.

"Excuse me," the man at the next table called out. "I couldn't help but overhear your question about ceviche."

"Oh. Yes. Do you have a favorite?" I asked.

"Amigas. Best ceviche on the island. I holiday here every year. I've tried most of the restaurants, and Amigas is the best. If you go, order the guava-berry margarita. Best cocktail you'll ever have."

"Thank you," I told him.

I ran the search, and bingo, Amigas was just across from another bank. Well played, Sandy. How excited she must have been, seeing the ceviche at that market booth, remembering the moment we'd been the closest, and pulling it all together with a shouted, "Amigas!"

The rain stopped, so I decided to visit the bank right away. I was now craving ceviche, and a guava-berry cocktail seemed intriguing.

It took a while to get there. The road was under construction, and I waited with several other cars, thinking about how difficult Sandy's task had been. Had she withdrawn the cash all at one time and then opened a safety deposit box in the same bank? Or had she driven around the island with large sums of cash? What was I planning to do once I found all three million? I hadn't thought that far ahead. The clues were all-encompassing. I didn't have the bandwidth to deal with the big picture.

I parked at the restaurant and crossed the street to enter the bank. I suffered another long wait to find the same box of cash. Six hundred thousand. I was now halfway there—one point five million less the six thousand I'd spent. I added the next key to the set, pocketed the clue, crossed back to the restaurant, and ordered the grouper ceviche and a guava-berry margarita.

#

The next clue was written hastily on paper with the bank's logo.

Anne, I've decided to use only banks from now on. I'm worried that the longer you take to follow these clues, the more exposed they are. Like the funds I just left at the airport. It seemed like a good idea at the time, but now, well, don't leave the money there. I'm tired of this game, but I'm almost done. Just two more trips. Love, Sandy.

This key was different. A stamped number: three-zero-four. There was no hidden meaning—just somewhere in the airport. If I hurried, I still had time to get to the airport, pick up the cash and stash it in the closest bank. If I could find it quickly enough.

The guava-berry cocktail was delicious, but I left it on the table with my half-eaten ceviche. Having a mid-day cocktail buzz was reckless; I needed a clear head. I followed route guidance, and forty minutes later, I parked at the airport.

I couldn't remember seeing lockers in an airport before; I didn't think it was typical for an airport to have them, but what else would the key open? I was standing near a ticket counter when a woman in a highlighter-yellow vest approached me.

"Can I help you?" she asked.

"Maybe," I began. "My friend asked me to pick up her bag. She gave me this key, but she didn't tell me where the locker was."

She gave me a strange look. "That key is for a locker in the employee lounge. Your friend works here?"

"Yes," I answered, as brightly as I could. "She does," I answered too quickly, and then I hoped she didn't ask for her name. Please, please don't ask me that, I thought.

"I can get it for you when I go on break."

No, that would never work. I needed to get it myself. "Can I just pop back there with you to grab it?"

She shook her head. "No, but you can wait there." She pointed to a restaurant. "Just there," she pointed across the hallway. "That's the door that leads to the employee lounge. I can't take a break for twenty minutes, so order a coffee and wait. I'll find you when I go on break, and you can give me the key."

I backed away a few steps. "Thanks," I said, but I needed to find another way in. I couldn't trust her with the key. I sat at a table just across from the door to the employee lounge and ordered a coffee and croissant. Both were bad decisions. The croissant was barely edible—Lucien had spoiled me for croissants, and the caffeine made me jittery, well, more jittery.

As I sat thinking, a man in the same brightly colored vest walked toward the door and touched a badge to a security panel. The door opened to a white corridor, and sitting in the doorway was a security guard. The only way I'd get past that guard was to get a job at the airport or trust the woman. She looked trustworthy. She had a cute button nose and dimples that suited her round face.

The biggest unknown was whether or not Sandy had left the money in a bag. She must have. An employee lounge didn't afford the privacy of a safety deposit box. She couldn't have risked being caught stacking cash into the locker. There would be a bag. But what if there wasn't? I was putting a lot of faith in Sandy's ability to follow conventions for bag drops.

I continued arguing with myself. Go, find another way. Stay, trust her. There were solid reasons for both, but I needed the next clue and the cash. I was halfway there. Another six hundred thousand would put me over two million. Possibly only two more drops to go. But if there were only two more, why did Sandy seem exhausted? And she'd said only two more to go. But at that point, she was completing the fourth, maybe the fifth? Something didn't add up. Sandy made it seem like she'd been doing this for months—not weeks.

Thirty-four minutes passed before the yellow-vested woman arrived. I still hadn't made a decision.

"Sorry about the wait," she said with a smile that deepened her dimples.

"No problem," I said. "I appreciate you doing this for me."

And I handed her the key.

"Be back in a few minutes!" she called out as she walked across the corridor.

I watched her open the door and disappear. A server appeared and asked if I wanted more coffee.

"No!" I shrieked and then more calmly said, "I've had enough, thanks. Just the bill."

I waited four minutes. Maybe the employee lockers were far down the corridor, or maybe she'd met a friend and stopped for a chat—perhaps the handsome man who'd gone in ahead of her. Or maybe she was running in the other direction with my money. Well, it wasn't really my money, but I needed it more than she did.

Eight minutes. I drummed my fingers on the table and tried to relax my shoulders. I took a few deep breaths without taking my eye off the door. What if she called the police? I imagined myself being walked out of the airport in handcuffs. But I had most of the money; I could tell the detective inspector how to find the rest. I'd show him the letter and the email, and it would all make sense. He'd believe me.

Eleven minutes. My nausea grew enough that I nibbled the stale croissant. I couldn't sit still much longer. I wanted to pace, but I couldn't risk taking my eyes off the door.

"C'mon," I quietly urged her. "C'mon. Please bring me the bag."

Twelve minutes. I paid my check. Breathe, Anne. Don't pass out at the airport. Not when you're so close. Then the door opened, and she walked out with a wide smile and a quick wave. A backpack swung from her arm in a casual arc.

"Is this it?" she asked. "I brought the key back just in case, but I need to return it if that's the right one."

I unzipped the backpack and peeked inside. It was full of cash.

"Yes! It's my friend's. Thank you so much."

"You're welcome," she answered and backed toward the door. "Gotta take the rest of my break now."

"Thanks again," I called out.

I clutched the backpack to my chest and fast-walked outside. When I reached the parking lot, I broke into a run and sprinted to my car. I threw the backpack on the passenger seat, climbed inside, and locked the doors. The heat was stifling, but I didn't care. I didn't look at the bag. I couldn't open it in the car; I was too exposed. I needed it in the bank, safely hidden away. I calmed down enough to drive and found the address of the bank by the snail—the closest one.

I rolled the windows down so I didn't pass out from heat stroke and let the wind dry the sweat from my face as I drove.

I lucked out and found a parking space right in front of the bank. I wanted to peek inside and count the money, but I needed to wait until I was inside. I grabbed the backpack and walked to the bank, but I was too late. It was closed.

#

I drove back to the villa, the backpack on the seat next to me. I had no other choice. I'd have to spend the night with it, but as soon as the bank opened, I'd drive it there and deposit the cash in the box.

I locked the front door behind me and tossed the bag onto the table in the kitchen. I needed a hiding spot. Should I hide it in several places? If I did that, would I have trouble finding it again? I searched the house, opening cupboards, and peering under the bed. No place was safe enough.

"Stop, Anne!" I shouted. I needed to calm down and think. I needed a glass of wine and something to eat, and then I'd be able to figure out what to do. I opened a cold bottle of Pinot Grigio and poured a generous glass. After a few gulps, I felt better and pulled items from the fridge to prepare dinner. I sliced a chicken breast in half and heated a skillet. I sliced mango, shallot, and bell pepper for salsa and boiled water for pasta. The backpack glared at me, so I pushed it onto a chair.

A loud knock sounded at the door, and I froze. I remembered the last time I heard a knock. What if the Police were here to search again? No, they didn't know where I was now. Wait, did they? Anne! Hide the backpack!

I opened the cupboard under the sink and forced the backpack behind the trash bin. Then I went to answer the door, wringing my hands and taking another long, deep breath.

"Lucien!" I exclaimed. "What are you doing here?"

"Because I wanted to see you. Are you alone?"

I felt a wave of relief, but my knees were weak, and I held the door for support. "Of course, I'm alone," I answered.

"You seem…on edge. Can I come in?"

"No, well, yes. I had too much coffee today." Truth. "Come in. Come in. I'm cooking. Have you eaten?"

I hurried back to the kitchen just in time to flip the chicken before it went from browned to burned. He followed me into the kitchen.

"Do you have enough for two?" he asked.

"Yes, of course," I answered, pouring him a glass of wine.

He wandered into the living room, and I heard him open the patio door. A welcome breeze made its way to me. "It's hot in here," he said, returning to the kitchen.

I was turned away from him, finishing the salsa and straining the pasta.

"Anne, darling?"

"Yes," I turned around slowly and forced a smile.

He wore a curious look. "Is something the matter? You seem out of sorts. Did something happen today?"

Pull yourself together, Anne. "No. Nothing like that. Like I said, I had too much coffee. It makes me jittery, and I'm tired. I was busy today."

"Busy doing what?" he asked.

"This and that. Oh! I bought a new hat! I'll show you." I looked for the shopping bag but realized I must have left it in the car. "Where did that go?"

He moved toward me. "Anne, it's something else. You're different tonight."

"Like I said, it's the—"

"The coffee. Yes, you said that." He placed his hands on my face. They felt so cool, and I closed my eyes and relaxed into him. "You're hot, Anne. Is your infection back?"

I sighed. "No, I feel fine, Lucien. I need dinner, and I'll be back to normal. I promise."

I wrapped my arms around his waist and let him hold me for a moment, and then I pulled away to finish dinner.

"Almost ready. Go wash up," I told him.

By the time he returned, dinner was laid out on the table, and I was seated, smiling, hands in my lap. Calm Anne as long as I ignored the backpack in the cupboard.

He suggested a walk after dinner, but I declined and patted the couch.

"I'm too tired," I said.

"Shopping wore you out?" he asked. He still seemed suspicious, but he sat next to me.

I yawned.

"You are tired," he said. "Maybe I should go."

I wanted him to go. I wanted to open the backpack and count the money. I wanted to find the next clue—possibly my last one. All I had to do was walk him to the door, but he smelled of aftershave. He was magnetic; his bulk created its own gravity, drawing me in. I snuggled into him and closed my eyes. The backpack wasn't going anywhere. It was safe.

"Don't go," I murmured.

He wrapped his arm around me and relaxed back into the cushions.

"I'm yours to command, Anne," he chuckled softly.

CHAPTER 13

Where was I? What had woken me? I lay still, listening, orienting myself, but the night was quiet. I lay alone in bed at the villa. I heard the distant crash of waves through my open window and something else. A low rumbling. Snoring?

I eased from bed and tiptoed barefoot into the living room. Yes, snoring—Lucien was asleep on the couch. Moonlight through the open patio door bathed him in blue light, and I watched his chest rise and fall rhythmically. A pleasant sound. Soothing, like a cat purring.

The clock in the living room read two-fourteen. What had woken me? I silently moved to the patio door and peered outside. All was quiet and still. I walked into the kitchen and carefully opened the cupboard under the sink. I didn't dare open the backpack while Lucien was in the house, but I touched it to reassure myself. It was still there, undisturbed. I closed the cupboard and sank onto the cool tile floor. I was still fully dressed. Lucien must have carried me into bed. How had I slept through that?

I counted back the hours—six hours of sleep wasn't enough, but I was wide awake. I noiselessly plucked my book from the kitchen counter and tiptoed back to the bedroom. I turned on the bathroom light and pulled it closed until a narrow strip of light crossed the bed. How long ago it seemed since I'd grabbed the book on the way out the door to the airport. Since arriving on the island only a few days ago, I'd only read a few pages. It wasn't the book's fault. What book could compare to what I'd experienced? And who knew what else was in store?

I tried to read, but my thoughts returned to Lucien. Considering anything long-term with him was delusional. He lived in Europe. At least, I thought he did. I couldn't remember if he'd told me where he lived. I thought back to our first walk on the beach and tried to remember his exact words. He said he came to Saint Martin often. I only lived a thousand miles away. Over a vast sea. I sighed. It was closer than Europe but might as well be China.

Maybe I could move. I could sell my house, and I'd be able to live off of the proceeds for a while. I could be with Lucien. An insane thought. Lucien hadn't shown interest in even a short-term relationship. He'd chosen the couch over my bed. Was that respect? More likely, it was a sign that he wasn't interested.

I was getting too far ahead of myself. I needed to focus on finishing Sandy's game, finding the money, and getting out of the mess she'd created. It was the only way to ensure any kind of life outside of prison. Not that Sandy thought I had a chance. Why had she told me to run? In the whole year she'd known me, how did she not realize what kind of person I was? I don't run away from things. Well, aside from running here to the island. An anomaly—definitely out of character. That decision was temporary insanity.

There was another reason to run. Someone had killed Sandy. If she had been killed because of the money, then I was putting myself in the crosshairs by chasing her clues. Perhaps I was already a target, but it was difficult to be afraid of a threat I couldn't see.

I closed the book. I needed sleep. I pushed the book away and closed my eyes.

A loud crash sounded just outside my window. I sat up, heart racing, and heard hurried footsteps. I flew out of bed to switch off the bathroom light. I squeezed my eyes shut to adjust to the darkness then I peered out the window. A dark figure stood several feet away outside my window. He scratched his head, and I recognized his shirt.

"Lucien?" I whispered.

He glanced my way. "Yup. It's me." Then he turned away and rounded the corner. I walked into the living room as he entered through the patio door. "Did you hear something?" he asked.

"A crash."

"Probably just a cat trying to get into one of the bins," he said. He yawned. "C'mon, back to bed with you."

He closed and locked the patio door, wrapped an arm around me, and pulled me to the bedroom. I silently agreed that it was probably a cat—or another animal. Nothing to be afraid of. But I shamelessly capitalized on it.

"Stay here with me, Lucien?" I was almost disgusted at myself for sounding so timid, but not quite because it worked. He nodded and lay down. He wrapped his arm around me, and I closed my eyes and lay next to him.

But sleep never came. I couldn't stop thinking about the backpack in the cupboard.

#

I could have made coffee, but when Lucien offered to run out to pick it up, I didn't argue with him. Instead, I watched him pull out onto the street, and I ran back to the kitchen to pull the backpack from its hiding spot.

I unloaded bundles of cash, stacking them neatly in rows on the floor next to me. All US currency. There were seventy-five bundles. Seven hundred and fifty thousand. Three-quarters of a million dollars sitting next to me. I replaced the money, stacking it neatly to get it to fit. Then I unzipped the front pocket and found another safety deposit box key with a tag that read, *That thing we laughed so hard about.* We'd returned to the vague clues, and I wasn't sure if that was better or worse than the airport fiasco.

I tucked the bag back into its hiding spot and put the key and note in my purse. There were four now—I'd lost the one from the airport, and they jangled as I moved my purse. I still had my hand inside the pocket, fingering the smooth wood of the charm on the keyring, when I heard the front door open. I zipped it closed and dropped my purse.

"Breakfast!" Lucien called out. It was adorable the way he announced his arrival before entering a room. I set two plates on the table, anticipating his croissant delivery. He didn't disappoint. The pastries were still warm from the oven.

"What shall we do today?" he asked.

I stalled, chewing slowly. We? Having him around all day would make it impossible to visit the last bank, and I was sure this one would be the last. I just needed a final seven hundred and fifty thousand to make up the three million.

"You don't have to work today?" I asked.

"No, I'm all yours, darling. How about we visit Pinel Island for the day? It's a quick ferry ride over to a beautiful beach. We can hike and snorkel. There's a restaurant there to grab lunch. How about it? We'll find you a snorkel on the way."

"I'm not sure…" I began. "How long would we be gone?"

He chuckled. "You have other plans?"

If I declined, he'd be suspicious. A snorkeling trip sounded amazing. And if we left quickly, perhaps we'd be back early enough I could still make it to the bank. The money was safe in the cupboard. No one knew about the villa except Lucien, and he'd be with me.

In the hall closet, I found a worn tote bag, and I wrapped the keys in one of my tank tops and dropped them into the bottom of the bag. On top, I set a beach towel, my sunscreen, and two bottles of water. I changed into a bathing suit with a clean tank top and cut-off jeans and piled my hair into a quick bun.

"Ready?" Lucien called.

I considered the backpack's hiding place again, but I couldn't move it while Lucien was in the house. I stared at the kitchen cupboard for a long moment. Then I heard Lucien's keys jangle from the front step, and I followed him outside and locked the door behind me.

#

Pinel Island was a vacation from my vacation. We took a ten-minute ferry ride across a bay. Once on the island—an oversized sand bar, really, Lucien found a couple of lounge chairs.

"Ready?" he asked. He waved two flippers at me and began unbuttoning his shirt.

Even though I live within an hour of the snorkel-worthy waters of the Florida Keys, I never venture into the water. Unless you count my community pool.

"I haven't been snorkeling in a long time," I admitted. "Not since I was a kid."

He pulled his mask over his head and let it hang around his neck. "There's nothing to it. I'll be with you every step of the way."

I didn't want to leave the keys unattended, but I was wearing a two-piece bathing suit that had zero hiding places.

"Are you worried about your arm?" he asked as if he sensed my hesitation.

I shook my head and followed him into the water, and he helped me adjust my mask and pull on the flippers.

"Let's go!"

I'd already inserted my snorkel, so I gave him a thumbs up and sank below the water. He took my hand and pulled me along next to him, propelling us along the surface of the water. We didn't have to swim far to find the first school of fish. Bright orange fish parted politely and continued on around us. We stayed at the surface for a while, watching the activity below. Breathing underwater was disconcerting, but I got used to the snorkel, blowing forcefully to clear the water. The farther we swam, the more there was to see. Much of the ocean floor was sandy, but we passed large rocks with entire ecosystems.

I thought of my father and the trips we'd made to the Keys. He'd taught me how to use a snorkel. Often, we'd drive to our favorite beach on Key West—the same beach my family had visited the day everything changed. After that day, I hadn't wanted to snorkel again, not for thirteen years, not until Lucien asked me.

I tried to focus on the fish, but memories of my father filled my head. When I was first learning to snorkel, he'd pluck me right out of the surf and toss me into a wave. I'd swim back and demand to be thrown again and again. We'd wander the beach for hours collecting shells. My mask fogged. I surfaced and realized I'd lost Lucien. I rotated a full three hundred and sixty degrees, but I was alone. I panicked and pulled my snorkel out, trying to breathe slowly but treading water furiously.

"What's wrong?" He surfaced next to me.

"Nothing," I lied.

But he didn't believe me. He reached out and pulled me close to him, wrapping my legs around him, and he treaded water for the two of us, his massive flippers easily holding us upright. "Should we head back?"

I shook my head. "I'm fine now."

He stayed close after that, subtly maneuvering us back to the beach. I emerged from the water and dropped the mask on the sand next to my chair. I lay wet and cool under the umbrella, catching my breath.

"There was a turtle," he said. "When I swam off. That's why. I didn't mean to scare you."

"I was okay. I think it was a shock coming out of the water to find myself alone—it just surprised me."

He took my hand and squeezed it.

"How about a drink? And then we can hike across to another beach if you're game to snorkel more, but we don't have to."

"Sounds great," I answered.

We each had a rum punch before we set out for the short walk to a beach on the other side of the tiny island. As I picked up my bag, I heard the muffled jingle of the keys. Safe. Hidden.

We snorkeled for another hour and then lay on the beach in the sun to dry. Lucien dozed, and I applied more sunscreen and watched him snore. Perhaps there was a future with him. I knew it couldn't be like this: the hot sun, the pristine beach, but maybe I'd be just as happy on a drippy British afternoon. Not knowing anything about him allowed me to fill in the gaps and imagine us in a perfect reality. And I did. While he slept, I stared at the water and imagined us on that catamaran again, sailing the world. Just the two of us. And I'd never be alone again.

But it was only a daydream. I knew very little about him. He didn't talk much; the quiet was comfortable. The fact that he didn't seem interested in knowing my thoughts meant I didn't have to share. For a long time after Chad, I wondered if I was capable of a normal relationship. With Lucien, it seemed possible.

When the sun was low in the sky, we returned to the ferry and arrived at my villa happy, tired, and sandy.

The front door was ajar.

I noticed it first and hesitated in the driveway. When Lucien saw it, he pushed past me, kicked the door open, and raced inside.

"Wait out there, Anne," he called out.

"No way," I said haughtily and followed him inside. Nothing seemed out of place. Maybe I'd just failed to set the latch properly. Maybe the door had simply blown open. But I knew I locked the patio door, and that stood wide open as well.

"Did you open that?" I asked.

Lucien shook his head. "No. Are you sure it was closed when you left?"

"Yes, I locked it. I opened the windows to let in the breeze while I was gone, and I know I closed the door and locked it."

"I'll check the bedroom. Stay here."

"Stop telling me what to do," I muttered under my breath. When he entered the bedroom, I went into the kitchen. Nothing looked out of place, but I opened the cupboard where I'd hidden the money and reached inside. Nothing there. I reached farther back, touching the wall, and pulled the bin out. Nothing. The money was gone.

"Anne!" Lucien called out from the bedroom. "You have to come see this."

I couldn't respond. I'd just lost three-quarters of a million dollars, and I had no idea who'd taken it. No one had ransacked the house. The search was careful. They'd known what they were looking for—perhaps they'd even known where to look.

"Anne!" Lucien called again.

I grabbed the beveled edge of the counter and heaved myself up off the floor. I followed his voice into the bathroom and looked where he pointed.

Across the mirror, someone had left a message scrawled in black eyeliner: *Find the rest.*

"That was an expensive eyeliner," I said.

Lucien caught my eye in the mirror. "Anne, what is this? What's going on?"

I didn't want to lie, and I didn't want to tell him the truth, so I just shrugged.

"Anne." He sounded angry, like he wasn't going to let it go. I had to make a choice. I left the bathroom and sat on the edge of the bed, and stared at my feet. He scowled from the bathroom doorway with his hands on his hips. "You found the money, didn't you?"

I nodded slowly. "Part of it. Not all of it."

"Why didn't you tell me?" His deep voice was quiet, scolding me. Or was he simply disappointed he'd missed out on the game? I didn't answer. "You don't trust me." It wasn't a question.

I couldn't argue. I didn't trust him or anyone else. Sandy told me not to.

"Lucien, it's not that I don't trust you." Another lie. "I don't trust anybody right now. I like you. I don't want to drag you into something…" I couldn't finish the sentence because I didn't know how it ended.

"I understand," he said. He kneeled on the floor in front of me. "I really do understand. You can trust me. I would never hurt you."

I wanted to trust him, but I wasn't sure I was capable of trusting anyone that much.

"Can you at least tell me what you found?" he asked.

Could I? How would I explain finding the money at the airport and leave out the rest of the clues? I had to explain the airport money, but I didn't have to tell him the rest, not yet.

"Yeah," I said. "But I need a drink first." That was happening to me daily now—needing a glass of wine. I do like a glass of wine with dinner, but I don't drink just because I'm stressed or sad. I was becoming that kind of a person.

I went to the kitchen and poured two glasses of wine. There was only enough left in the bottle for two small portions. I took a sip and hoped it would fuel my creativity; I needed an answer.

Lucien followed me into the kitchen. "I'm going to walk the property. Make sure no one is still hanging around. I'll be back. Keep the door locked, okay?"

I nodded.

Chapter 14

I'd finished my glass and started in on Lucien's by the time he knocked on the patio door. I let him in and collapsed on the couch.

"I didn't see anyone," he said. "Whoever was here is long gone. Now, tell me. What did you find?" he asked. He remained standing, glaring at me.

"A backpack. With seven hundred and fifty thousand dollars in it. I was trying to decide what to do with it."

Lucien whistled. "That's a lot of money."

I nodded. "Yes, but it's gone. That was my way out of this mess."

"What else aren't you telling me? Do you know who took it?"

I looked up at him, surprised by the question. "Of course not."

"How did you find it?"

That was the question I was hoping to avoid. The one I didn't have an answer for. "I remembered something yesterday—something she told me a few weeks ago. I had a hunch, and it paid off." Vague. Well done, Anne.

Lucien seemed to accept it. "And the rest of the money? Do you know where to find it?"

Yes, but I wasn't going to tell him that. "I have to figure it out. And quickly. Do you think the message on the mirror is a threat?"

"Definitely."

Then why wasn't I more afraid? Because I didn't know who'd written it?

"We should move you out of here," Lucien said.

"I don't want to go anywhere. This place is paid for a whole week."

He sat and put a protective arm around me, and I shrugged it off. "Look, I'm not helpless. I *can* take care of myself, and I understand if you want to take off. You didn't sign up for this. You got dragged into this simply because you helped me buy shrimp."

"Anne, I'm not going anywhere."

His tone was patronizing, and it irritated me. "I only found that money when I had space to think. I need that if I'm going to find the rest."

He nodded. "I understand."

"But…" I didn't want him to go away. "I can't do anything about it tonight. I'm too tired. I need a shower. So do you, by the way."

He cocked his head to one side. Curious, I hoped. "Are you inviting me to join you?"

Yes. C'mon Anne. Be brave. Ask for what you want. "Join me in the shower?"

I watched his reaction, wishing I could read his thoughts. I loved his mystery, but at that moment, I would have sacrificed the mysteriousness to know his thoughts. He didn't answer right away, and I could tell a battle was raging within him. I let it play out.

"Anne."

So much rejection in one word, but I couldn't just let him leave with dignity. I needed to know why.

"Are you married?" I blurted out. It was a fair question. It had occurred to me early on, but I'd been too shy to ask. He didn't wear a ring or a telltale tan line, but something was holding him back.

He chuckled softly and shook his head. "No, I'm not married."

"What then?"

"Anne-"

I cut him off. "Don't do that. Keep saying my name like that. Like I'm something that needs managing. I'm not a starry-eyed girl. I'm a woman, independent and capable of knowing my mind. I'm not asking you for a relationship—at least not right now. Just sex. Just the kind of sex you have after you've just lost three-quarters of a million, and someone has written a vague threat in your best eyeliner. Maybe it's only a one-time thing. Probably is, but I'm going into this with my eyes wide open. Stop treating me like I'm some fragile thing."

He leaned away as I spoke. Surprised. So was I.

But he leaned back toward me and said, "I don't think you're fragile at all. I think you're exceptional, actually. Have you even stopped to think about what you've been through in the last few days? A bike accident. Your friend was killed! You just got robbed, and you're taking it all in stride. You're not at all fragile."

"You forgot about the sepsis."

"That's what I'm talking about. Just a few days ago, you were in hospital. Today, you went snorkeling. You're tough. Probably the toughest woman I've ever met. It's very sexy."

I smiled. Waited for the but.

"But." And there it was. "I just got out of a complicated relationship. I'm still grieving a bit. Not as much since I met you."

He paused again, and I held my breath. Was there a but to the but?

"If you accept my situation is complicated…"

He never finished the thought. At least not with words. He kissed me fiercely, and I knew he'd changed his mind. There would be no return to the respectful, stand-offish Lucien. He gripped me hard enough to hurt my arm and pulled me onto him.

His hands were everywhere at once in a frenzied attempt to experience all of me. I pulled away and removed my shirt, dislodging dried sand and brushing it away. He lay back on the couch, watching me, and I moved slowly, but he wasn't patient. He lunged and yanked off my bikini top, and we became a tangle of limbs and fumbling fingers. He pushed inside me too soon, grunting with the effort. I clung to his hips, trying to slow his rhythm, to wait for me, but my hands had no effect. The couch screeched and threatened to topple, and he went silent and still for a second before he began to tremble. With a final thrust of his hips, he erupted in a long roar, a victorious cry. I lay underneath him, trying to catch my breath.

"That was—" I was cut off as he struggled to roll underneath me on the narrow couch. The wicker complained but held us.

"Sorry," he said, breathing heavily. I kissed his bare chest, and he tasted of seawater. "It's been a while," he explained. "And I wanted to do that every time I've seen you. Had a hair trigger."

We lay together until his breathing returned to normal, and then we showered, taking turns lathering the soap and removing the salt water and the sand. We fell into bed, still damp from the shower.

The second time, he was patient, allowing me to almost reach a climax and then pulling back, making me wait, building it further and further each time until I couldn't be stopped. And then there was a moment where I didn't worry about the money, the police, or anything. Then we slept.

#

Lucien left after we'd shared his usual breakfast: coffee and croissants.

"Call me if you need me," he said. I could tell he was holding back. He probably wanted to tell me not to do anything stupid, but he'd learned his lesson last night. And I'd learned something about him. At his most intimate, he was still shielded, unreadable. Sex was a release—nothing more. Even while he was deep inside me, I felt no connection to him. It made me feel hollow.

Something else bothered me. Why hadn't he suggested calling the police? As soon as he realized the house had been broken into, it should have been his first thought. I'd thought of it and dismissed it immediately because I couldn't explain to the police that the only thing stolen was the money I wasn't supposed to have. They wouldn't have listened to the rest of the story. I'd be in cuffs. Had Lucien worked through all of that in his head? It was possible, but it still bothered me that he hadn't even mentioned it. Of course, I hadn't given him much of an opportunity. Shamelessly throwing myself at him.

Jeez, Anne.

I walked to the beach. I had to decipher another of Sandy's cryptic clues—the latest one especially cryptic. *That thing that we laughed so much about.* We laughed all the time, about everything. How could I narrow it down? What was the last thing we laughed about? The last night I saw her, we shared a bottle of wine and Thai leftovers. There was nothing particularly funny that night.

I couldn't focus on memories of Sandy. I'd walked past the imaginary boundary of protection I'd erected around the villa. I did that sometimes—ignored reality that was too frightening in order to give myself time to process. I'd holed up with Lucien all night and pretended everything was okay, but it wasn't. I was in serious trouble. Someone knew I had the money. The search of the villa had been precise, methodical, my things barely disturbed. That meant whoever it was, knew they had time. How? And what was I planning to do about it?

I plopped down on the sand. The tide had cut a shelf into the beach, and I sat atop and watched the waves. The tide was going out, and I wanted to go with it. Run away. I had money—a million and a half. I could rent a boat, get to another island, and find a flight.

Take the money and run, Sandy had said. At the time I read her email, it was a crazy idea, and now I was actually considering it. Was it enough money? Once I started, there'd be no turning back. It didn't seem like enough to last the rest of my life.

There was another option—find proof that I was innocent, and Sandy had the proof. Another insane idea, putting a dead woman at the crux of my plan, but so far, she'd shared more with me since she was killed than she had when she was alive.

I had two options. Stay and hope that Sandy gave me something to prove I was innocent or run with limited funds. Anytime I needed to make a huge decision, I'd list the pros and cons. And this was a big decision—running versus staying—potentially a life or death decision.

I grabbed a long stick from a pile of driftwood and drew a line across the wet sand at my feet. I added a P for the pro column and a C for the con. I'd never be able to settle down and have a normal life, so I drew an X in the con column. Running would keep me out of jail. I'd travel, but out of necessity and on a budget. I hesitated to draw another X, and I had my answer. I didn't want to run.

One brazen wave erased the grid, and there was no point in redrawing it. I was going to stay and fight to have the life I wanted. I threw the stick into the sea and walked back to the villa. I had more banking to do.

#

That thing we laughed so hard about.

What was Sandy trying to tell me? It must have been something she found funny, and she had a warped sense of humor. Like that time we went for a hike in Everglades Park. She'd seen a group of tourists on the wrong side of middle-aged. They stood out in the park in their floral-print poly-blend tops and their white cropped pants. We could smell the perfume a half mile off. I didn't understand why it had bothered Sandy that day. The tourists were always there. But that day, Sandy had a mean streak. She walked us right up behind them and broke into a run, sprinting past them and shouting, "Gator! There's a gator!"

The covey of women shrieked and ran, their sandals slapping against the wooden planks of the path. The women were soon out of sight, but I hung back, embarrassed by Sandy's cruel prank. Tourists went to the park to see alligators, and when they arrived and walked on the path, just feet from alligators sunning themselves, they stayed on high alert. It was instinctive—the fear. And useful. It made you wary. Even the soft ladies, giggling nervously, kept one eye peeled as they passed the prehistoric monsters.

I walked back to the car, ignoring Sandy's cries to slow down. I could hear her laughing as she jogged behind me.

"Why did you do that?" I asked.

She waved away my concern. "They deserved it."

"You don't know anything about them. How would you know?"

She stopped laughing. "How many times have we come here? The tourists are always the same. They come here lookin' for gators, and they're shocked when they actually see them. They shriek, snap photos, and go home. It just pisses me off."

"Why? You're not even from here. Why do you care?"

She plucked a leaf and twirled it between her fingers. It was a rare pensive moment for her, so I waited for her to speak. "I grew up here. Not close by, but in Florida. Somewhere you've never been and you'd never go. The kind of place those people disembark from a bus to ogle people like me like they're gators. Like we're something to fear." She began shredding the leaf. "And my pa loved them. The tourists. Put on a show. Except it wasn't. It was our life, and those tourists made a mockery of it. I got out and never went back." She tossed the leaf, and her voice returned to normal. "That version of me is gone."

I was too surprised to answer. It was more detail than she'd ever shared. Since that day, she never brought it up again. She closed the door on it, and I respected her boundary because she never asked me about my family either. I liked it that way.

But that wasn't the right story. We hadn't laughed together. The truth was when she did laugh, really laugh, I wasn't always joining in. Sometimes I did that with her—put on a show. I knew I didn't need to because she knew the real me, but sometimes I felt like I was too serious for her, so there were times I pretended. Not because I wanted her to think I was more fun than I am, but there were times when she was enjoying herself so much that I didn't want to take it away from her.

I remembered one of those times—when I pretended.

We'd had a late dinner together and went to a bar for a drink afterward. We were dressed up, not club-style, but we both made an effort. She looked good that night, and we'd hooked a couple guys. They looked younger—in their twenties. One of them was drunk, really drunk, and the other looked embarrassed to be with him. As we talked, we learned they were brothers, and the older one was stuck taking care of his drunk younger brother. Sandy was drawn to the drunk guy. She could always spot an easy target, and she ordered shots for the four of us. The poor guy never knew what hit him.

Sandy suggested we go to another bar—a place known for having bull riding, and she signed the drunk guy up. He was totally on board, and she kept buying him shots to sustain his courage. By the time it was his turn, he could barely walk, but somehow, he made it up onto the bull. The older brother and I watched slack-jawed as he stayed on that bull for the full three minutes.

Sandy clapped and screamed as he held on, and she laughed so hard. I'm not sure I've ever seen her happier than in that moment. It was like she felt this weird pride that she'd discovered his hidden talent. She'd set him up for a painful fall, and instead, he'd become a legend in the bar. She loved that moment.

We stayed out late, drinking too much, and watched Sandy and the guy retell the story over and over to anyone that would listen. We laughed along, the older brother and me, but my heart wasn't in it. We only laughed because her laughter was so infectious. She'd bring it up occasionally, remembering that one happy moment.

"Remember that dude who rode the bull?"

"Of course," I answered.

"So funny. We laughed so hard about that."

Were those her words? Or was my brain overwriting the memory to find a match? It was an odd clue for Saint Martin, but I ran a search anyway. There was no reference to bull riding on Saint Martin Island. Just bulls? Nothing.

Two of her clues had been in French. Escargot and Emeraude, and I needed a translator. My French wasn't extensive enough to know the word for bull. I looked it up. *Taureaux.* It sounded familiar, so I ran a search. Taureaux Tavern. A restaurant I'd passed the day before.

Sandy's mind made strange connections. I could imagine her standing outside the bank, scanning local shops and restaurants, searching her memory for a shared story. Why couldn't she just say, "Bull riding night." Why did it have to be so obscure? I sighed and closed my laptop. So far, I'd figured out her vague clues, so her stories were working. She'd primed me, reminding me of these moments frequently during the last few months—making them easy for me to remember. Why? Had she known she might not be here?

Chapter 15

This time, suspicious that someone was watching me, I wanted to get into the bank discreetly. I packed a shopping bag with a few supplies and began my approach to the bank in a shop around the corner, playing the part of a tourist. At the back of the shop, I casually put on the black visor and my raincoat and exited quickly. Then, I went into another shop and did the opposite.

In the next shop, I pulled a bright green blouse over the top of my clothes, changed into the floppy straw hat, and bought a duffle bag for my props, stuffing the shopping bag inside. I exited through the back door and walked quickly to the bank, hoping it had been enough.

Inside the bank, I made a big show of being overheated, slipping back out of the green blouse, taking off the hat, and stood waiting for the safety deposit boxes. My French phrases regarding accessing safety deposit boxes were well practiced, and soon I was in a room with a new box stuffed with cash. More than I'd seen in any of the other boxes. More than the backpack.

I counted out one point three million. If I still had the money from the backpack, I'd have well over three million. Whatever Sandy was doing was not limited to the wire transfers I'd known about. My assumption that

I was looking for three million dollars was wrong. There was more.

There was another key in the box—this one as strange looking as the one from the airport. And a note.

I bought a boat! I moved into it today. It has two staterooms—one for each of us. I can't wait to show you the islands. The places we'll go! This key is for a locker at the marina. Your boat key is there. See you soon! I gotta catch a flight out of town.

I crossed the street and entered another store, browsing and thinking. A no-named marina? I shifted a handful of hangers along a metal rack, causing an angry screech, and the sales lady frowned.

I left the shop. Why couldn't Sandy make something easy? This was an island famous for boating. There had to be twenty or so marinas.

My phone buzzed in my pocket, startling me.

Luke texted, *Reminding you about your doctor's appointment Monday.*

What time? I answered.

9 am

My phone was quiet, and then he asked *Busy tonight?*

I'd sent Lucien away, and for the first time since I'd met him, the thought of him didn't spark anything inside me.

No plans, I texted back.

Dinner? My place at 7.

I sighed. Was I so desperate for company that I was going to step from Lucien's bed right back into Luke's? No.

At the street corner, I paused and stared at my phone.

OK, I texted.

First, I had to find Sandy's boat. I searched the internet and found three marinas within walking distance.

I was tired of Sandy's clues. I wanted to do something more—something to draw out the person that had written the message on my mirror. The unknown threat was festering, making me anxious and jumpy. I needed a new plan. A sting operation. I laughed out loud and glanced around, but nobody looked in my direction.

Someone must have followed me. They saw me with the backpack—either at the airport or rushing from my car into the villa. When I left for the beach, they knew they had time. That meant if someone was watching me, I could set a trap. Withdraw funds, make a big show of leaving the bank. Act shifty. That wouldn't be difficult. I looked over my shoulder again. I looked shifty without trying. Then what? The first step would be to figure out who it was. Then I could make a plan.

#

The first marina was small, and they didn't have lockers, so I went to the next one. It was close, a five-minute walk along the water's edge. A boat passed by, a throaty rumble of motor constrained to a snail's pace within the harbor. A man sitting on the back deck nodded a greeting as he cleaned a fishing reel with a greasy rag.

Just outside the gates of the marina, a group of people stood in front of an official-looking building. The large flag waving overhead was a reminder that I was in a foreign country, unable to leave without permission. Trapped. I walked past, holding my breath as if my photo was plastered on a bulletin board inside. Once I stepped into the marina gates, there were several buildings, all labeled in English. I went inside the one marked *Office.*

A kid sat behind a counter. He was bent over his phone, scrolling with his right index finger. I used the same tactic that had worked at the airport.

"My friend asked me to grab her bag from her locker. I have the key, but I have no idea where to find the lockers."

The kid seemed eager for a chance to stretch his legs. He jumped up and walked around the counter.

"Locker rooms," he called out in a funny accent that wasn't French. Dutch maybe?

We walked outside, and I followed where he pointed. "The green building. Did she give you a key card?" He showed me a white plastic card that hung from his neck on a lanyard.

I shook my head. "She probably forgot."

"Yeah, no worries. I'll let you in."

Once again, Sandy had stowed the money behind a locked door and hadn't provided me with a key, but I couldn't be angry with her because I was accessing it easily. She'd capitalized on the kindness of the islanders. Since she wasn't the kind of person to assume the best of anyone, I knew she'd spent enough time here to get to know the locals. She knew they'd help me.

The kid chatted while we walked. He told me where to purchase supplies, that the ice machine was down for repairs today, and where to launch a boat. He even described the services they offered in the boat yard as if I was a prospective customer. I nodded while he spoke, but I walked quickly, impatient to find the locker. After he unlocked the door to the women's locker room, I thanked him and closed the door behind me.

The locker room smelled moldy. Louvered windows along the top of the walls didn't provide sufficient airflow. There were three showers, a bank of sinks, and two toilet enclosures. I peeked underneath the doors, making sure I was alone. I found locker number seventeen, the number stamped on the key, and unlocked it.

Another backpack. I sat on a bench and unzipped the largest section. There wasn't much cash inside, maybe twenty bundles. How skewed had I become in a few days? I was holding two hundred grand, and it seemed paltry. There was another note and another keyring that held a safety deposit box key, a small gold key, and a white plastic key card like the kid had used to open the door. It also had a bright yellow spongy thing—the kind found on boat keys to keep them afloat in case they fell into the water.

Anne,

Slip C9. She was called Second Chance before I bought her. Fate, I thought. Because my life is all about this second chance. After you forgive me, of course. The slip is paid for through the end of the year, but we won't be able to stay long. Find the rest of the funds and leave. Your next clue is The Premier Ink.

See you soon, Sandy

Second Chance. Slip C9.

I dropped the note into the backpack, zipped it, and stuffed it into the locker. I moved the newest bank key onto the keyring with the others and pocketed the boat keys. I stepped out of the dingy locker room and into blinding sunlight. I paused to dig my sunglasses from my bag, stepping back under the shade of the roof.

I considered returning to the office to ask the kid where slip C9 was when I noticed a sign with a huge A. Farther along the path was a B, followed by the one I wanted—Dock C. I hesitated a second longer to pull on my sunglasses and froze.

Lucien walked right past me.

My tongue formed his name, but something in the back of my brain held me back in the shadows, and he walked past without seeing me. I watched him stride to the gate marked C. He paused and pulled out his phone. A minute went by, and I stayed in place. A man approached the gate and let Lucien inside. They shook hands and walked along the dock together. They walked out of sight behind the boats on my side of the dock. I broke cover and jogged to a trash enclosure, rounding it, staying out of sight, and watched the two men board a boat. They seemed to be having an intense conversation. The other man gestured wildly with his hands. I walked closer, keeping the gate between me and the boat.

Another man walked out of the cabin, and I froze again, pinning my back against the trash enclosure. Terry.

The back of the boat read: *The Second Chance.* Sandy's boat. A lifetime of seconds went by before I moved again. I walked out of the marina.

Lucien knew Terry. Lucien knew where Sandy's boat was. Lucien knew so much more than he'd let on. I'd kept secrets from Lucien, but I should have been more cautious, and I was angry with myself for lusting after him like a teenager.

I found my car and drove to the villa. It took me seven minutes to pack my clothes and toiletries. I left the food. I left the front door key on the counter and the door unlocked. It didn't matter; I wasn't going back.

Had I been on the mainland, I probably would have driven for hours, but I was on an island. So, after twenty minutes I ran out of road.

I pulled the car into the parking lot of a different marina. I wanted to cry or scream, but nothing came. Lucien had been watching me. How had I not seen it? He was evasive and vague. He'd never answered any of my questions. Instead, he'd offered support. "I would never hurt you, Anne." It was all an act, and I'd fallen for it. I'd slept with him. Worse than that, I hadn't succumbed to his manipulative advances; I'd thrown myself at him. He was probably somewhere laughing at ridiculous Anne.

I was overheating in the car, so I got out and glanced around. There was a restaurant across the parking lot, and I really needed a drink. But halfway there, I stopped. A cocktail wasn't the answer. I needed a plan. I knew Lucien was involved, but he didn't know that I knew. Could I use that to my advantage? Go back to the villa, pretend I didn't know? Turn the tables on him?

I walked across the parking lot, but I walked past the restaurant and onto a dock. I kept walking, and when the dock ended, I followed the path as it meandered through tourist shops and restaurants, wanting to be lost in the crowds.

I couldn't go back to the villa, and I couldn't confront Lucien. I wasn't capable of lying well enough to hide what I knew from Lucien. He was an exceptional liar; he'd certainly be able to tell if I was lying. I couldn't go back.

But I still had an advantage: they didn't know what I knew. I could text him, tell him I was still searching—ask for more time, and I could watch them.

Why had I run away from the marina? I needed to know what they were up to, and I needed to know who the third man was. I turned around and fast-walked through the shops until I found a pair of binoculars. I bought them and jogged to my car. I had a new plan.

#

I returned to the marina, but this time, I drove past and into a bigger parking lot for a restaurant and dive shop. It was next to a shopping village, swarming with people. It was the perfect place to be lost in a crowd. From my car, I didn't have a good vantage of the boat, so I walked closer to the marina. I found a bench just outside the gate. There was a constant stream of foot traffic to hide behind. I could see the boat, but nobody was in sight. I'd missed them, so I settled in to wait.

I studied the passing faces, but I felt exposed on the bench. I shifted nervously and kept glancing over my shoulder. The threat was tangible. I couldn't ignore it now. I knew who they were. I knew they'd killed Sandy and Mr. Sampson, and they would kill me for knowing as much as I already did.

Was there a way out of this mess? Sandy's words rang in my head. *Take the money and run.* She'd known all along. But I now had the upper hand. If I followed them and figured out what was going on, I could formulate a plan. One of them was a murderer. If I could figure out who it was, I could get the police involved. My stomach lurched as I realized Lucien could have left me that night, murdered Sandy and then arrived the next morning with coffee. I pushed the thought away.

My phone buzzed. Luke. *Remember my address?*

I looked at my watch. I was supposed to be at Luke's in thirty minutes. I considered canceling, but then I remembered I had nowhere to stay.

CHAPTER 16

I made it to Luke's house early, and my mood temporarily improved when he answered the door wearing an apron. Laughing at him eased some of my tension.

"Don't make fun of the apron," he said, waggling his index finger at me.

"I wouldn't dare," I answered. "You look very serious. Can I help?"

He handed me a bottle opener and a wine bottle. "This is your one job. Open a bottle, pour yourself a glass, and sit." I did exactly that. "What have you been up to? Enjoying your vacation so far?"

I laughed and couldn't stop. It was cathartic. He watched me with a concerned look. I must have sounded hysterical, laughing at such an innocent question. When I finally regained control, I took a deep breath.

"To be honest, there haven't been very many moments lately that felt like a vacation." There had been some. The first beach I visited with Lucien. Snorkeling with Lucien. But all of my vacation memories were lies. Lucien was using those times to get close to me, and each one of those memories was spoiled.

Tears streamed down my face. Luke was busy at the stove, but my silence distracted him, and he glanced over and saw me crying. He pushed a pan onto the countertop and grabbed a paper towel, and then he was on his knees in front of me.

"Shh. It's okay. Whatever's happened, I'm sure it's not that bad."

I sniffed. "It's pretty bad."

"Want to talk about it?"

"I'm okay. Today's been a roller coaster, that's all. Finish cooking, please. I don't want you to burn my dinner."

I dried my eyes, sipped my wine, and sniffed again. Then I walked out to the patio and collapsed into a chair. Maybe coming here wasn't such a good idea, but where else could I go? I needed a place to stay. And this time, I didn't have a pile of cash in my pocket.

Luke joined me on the patio. "Dinner's almost ready," he said. "Want to talk about it?"

I shook my head. "I want to talk about anything else." I smiled softly. "Tell me about your project—the house. How's it coming along?"

"Finished the wiring today, and more dry wall went up. You should come back and see it again."

I nodded.

"C'mon, let's eat."

"I think I skipped lunch," I told him. The last time I remembered eating was the croissant Lucien brought me this morning. My stomach growled.

"You like seafood, I hope."

"Sure," I said.

"Triggerfish. Ever tried it?"

"I don't think so. It's local here?"

He nodded. "I caught it this morning."

"You caught this yourself? And then you cooked it?" I had to admit, that was impressive.

"Yep." He set a plate in front of me. A fillet drizzled with a yellow sauce, rice, and peas. "Eat up."

I took a bite. The fish was delicately flavored and slightly sweet. The sauce was garlic and saffron. It complemented the fish, not overpowering the flavor.

"Do you like to fish?" he asked.

"I don't really fish, no. I used to when I was a kid. We went out all the time, but after my parents died, I guess I just never had another opportunity. It wasn't the sort of thing I did on my own."

"When did your parents die?"

"A long time ago. When I was seventeen. And you?" I asked, redirecting the conversation. "Do you fish a lot?"

"I try to. Work gets in the way. That house has consumed me. I'm there twenty-four-seven."

I took another bite. He was a good cook.

"Where are you from?"

We'd skipped that part. I knew what he sounded like when he snored because he'd spent the night next to my hospital bed, but he didn't know where I'd grown up. "Homestead. It's a little town outside of Miami."

"All your life?"

I nodded.

"When I was younger, I envied people like you. That came from one place and stayed there. I was shipped back and forth on a regular basis. I liked it here, and I liked California, but the bouncing back and forth was hard."

"Does your mom still live there?"

"Yes. I rarely see her. She sometimes says she'll retire here, but I'm not sure she'll ever retire. She's a teacher, and she loves her job."

"And your dad?"

He pushed his chair back and went back to the stove. "More fish?"

"Please," I answered.

"My dad lives here. He has a family. Two kids, much younger than me—still little kids. I see them often, but they're busy. He runs a charter company for tourists."

I ate until I was stuffed. We chatted about his family, his half-brother and sister, his aunt, who lived on a neighboring island. He was easy to talk to.

When the bottle of wine was gone, he said, "I ate too much. Let's go for a walk."

We went barefoot onto the sand.

"How's your arm?" he asked.

"Doesn't hurt anymore." I paused. "Thanks for taking care of me. Both times."

"My pleasure," he said, and then we were both quiet for a while.

The beach by his condo was massive. It took several minutes to walk to the water. Once there, we walked in the surf.

"Want to talk about it yet?" He spoke softly, careful not to stir up my erratic emotion from earlier.

"Today was hard. I found out someone that I thought was my friend had betrayed me. Since I arrived here, I found out my best friend was using me to embezzle money from the company where I worked, and then she was killed. And my boss was killed. I'm stuck here. I'm all alone, and I have to figure a way out of this." He didn't answer. "Sorry you asked?"

"Not at all. Just processing. That's a lot. She was killed because of the money?"

"I don't know."

"Was your boss in on it?"

Was he? He couldn't be. He was the one that had asked me about it. "No, I don't think so. I think he started asking questions, and he was killed for that. But that's just a theory."

"Are you in danger, too then?"

I nodded. "I have to find the money. Until they have it, I think they can't touch me."

"How do you do that?"

I shrugged. "Can we go back to not talking about it?"

He chuckled. "Of course. What do you want to talk about?"

"Can you help me find a place to stay tonight?"

"Where have you been staying?"

"I rented a villa, but I can't go back there."

He stopped walking. "Stay with me. I mean, if you want. I'm not being forward. I have a guest room. It's all yours."

"That's nice of you, but I just explained that I'm being chased by someone that wants the money badly enough to kill anyone that gets in their way. And you're inviting me to stay?"

"When you put it that way, it sounds like a bad idea."

I smiled. He had a disarming humor. Staying with him was probably a bad idea, but he was nice, and I felt comfortable with him. "One night, and then I'll find a new place tomorrow."

"Deal. Now that's settled, let's head back and open another bottle. If I were in your shoes, I'd want another drink."

"I'm not wearing shoes," I teased.

He laughed, and I joined in, and this time I wasn't hysterical.

Luke's guest bedroom was a twin bed in his home office. He cleared off the bed and put on clean sheets. After another bottle of wine, I was tipsy and exhausted, and I fell into bed and was asleep immediately.

#

Sunday morning was lazy. I slept in, emerging only after noise from the kitchen roused me.

"Pancakes!" Luke announced. "Brain food. You seem like you have some issues to work out today, and you can't do that on an empty stomach. So, I made banana pancakes."

"Thanks," I mumbled.

I sat at the table, and he dropped a plate with pancakes in front of me. Syrup oozed down the stack. "I hate syrup," I complained.

"Weird," he said. "Good thing I made extra." He whipped the plate away and replaced it with another stack. "What do you put on your pancakes?"

"Well, I don't really eat pancakes, but I guess I just put butter on them."

"What red-blooded American doesn't like syrup?"

"Me," I answered with my mouth full. The pancakes tasted of banana and brown sugar. "Wow, these are good."

"Coffee?"

"Please. Can I ask you something?"

"Of course," he said. He joined me at the table with his plate.

"Why are you being so nice to me? You saved my life—like twice, and you let me stay here. Now you're serving up homemade pancakes."

He grinned. "Well, other than the fact that you provide me with so many opportunities to be a hero, I kinda like you."

"But I wasn't very nice when we met."

He chuckled. "No, you were a mess. You were bleeding, clearly in shock, and still too proud to accept help. I liked your attitude. I still do. You've had a rough time here. Anyone else would be a mess, crying, wringing their hands, but you're solid. Totally in control."

"I cried last night."

"For two seconds. Look at yourself now. A lot of people would have just eaten the syrup to be polite, but you didn't. You turned your nose up at my expensive maple syrup that I imported from the States. You know yourself, and I respect that."

I smiled and blinked away fresh tears before he continued, "I don't doubt that whoever is after you is going to regret ever taking you on. You're a force to be reckoned with."

"Thanks," I said.

"So, what's your plan for the day?"

"Surveillance."

"Like a stakeout?" He sounded excited.

"No, like I'm going to stare at a boat all day until something happens. I think it will probably be very boring."

"You need a partner?"

I shook my head. "Too dangerous."

"Well, if you don't invite me along, I'm just going to follow you and maybe spoil your cover."

"You wouldn't!"

"Yeah, I wouldn't. I get that the stakes are high, but I can help. I have a perfect surveillance vehicle."

"Your truck?" I asked, but he shook his head. "I don't need a partner," I told him. "I thought I had a partner yesterday, but it turns out he was on the wrong side. Don't you have to work today anyway?"

"Nope." He sat there wearing a smug look. Like he knew something I didn't know.

"Okay, tell me. What's your vehicle?"

"I have a van. It's not mine, but we can borrow it for the day. Sometimes I use it for jobs. It belongs to a buddy of mine. It's perfect for a stakeout."

"It's not a stakeout," I argued. But having a different car was a good idea. I'd be completely hidden. "Okay, you can come."

He clapped and jumped from his chair. "I'll be in charge of snacks!"

I laughed. So ridiculous to talk about snacks when I was about to follow a murderer around the island.

#

I understood Luke's need for snacks after two hours. We were parked in the marina lot. Luke had sweet-talked his way through the gate, and he'd parked in a spot with a perfect vantage of *The Second Chance*. So far, we hadn't seen anybody, but Luke had eaten two granola bars, a bag of chips, and an apple. I wasn't sure he'd brought enough snacks to last the day.

"Who are we watching?" he asked.

He'd brought a camera with a telescoping lens and a pair of binoculars—much better than the ones I'd bought. He was full of surprises.

"I don't know who they are. I know that Sandy bought that boat."

"The Second Chance," he interjected.

"Yes, she gave me keys to the boat."

"If you have the keys, why are the bad people on it?"

"You are quick to take sides. How do you know they're the bad ones? Maybe you have it backward, and I'm the bad guy here." He ignored me and kept staring through the binoculars. "The bad guys must have keys too. Sandy was working with them. She's one of them."

"And how do you fit into this?" he asked.

"No idea. I don't even know what *this* is."

"So, how did you get dragged into it?"

"I came here because Sandy invited me."

He dropped the binoculars and looked at me. "No, I get that part, but why do they think you're involved?"

Could I trust him? He was adorable and helpful. And if I told him anything more, I'd be putting him in danger as well, but he was here, on my stakeout. He'd saved my life a couple of times, he'd fed me, and given me a place to sleep.

"Because Sandy put all of the money in banks in my name."

"Why?"

"I don't know. She keeps leaving me notes. She wants me to play this stupid game, follow her clues, but she isn't giving me any way out of the game. Each time I figure out one of the clues, there's just another clue to follow. I have no idea why she put all the money in my name."

He was quiet after that and another hour passed. There was no activity on the boat, and Luke was running out of snacks. I began to think about the next clue. *The*

Premier Ink. Ink meant tattoos. I'd seen Sandy naked; I knew her only tattoo was the dove on her shoulder blade. I didn't have any tattoos, but we'd talked about getting one together.

"What would you get, Anne? As a tattoo?" she'd asked.

"I wouldn't. I hate needles."

"Oh, play along. Imagine it's a fake one if you have to, but what's important enough to you to tattoo it on your body?"

I had a fleeting thought, but it came with unwanted emotion, so I said, "Nothing."

She was wistful. "Do you know what mine means? The dove?"

"No," I'd answered.

"Freedom. And hope."

"Well, I guess it worked. You're the freest person I know."

While Luke kept watch, I ran a search for tattoo parlors on the island. There were several, but the list was short enough to run through. Superior Tattoo. A bank across the street. Easy clue. Was it too easy?

"You're quiet," Luke said.

"Yeah, wondering why we're still sitting here. Nothing's happening, and I need to find a place to stay."

"Surveillance takes time. You have to be patient. And I was thinking about your housing issue. I have a friend with a place here. He's not here often, and I have his keys. I'm sure you could crash there for a few nights. I'll text him and ask."

"What kind of place?" I asked.

"Oh, you're homeless *and* picky?"

"No," I chuckled. "I'm not picky. Just wondering."

"It's a condo at the North end of the island. It's a nice place. Clean. But you can always just stay with me, too."

I couldn't. As much as I'd enjoyed spending time with him, I needed my own space. "Text him," I said. "Please."

At lunchtime, Luke left me alone in the van to go get food. He came back with an assortment of junk food from the little market in the marina. I declined all of it. I was still full of pancakes. He left two more times: to get water and to use the restroom. He was terrible at surveillance.

There was no activity on the boat. Mid-afternoon, my phone rang with an unrecognized number, and I sent it to voicemail. A full minute later, it buzzed with a notification of a new message. I listened while I stared at the boat.

"Hi, this message is for Anne Wilson. My name is Susan Jorgensen. I'm Gilda's mom." There was a pause. "I'm here in Saint Martin. I, uh, wondered if you'd meet with me. It would be nice to talk to one of Gildy's friends. You can call me back on this number, or you can also reach me at the Grand Case hotel. I'll be staying there for a few days. Thanks, bye-bye."

Sandy's mom? Why was it strange to find out she had a mother? Of course, she had one, but she never spoke about her family. I'd always assumed they were no longer a part of her life.

"You okay?" Luke asked. "Who was it?"

"Sandy's mom. She's here on the island. She wants to meet with me."

"You should. Maybe she has some of the answers you're looking for."

"I doubt it. They weren't close. Or maybe they were. I didn't even know Sandy's real name."

"Still. There's nothing going on here. I'll keep an eye out while you make the call."

I pulled my hat on and stepped out of the van. I walked out of sight behind the building with the locker room and dialed the number.

"Hello? Mrs. Jorgensen?"

"Oh, call me Susan, honey. Thanks for calling me back. The nice policeman told me you were still here. I thought maybe we could have a drink. It would be nice to talk to someone that knew Gilda. Can you meet me here? In an hour, maybe?"

I was curious. So very curious.

"Okay."

She repeated the name of her hotel, and I promised to come within an hour.

I walked back to the van and told Luke. "Want me to come along?" he asked. And I did. I wanted the company.

CHAPTER 17

Sandy's mom didn't look at all like the tourists that visited the Everglades. She had a runner's build. She wore skinny jeans and a simple white T-shirt. A tiny gold heart hung from a thin chain around her neck. She seemed too young to be Sandy's mom. She greeted me with a quick hug and insisted I call her Susan, but I called her Mrs. Jorgensen instead. The three of us ordered drinks and sat on the hotel's patio. I opted for a boring Sauvignon Blanc, Luke ordered a beer, and Mrs. Jorgensen had a dry martini.

I introduced Luke, and he knew exactly the right thing to say, "I'm very sorry for your loss. I didn't know your daughter, but I know she and Anne were close."

Mrs. Jorgensen smiled and patted my knee. "I'm glad she had you, Anne. She never had many close friends."

"When was the last time you saw her? It's just that she never talked about her family." I said.

"Years," she answered. "Not since she got out of prison."

A gasp caught me mid-sip, and wine went up my nose.

"You didn't know," she said. "I'm sorry to surprise you like that. I just assumed she'd told you."

I shook my head and gulped wine to stop coughing. "She didn't tell me. Why was she in prison?"

Mrs. Jorgensen leaned forward and spoke quietly. "One tiny thing can change your life forever." She paused, and I held my breath. "Not exactly tiny, though. She served eight years, a harsh sentence. She'd just turned nineteen. Still a kid, really." Her voice trailed off, and Luke and I stayed silent, too surprised to answer. "When she got out, she came home for a couple of months, but it wasn't any good. She never got along with her father, and our town is too small to forget something like that. So she left, and I haven't seen her since. The first couple of years, she sent cards at Christmas and birthdays, but nothing lately."

"I'm so sorry," Luke said. "It's like you're losing her all over again."

She nodded. "Exactly. At least before I had hope that she would return. Now…So, it's good to know she had a good friend."

Was I a good friend? If she hadn't told me this one huge thing? If she never talked about her family, her childhood? Were we close? Or were we simply companions? Two people trying to ignore their past, living fully in the present, hoping for something better.

"What was she like?" Luke asked. "When she was younger."

Mrs. Jorgensen lit up with the memory of her daughter before *that thing* that changed her life. "My Gildy was never meant to be stuck in a small town. She had dreams, you know? She was smart. She could've gone to college. Just like her daddy. He was a charmer." She stopped and smiled sadly. "He charmed everything. I thought when he died, maybe she'd come home again, but I suppose there was nothing there for her. She wanted something more than she could find there."

We stayed for a while longer and listened to her stories about Gilda Jorgensen, but the girl she described seemed like another person than the Sandy I knew. I considered telling Mrs. Jorgensen about my Sandy. Perhaps knowing who she had become would have given her some comfort. But I didn't know Sandy well enough to understand why she'd stayed away from her family, so I left it unsaid.

We left the hotel and climbed back into the borrowed van.

"Feel like a quick detour?" Luke asked.

"Sure," I said, still sad for Mrs. Jorgensen's loss and my own, but behind the grief was a feeling of disappointment in myself for not being a better friend. I was still angry at her for putting me in the middle of whatever she was involved in, but maybe it was time for me to let go a little and forgive her.

Luke drove to his job site, and I was surprised by the progress they'd made in a few days. Wires and pipes ran through the skeletal walls of the living room and dining room, but most the other walls were now covered with drywall. The layout was simple, but the rooms were large, and the ceilings were tall—maybe ten feet. The open space past the kitchen was now filled with large cardboard boxes.

Luke pointed at them and said, "Cabinets get installed this week. Then, the flooring goes in. And the windows. So much happens in the next two weeks."

I walked outside to admire the view. I remembered it from my last visit, but my head wasn't spinning this time. I stood on the edge of the slab, confident that I wouldn't tumble down the cliff face.

One side of the patio was cluttered with various pieces of wood—the cast-offs from the scaffolding. I peered down at the strange wooden structure. After about ten wooden steps, it became an open framework that dropped forty feet. The tallest part of the frame was connected to cables that ran to anchors in the exposed side of the concrete where I stood. Several ropes hung from the framework. They disappeared out of sight behind a boulder. Chisel marks scarred the surface of the first section of exposed stone where two steps had been carved into the rock face.

"Want to go down?" Luke asked.

"You're cutting steps into the rock?" I asked. He grinned and hopped down the wooden stairs to land on the top of the stone. "I don't get it. Why do they go straight down? Instead of along there." I pointed beyond the driveway. It was thick with brush, but a path could have been cut into the hillside. A switchback or two would have made a gentle-sloped walking path.

"I'm trying to build with a minimum of disturbance to the environment. I almost decided not to have beach access at all, but I free-climbed it a few times and found a path to cut stairs that should have a minimal impact. The steps will just become part of the wall."

"You free-climbed that?" I asked.

"It's not as steep as it looks. Around that boulder, you can almost slide in a few places."

"How long will it take to carve the steps?"

"A while," he said. "Couple weeks, maybe. The rock guy spent all day yesterday on this." He stomped on the step. "But he said he was getting a feel for the stone. And he spent a lot of time hanging from the scaffolding."

"He hangs?"

"Yeah, we harness him, and he moves down the cliff using that pulley system. Cool, right?"

It didn't look cool. I couldn't imagine hanging over a cliff while carving stone. It seemed insane.

"Come down here. You can just see the beach from this spot. Hold the rope if it makes you feel better."

The rope didn't make me feel better, but I held on and descended the steps.

"That's it," he said as I joined him on the stone step. "Now, hold on to this rope and lean out a bit."

I gave him an exasperated look, but I followed him.

"Wow," I said. "It's a little cove."

"The steps will come around that way." He pointed to our left. "And drop down on the beach. There's a sheltered part in the rock, like a little cave. I want to build a kayak stand in that. Those rocks curve and shelter the beach enough that you can launch a kayak from there, and as long as you line it up correctly, the waves put you right back on the beach."

"You make it sound like this is your house."

He laughed. "This is my house."

"Oh," I said, surprised. "I thought it was a job site."

"Yeah, mine. I built four of these as spec homes, but this one's mine."

I'd completely misjudged him.

"Okay, let's grab your things and get you settled into your new place. We can grab something for dinner on the way. The best pizza place on the island is on the way."

"You eat a lot," I said.

I climbed the stairs and turned for a final look. The view was still dizzying.

#

Luke's friend's condo was a minimalistic penthouse. White furniture and stainless steel appliances made it feel sterile and not very comfortable, but it was a safe place to land for a few nights until I made a new plan. I followed Luke in my car and parked it in the garage. Luke ate a few slices of pizza and then left with a quick goodbye.

"Call me if you need help. I enjoyed our stakeout, but I won't waste my breath telling you to be careful. I get that you have to figure out how to get yourself out of this, but remember, I'm only a phone call away."

I sat on the balcony and watched the sun set. I'd wasted the day. The plan to follow Lucien and Terry had failed. The meeting with Sandy's mom had been intriguing but unhelpful. The only positive note was that hanging out with Luke had calmed my nerves. In twenty-four hours, I'd gone from hysterical to level-headed.

I still had another option. I could use the fact that I knew Lucien was involved. I had his number. If I used a new phone, I could text him—somehow bring him out to meet with Terry at the boat. But to what end? To put him on alert? He might suspect me because I'd gone dark. I never sent him a message. I'd chickened out—thinking he would be able to see through my lies. If I flushed them out, I wouldn't be able to follow all three of them anyway. I'd have to choose one.

I ran through possible scenarios. Texting Lucien, watching them gather, following one of them, but my imagination was as limited as my knowledge, and each plan ended in another dead end. Watching the boat didn't get me anywhere. I needed to get on the boat. If Sandy had lived there, something would help me figure out what she was up to. I also had another bank to visit. It was only a couple minutes from where I was staying, so I could visit the bank when they opened and then return to the boat.

Then I remembered my doctor's appointment and altered the timing. First the doctor, then the bank, and finally the boat. It was as good as any plan I was going to come up with.

I went inside and locked the condo. The bed was too soft, but after staring at the ceiling for an hour, I drifted to sleep and woke at dawn. I watched the sunrise from the balcony, hoping that today was going to be the day where everything changed.

#

The doctor was pleased with my recovery. I still had two days of antibiotics left, but he said there was no need for another follow-up unless I had problems. I didn't tell him that I already had more problems than I could handle.

After the doctor appointment, I followed the familiar protocol at the bank and waited. Nobody was in a hurry. The box held a million and a half dollars, another key with a clue, and four pages of handwritten scrawl—Sandy's drunk letter. I hoped drunk Sandy would be more enlightening.

I pocketed the key, the clue, and the letter. I left the money and walked back to my car. Then I drove back to the marina and parked in the restaurant lot next door. I used the binoculars to peek at the boat, but nobody appeared right away, so I opened the letter.

Anne,

I've written this letter so many times. In this particular instance, practice does not make perfect. Because I still can't figure out how to say the words.

I could tell she was drunk when she wrote it. She used unnecessary phrases like "particular instance" and "impossible situation" when she drank too much.

When you want to make up for ruining someone's life, how do you put a number on that? Any amount puts a price on happiness, and I do know deep in my soul that no amount of money can repair the damage I've done. I want you to know that I always knew anything I did would never be enough. But I want you to know how hard I tried. I want you to know that I've been consumed by this for years. It's all I've known, this one single goal to change your life again, but for the better this time.

You're amazing. So strong and independent. The one and only time I asked about how you felt about losing your family the way you did, do you remember what you said? You told me that it taught you how to survive. It made you who you are. And you said it with a pride that I've never felt in my thirty-three years. I've never met anyone like you.

In case you never speak to me again after this, and you have every reason not to, by the way, I want you to know how much I enjoyed the past year. You were the sister that I never had, the college roommate I never knew, the best friend I always hoped for. You were my person, Anne Wilson. And I didn't deserve you.

I set the pages down without finishing. It was out of character for her to be that drunk chick that professed her endless love for everyone and the lamp post. Drunk Sandy drew inward and spoke with an overly serious tone as if alcohol enhanced her control instead of loosening it, but this letter showed a different person—an emotional person. I didn't know her this way in life, and I didn't want to know this side of her in death.

I picked up the binoculars again and watched the boat, adjusting the plastic eyepieces against my face. The binoculars made my head hurt, and my neck was stiff from slouching out of sight. I wanted to scream. Sandy's apology didn't help me. I needed proof that I didn't kill anyone—not another key. How many more keys were there? When would this end?

I rolled my shoulders and reset my line of sight on the boat as Terry and another man appeared on the dock. I'd almost missed them. I followed their progress through the gate and panicked when I lost them behind a building. I scanned the lot and caught them getting into a red convertible.

Lucien.

As the car flipped a U-turn and sped away, I grabbed the boat keyring and ran into the marina. I only needed a few minutes on the boat. At the C gate, I hesitated, my hand on the knob. If either man returned while I was still aboard, I could slip over the side and swim away, but my phone was in my pocket. I backtracked and used the white keycard to open the women's locker room and set everything from my pockets inside the locker. I added the locker key to the key chain with the boat keys and hurried back to the C gate.

The gate slammed shut behind me with a loud crash, and I slowed to a walk and passed *The Second Chance* with a casual sideways glance. The cabin was empty. I paused on the dock, rotating, scanning the neighboring boats, but nobody was around. My heart skipped a beat when I stepped aboard *The Second Chance*, and the boat shifted under my weight. But no one appeared or called out. I unlocked the door and went inside.

CHAPTER 18

The door closed behind me. The sudden silence was disconcerting, and I stayed in the doorway, listening, but all of the harbor noises, the hysterical screeching of gulls, and the clanging halyards were muffled inside the cabin. I let out my breath and moved farther inside, past the kitchen and into a living area with an L-shaped white leather couch and a shiny mahogany table. Clean and uncluttered.

Toward the front of the boat was a cockpit, or whatever the boat version was called. There were no papers and no personal effects. A set of carpeted steps led below. I stood at the top and listened.

Only a few minutes had elapsed since I'd climbed aboard, but I looked out at the marina, scanning the path beyond the gate, searching for signs of Terry, Lucien, or the other man. I needed a lookout and thought of Luke, but I didn't have my phone, and I regretted leaving it behind. I hadn't even told Luke where I was going. But there wasn't time to go back. I needed to search the cabins below deck and get off the boat.

I descended the steps and found two bedrooms. The one on the right had rumpled bedsheets with clothes strewn across the floor. I searched that one first. The clothes and toiletries were Terry's. He had a slight build. No mistaking Lucien's extra-large, button-down shirts with Terry's narrow T-shirts.

I walked into the next cabin and into a cloud of Sandy's scent. I could *smell* Sandy—her lotion, an earthy mixture of grapefruit and algae. I closed my eyes for a moment as if I could conjure her by smelling her, but the room was empty, and her scent was the only evidence she'd ever been there. There were no pictures, no clothes. Terry, or someone, had cleared Sandy's belongings. I sat on her bed and hugged her pillow. Another dead end.

The boat lurched, and I jumped from the bed and crouched at the bottom of the steps. Overhead, the door opened and slammed, and then footsteps hurried overhead. I silently crawled up the carpeted steps on hands and knees. There was a scratching noise, a small cough, and a series of clicks. And then the engine turned over, and the boat was moving.

#

I lost my balance when the boat lurched and slammed into the wall. I grabbed the railing to stop myself from falling down the steps.

Why was the boat moving? No, that didn't matter. I needed to get up top and outside and overboard. I climbed the remaining steps and peered into the cabin. I couldn't see anyone. Anyone driving the boat would be in the cockpit, but a low wall separated it from the back area. I could crawl along the floor unseen. He'd notice the door opening, but by then, I'd be three long strides from going over the side.

Was it safe to jump from a moving boat? Probably not, but was it safer than staying on a boat with Terry? I craned my neck around the opening to the stairway, trying to get a look at him.

"You can come out," Terry called. I flattened myself against the stairs. "I installed a camera on the door. I figured you'd make it here eventually. It saved me the trouble of tracking you down. You should come sit. It'll be safer if you're sitting down. We wouldn't want you to get hurt when I speed up."

We were still in the harbor. I sprang up and sprinted to the door, but the catch stuck. Locked. I fished the keys from my pocket and lost my balance as the boat slowed. I turned to make sure he was still driving the boat, but he stood right behind me, holding a gun.

"Up front. And hurry. I need to get back to the wheel."

I stepped past him and strode to the cockpit, considering my options. I could grab the throttle and drive us into the rocks, but I doubted that would go well for either of us. He pushed me into the seat, put the boat back in gear and grabbed the wheel with the hand that wasn't holding the gun.

"Let's take this baby out of the harbor and open her up. See what she's capable of."

He passed the breakwater and sped up, and I was glad I was seated. We hit the first wave with a jolt that almost knocked the gun from Terry's hand, but then the boat found another speed, and it seemed like we weren't hitting the waves but flying just above them. Going fast. Within a minute, the harbor was no longer within my reach.

"We're just going to hang out here and have a nice little chat."

He kept driving until we were far from land. I couldn't see any other boats.

"What do you want from me?" I asked.

"The money, Anne. Where did you hide it?"

"You already took what I found."

"Now, I know that's not true. You may be a prude bitch, but you're smart. Lucien told me you've been visiting banks. He thinks you're still looking for it, but I think you've got him snowed. You figured him out fast enough. I'm impressed by that. Women never see through him. Even Gildy, the most suspicious person I've ever known, was head over heels for Lucien."

Sandy? With Lucien?

"What was that look? Jealousy?" he sneered. "Maybe I gave you too much credit. You fell for him too, didn't you?"

I stayed quiet, searching the boat for an escape. On the front, strapped to the deck, was a dinghy. If I could overpower Terry and get the dinghy in the water, I could escape. I searched the coastline. From where we sat, it looked rocky, but I could follow it back to the harbor.

"Where's the money?"

"I don't know," I said.

"I can see you staring at that dinghy like it's your lifeboat. It's not. There's only one way out of this. Give me the money. All fifteen million."

"Fifteen million?" I cried. "You stole fifteen million?"

He laughed. "Is that what you think we did? Steal it?" He kept laughing. "I wondered if Gildy had told you everything. You acted like you knew what was going on, but you're as much in the dark as she told me you were. How much money did you think you were searching for?"

"Three million," I lied. I knew it was more. I'd found more, but I never dreamed it was fifteen million.

"How much have you found?"

"Just the money in the backpack."

He waggled the gun at me. "Don't lie. I get mean when people lie to me. You don't want me to get mean, do you?"

"I'm supposed to follow the clues, but Lucien…" I let my voice trail off.

"You two were too busy playing house to find the money. Well, no more beach days for you. Time to get the money. What's your first clue?"

I stayed quiet. He couldn't get to the money without me.

"You need me."

"I know I do, sweetheart." His voice was cold. A shudder ran up my spine. "I think it's time we find a little motivation for you. All this time, Lucien's been protecting you, coaxing you, building you up, but his way didn't work. So, now it's time to try my way. You won't like it."

At work, I'd thought of him as a nervous kid, but this Terry was a different person. I hadn't known him well—our interactions were brief and limited to conversations about his customers. He seemed older now. And colder. I hadn't considered him capable of murder, but now…he scared me.

He opened a compartment and took out a pair of pliers. He set them on the seat next to him, and the way he looked at them frightened me more than the gun.

"We're going to play a little game. I'm going to ask you a question, and you're going to answer me. If I don't like your answer, I'm going to hurt you. Ready to play?"

"What if I don't know the answers? Like you said, I've been spending my days at the beach with Lucien instead of following the clues."

He sneered again. "You've been following the clues. I know what kind of person you are, Anne Wilson. You have to be the smartest person in any room. You're smarter than Gildy. I know you are, so don't try to play dumb."

I stayed quiet again.

"What was your first clue?"

I closed my eyes and thought about the bank where the clues had started. "She told me to find a snail."

"What does that mean?"

"It's how she hid everything from you. Each clue is a memory that we shared. Nobody but me can follow the trail."

"What does it mean? The clue about the snail."

"There's a restaurant on the island called Escargot."

He was getting angry. "So, what does that mean?"

"It's next to a bank," I said.

"And that's where the money is?"

I shook my head. "Inside a safety deposit box in my name, I found three hundred grand."

He sat back down. Deflated. "It's all in cash. That's why I can't find a trail."

I didn't know if that was a question. "Yes," I answered.

"How much?" he asked.

"How much what?"

"How much have you found so far?"

I hesitated, and he noticed. He swung his hand, and the gun connected with my jaw with a sickening pop. I cowered, covering my face, and tasted blood in my mouth.

"One more time. How much have you found?"

The taste of blood gagged me, and I coughed and spat blood across the window. It dribbled down my chin, and I wiped it away with the back of my hand.

"The first three banks had a total of one point five million," I said. I swallowed painfully and gagged again. "Can I have some water?" I asked. I didn't want to throw up.

"One more question. How many banks are there?"

"I don't know!" I cried. I held both hands up, expecting another blow. "I swear. I don't know. I haven't followed all the clues yet."

He handed me a water bottle. "Because lover-boy Lucien has been wasting your time. He's been trying to romance the money out of you. Tell me this, were you ever going to share the money with him?"

"No," I answered. "I wasn't going to keep it. I was going to give it back. Clear my name."

He laughed again. "You don't need to clear your name. You never did anything wrong. Mr. Sampson poked his nose where it didn't belong. I should thank you, you know?"

"Why?"

"Your reaction that day—that's what set all this in motion. Mr. Sampson called you into his office, and a few minutes later, you were emailing everyone in the department. Without the head's up, I wouldn't have known he was on to me. I wouldn't have known to get out of there. I was already starting to suspect Gildy was hiding something from me, but that night I knew. I checked the accounts and found out she'd taken all of it. Everything changed that night."

I caused this?

"Give me your phone."

"I don't have it. I left it behind in case I had to go overboard."

"You see, that's the kind of thing I'd expect you to say. You think things through. Not like Gildy. But I don't believe you. Stand up."

I stood up, pressing my hand to my face. It throbbed, but the bleeding had stopped. I probed my teeth with my tongue, and everything seemed in place. Terry patted my short pockets, pulling out the boat keys and tossing them onto the ledge behind me.

"You won't need those any longer. By the way, she put the boat in your name, so I'll need you to sign it over."

"Okay," I agreed. I didn't want the boat anyway.

"Now, go downstairs and clean up your face. You're a mess. And get something to clean the window. I need to anchor the boat. We can't just float on this side of the island. We'll end on the rocks before too long. But once we're anchored, we are going to continue our chat, and I want answers."

I went down the stairs, relieved to be out of his reach. I went into Sandy's bedroom and closed the door. Her scent made my bottom lip tremble. I found a washcloth in the bathroom, wiped my bloodied face, and pressed the cold cloth against my bruised skin.

The boat began to move again. I sat on the toilet and braced myself against the shower door with my foot. There was only one option. I had to tell him about all the banks. He had to let me off the boat to visit them; I was his only access to the money.

I stayed in the bathroom until the boat stopped moving. Then I ventured back upstairs. He glanced at me as I used the washcloth to clean the blood from the window. He was pushing buttons and levers, focused on whatever it took to anchor a boat.

The sky had darkened with ominous gray clouds, but I brightened when I saw a lone catamaran behind us. I estimated the distance between our boats. It was a long swim—well beyond shouting distance. The shore was even farther, too distant to see whether there was a beach.

"Why are we anchoring here?" I asked.

"So I don't have to wave a gun around. Actually, there's no point in waving it around. It's not even loaded. You can go overboard if you want to. If you make it to shore, you'll be stranded. You can't climb that cliff. I promise, once you answer my questions, I'll take you back."

"All you want is the money?"

"All I want is the money. It was supposed to be split three ways—me, Gildy, and Dominik, but now Gildy's gone. So, now I want half. Seven and a half million. Where is it?"

I shook my head. "I haven't found that much yet. It's in small amounts. Why doesn't Lucien get a cut?"

He threw me a sour look. "What is it about that guy? Gildy was the same way. Everything was always about Lucien. Dominik brought him in, so he can pay Lucien out of his share."

"Who's Dominik?"

He gave me an annoyed sideways glance. "I'm the one asking the questions, remember?" But his tone had softened. He had the upper hand; he'd relaxed. So I pushed a little.

"What do you mean you didn't steal the money?"

"You know the saying, if I told ya, I'd have to kill ya?"

I nodded.

"Are you sure you want the answer to that question?" he asked, but then he continued as if he wanted to explain it to me. "Gildy came up with a foolproof plan, and it was working until Mr. Sampson poked his nose where it didn't belong. Fine with me, though. Now that Gildy's gone, I have enough to go where I can't be found. I'm taking this boat and the cash."

"I'll find it. I just need a few more days."

"How much have you found? The truth this time."

I did the math in my head. "Four and a half."

I stared at the water. I could swim to the beach. The water was warm, and the current would push me toward land. The only unknown was the beach. I couldn't see where I was. I knew there were areas on the island where the closest road was miles from the beach. I had to assume that's where Terry had anchored.

I walked to the back door and tested it. It opened. He'd unlocked it to work on the anchor. I stepped outside, testing my leash. Terry watched me but didn't argue. It was windy, and the air was charged the way it gets just before a storm. If I went in the water while he was fiddling with the anchor, he might not notice right away. It could give me a head start. And he'd have to pull the anchor in order to follow me, which would give me even more time. I stretched my right arm. It was still stiff from the surgery, but it was healing well.

I watched him bend over the controls once more, and I stepped over the swim step door and slipped into the water. I hoped the small splash I made would be concealed by the sound of the waves slapping against the hull. I pulled away from the boat, kicked off my shoes, and began to swim.

I swim daily, Monday through Saturday. Most days, I go through the motions, swimming laps until my time is up, but every once in a while, I let the person in the lane next to me set the pace. Sometimes they notice, and it becomes a race. As I pulled away from the boat, I swam like the person in the lane next to me was also fighting for their life.

But this wasn't my community pool. The incoming storm blew indecisive winds that turned the sea into choppy blackness. Regular breaths were impossible; water sprayed from all directions. The waves were unpredictable—propelling me forward and then pushing against me. A few times, I stopped swimming completely and treaded water, coughing and watching the boat. It grew farther away, and the shore grew closer.

I'd crossed half the distance when I heard the whining sound of an engine. Not the deep grumbling inboards of the boat. This was smaller—the dinghy. Then I heard shouting.

"I don't want to run over you, Anne. I know you're out here."

His voice bounced off the waves, distorting the distance. I pulled my arms through the water with all the strength I had, hoping the darkened skies would keep me hidden. He kept shouting; he was getting closer. He seemed to be driving back and forth in arcs around me. When his voice sounded like it was right behind me, I stopped swimming and became a periscope, holding myself low in the water, spinning, and scanning. He passed several feet from me, still shouting.

"Come out, come out wherever you are."

I stayed still, bobbing in the waves until his head turned my way, and then I ducked underwater until I could no longer hold my breath. When I resurfaced, he had moved past. I treaded water, afraid to break the surface and give away my location. I bobbed along in the waves, hoping the storm wasn't angry enough to push me out to sea.

When his voice faded, I began to swim again. And then there was no need to worry about making any sound. The sky opened up and released rainfall so heavy it became difficult to distinguish between ocean and sky. I swam with the waves, trusting they knew where we were headed, but I could see nothing.

Every couple minutes, I stopped to bob in the water, keeping my line of sight as straight as I could, straining to push myself high enough in the water to spot the shore, but the rain was a sheath, hiding me and hiding my goal.

I cried angry, helpless tears, but they mixed with the constant water around me. When my arms tired, I kicked my legs furiously as if I could propel myself above the storm, but there was no escape. The rain was relentless. I lost my bearings. There was no point in swimming. I floated on my back and closed my eyes against the rain, and surrendered myself to the storm.

When Terry found me and dragged me into the dinghy, I lay in a heap in the corner, gasping for air and hating myself for feeling grateful to him. He drove for only two minutes before he slowed and jumped over the side. I sat up, confused until I realized we'd gone ashore. I'd been so close. I'd almost made it.

Standing on the beach was our welcome party: Lucien.

CHAPTER 19

Lucien hauled me from the dinghy and marched me across a rocky beach, up a concrete path, and into a house. He wrapped a towel around me, and I used it to wring out my hair.

"Jesus, Anne," he whispered. His deep voice, the same voice that had made me shiver with pleasure, now made my skin crawl. "You could have drowned out there. What were you thinking going into the water in the middle of a storm?"

"I thought I was trying to escape."

Lucien stroked my bruised cheek, and I slapped his arm away. "What happened to your face?"

I pointed to Terry.

"You hit her?" Lucien bellowed.

Terry sneered. "I got more out of her with one smack than you did with a week of cuddling. She's got four and a half million already. Almost a third of the way. And she hid all of that from you."

A dark scowl crossed Lucien's face as he turned back to me. "You found that much? Why didn't you tell me?"

"Because you're on the wrong side."

"When did you figure that out?" he asked.

"Does it matter? Look, I want to get out of these wet clothes. Can someone take me to my car? I can't help you guys until the banks open in the morning anyway."

Terry laughed. "There's no way you're leaving my sight again. Until you hand over the money, I'm stuck to you like glue, sweetie."

"Don't call me sweetie," I spat.

Lucien glared at Terry. A door slammed in another part of the house, and Terry jumped.

"You called him?" Terry whispered loudly.

"Of course I did," Lucien answered.

Footsteps approached, and three of us stared expectantly at the door. A man strode in—the man I'd seen with Lucien at the boat. He was older than me, mid-forties and dark—a few shades lighter than Lucien's ebony skin. He had a wide face with short brown hair that stuck up in the front in a trendy style that matched his hipster vest.

"Welcome to my home, Anne," he said. "I'm Dominik. I guess you know everyone else. Has anyone offered you something to drink? No? How rude, boys."

He was unexpected. His words were friendly but carried a sinister undertone. He strode into the next room, and I heard a fridge open and bottles clinking. Then he returned with two Pellegrino's and handed me one.

"Only other thing we have is beer. I thought you'd prefer this."

I accepted the bottle and took a long drink. The bubbles burned my throat, but the water was deliciously cold. He sat across from me.

"I think we were all hoping that we'd never meet—me and Terry, I mean. You got to know Lucien pretty well, right?"

He cocked his head to one side and gave me a knowing glance. I glared back. If he was baiting me, I wasn't going to give him the satisfaction.

"I still don't know for sure if you were in on Gildy's scheme or not. Lucien's convinced that you weren't, but Terry and I are on the fence. The best way to convince us is to hand over the money, and we'll all go our separate ways."

I nodded.

"Good girl. See how easy that was, boys?"

"Dom, she's only found four and a half," Terry said.

Dominik nodded. "We're going to need you to work a little faster. If you do, I won't have to ask Terry to provide motivation. Terry's kisses aren't as sweet as Lucien's, are they?" He stood up, signaling the end of the one-sided conversation. "Terry, tie her up. We have a new problem, and I don't want to discuss it in front of her. She's caused enough trouble already."

"I'll do it," Lucien offered.

Terry and Dominik went into the other room, and I recoiled as Lucien approached. I would've have preferred Terry over Lucien.

"Don't touch me," I hissed.

"Anne, I'm on your side," he whispered.

"You slept with me. How could you do that? And you were with Gilda before? That's the relationship you were getting over? She's been dead a week, and you jumped into bed with me? How could you?"

I heard the jealousy in my voice, but I didn't care. His betrayal was so layered and complex, but the worst part was his disregard for Sandy's memory. Perhaps I *was* Sandy's friend above all else.

He used a roll of duct tape and fastened my hands together. "Will you promise to sit still? I can get you out of this," he said. He sounded tired.

"I don't want your help," I answered. "And no, I don't promise to sit still. I'll run the first chance I get."

He sighed, "I have no choice then. I'll have to tie you up."

He walked to the window, reached for the cord hanging from the blinds and yanked it hard enough to pull it off the wall. The blinds broke and crashed to the floor, but he didn't seem to care about the damage. He used the cord to tie me to the chair, wrapping it around me three times. It was a thin cord, and it dug into the skin of my arms. He knotted the cord behind me, and then he left the room, shutting the door behind him.

I wiggled in the chair, testing the strength of the cord. He'd wrapped me around the abdomen, pinning my arms to my sides, but as he'd pulled tight, I'd fought. When I pulled my right arm into my body, I could move my left arm enough to push the cord up. I rocked back and forth that way, left arm, right arm until the cord began to move up my torso.

It was a painful process that caused repeated rope burns along my arms. As it moved up my right arm, it reopened the scabs, and my arm began to bleed, but soon, the cord was high enough that it loosened around my neck, and I slid out from under it and onto my knees on the floor. I raised my hands and tore at the duct tape with my teeth, and then I was free. I opened the door and stepped out into the rain.

#

I ran. Down the concrete path and to the beach. I turned right and left, gathering my bearings, but I knew where I was. The steps I'd come down were the steps where Lucien had appeared so gloriously ten days ago. This was the same beach where I'd walked with him and daydreamed of our future together. How everything had shifted. The beach was no longer idyllic and safe. The sky and the sea were now dark and menacing.

I heard voices behind me, and I ran. I turned right, sprinting along the beach. I knew it was a dead end, but there were other houses. I just needed to find another path, but the darkness was my ally and my downfall. I tripped on a rock and fell, scraping my hands. I was up and running again searching for a path, but finding nothing but dark rocks and darker trees. I couldn't hear anything but the rain and the wind. I reached the rocks at the far end of the beach. I'd missed any other houses.

I thought of the catamaran anchored nearby and tried to remember what the ocean was like that day I'd stood with Lucien and stared at the waves. The water had been mostly turquoise, darkened in some places, and I knew those shadows were rocks under the surface. But most of the water was clear, and the rocks were on the seabed, so if I stayed at the surface, I could swim around the point. I hesitated on the beach, staring up at the towering dark shapes, wondering if climbing was a better choice, but the rain was lighter, and swimming was my strength—not climbing.

I heard voices again and waded into the water, sinking low to stay hidden. I walked in a crouch on the sandy bottom toward the bobbing catamaran. It stood out, white against the black sea and the black sky. It seemed unoccupied—no light shone from the windows.

I knew there was a beach on the other side of the cliff—the bay that stretched for an eternity, full of houses and resorts. I only needed to get around the rocks, and I could run along that beach to find help.

The water grew deeper, and I lost my footing. I hoped I'd gone out far enough to round the rocks, and I began to swim parallel to the beach. The towering rocks were darker than the sky, and the rain had eased enough that I could see their hulking shapes. I swam slower this time, focused on the water ahead. The waves pushed me toward the beach, moving too fast, fast enough that I knew I could slam against an unseen rock hard enough to snap bones.

My path remained clear, and I kept swimming. I flinched as a rock grazed my thigh, but a wave lifted me up and over it. I wished for a moon, but the storm wasn't accommodating. There was no light, only degrees of darkness. The shapes on the shore softened into something different, and I altered my course and headed straight to the beach. I was tired again, running out of adrenaline.

About fifteen feet from shore, my left shoulder slammed the first rock. I reacted too slowly, rolling within the wave, and hitting the next one with my other side. The second time I dropped my legs and found solid ground. The waves kept coming, forcing me forward, but my footing was solid, and I ran between the dark shapes. When I reached the surf, I slipped and fell, but all I found underneath me was sand. I lay there for a while, heaving, letting the surf crash over me and wash my bleeding shoulders.

Had I not heard the whine of the engine, I might have stayed there until the tide forced me higher, but I sat up to see a wide beam of light dancing across the waves. The light showcased a minefield of jagged rocks. I'd been lucky to only hit two of them. I needed to find cover. The rocks that had tried to kill me were now the barrier that would keep the dinghy offshore, but with a light, they could navigate the rocks.

The beach was a small cove—not a giant bay. I didn't need to reach the end to see the cliff face. It loomed high overhead. I was trapped.

The cliff became a small, sheltered cave. I stood inside out of the rain and knew where I was. Luke's cove.

#

I had to choose: swim or climb. Swimming had gotten me this far, but I couldn't hide from the light in the dinghy. I'd be too exposed. Luke had free-climbed these rocks—in the daylight, not in the middle of a storm, but if I could scramble up high enough to grab the ropes, I could pull myself up the rest of the way. I stood under the shelter, reluctant to choose.

The whine of the engine was closer, and I heard Terry shouting but couldn't understand what he said.

Lucien's deep voice answered, "Go slowly in case she's in the water."

The first rocky ledge was an easy step. I stood on my toes and reached overhead, feeling the stone, searching for natural handholds, using my grip to shift my toes, one foot at a time. My shoulders throbbed, and my right arm burned, but I ignored the pain and heaved myself onto the next ledge. About a foot to my left, I found a three-foot section that sloped enough to inch up the stone like a worm.

I lay against the wall, panting, and peered above me. The next section was a vertical series of linear shelves. I moved my hands across the surface, scratching my fingers as I searched for places to grip. My progress was more horizontal than vertical, but it paid off when I found another sloped area, and I scrambled up a larger section, about five feet, with a ledge at the top wide enough to turn and watch the dinghy in the water below me.

Lucien jumped from the boat onto the beach and walked toward the wall. He stood below me—only a few feet away, but away from the light in the dinghy, it was too dark to see where he was looking. I flattened myself against the wall and froze.

For someone his size, he moved quietly. He disappeared into the cave.

"Nowhere to hide," he called out. I held my breath, unsure if was talking to Terry or if he'd spotted me. "Shine the light in here."

I let out the breath. He hadn't spotted me. But if I stayed in place, Terry's light would reveal me. I turned back to the wall and began to climb again. The process was methodical. I searched for hand grips and then held my body in place while my toes found new holds. The pain in my shoulders was replaced by muscle aches in my calves and my forearms.

As I grasped a section with my right hand, the stone broke away, and I lost my grip and heard the rock cascade down the wall. My fingers floundered along the surface, searching for something solid. Another piece broke away, and I gasped and clung with my toes. But then my hand found a gap in the stone above me, and I reached inside and heaved.

"What was that?" Lucien called out. "Shine the light again. Higher this time."

I froze and listened, unable to turn my head to look below me. I hung from my right arm and pulled my legs higher, resetting my toes. I reached higher with my right hand, but all I found was open space. Thinking it was a wide ledge, I hauled my body up, and for a moment, I was relieved to sit, but a rustling sound from within the black hole made my blood run cold. Something alive was in there. A high-pitched screeching followed, and then a fluttering.

As they came at me, I drew my arms over my head. I couldn't see them emerge from the blackness, but I could *feel* them. Flapping wings. And I saw their shape against the dark sky.

"Just bats," Lucien called out.

I pulled my legs up as the light darted along the wall below me. I followed the progress of the bats as they flew in a wide arc. They were headed back. And I was sitting in their front door.

I wished for a bolt of lightning to light the stone— just one quick flash of light to show me a path forward, but lightning would also give me away. I stepped off the ledge and cowered against the wall as the bats returned to their roost.

"There's no way out of here. Come back and pick me up," Lucien called out. His voice echoed within the cave below. Then the dinghy engine roared as Terry motored back into the cove, and when the engine quit, I heard a scratching sound as the rubber hit the beach.

"Dom called. He's driving the coast road above us, but he hasn't seen her yet. She swam farther than we thought."

"Or she's climbing," Lucien said.

I heard the dinghy squeak as he settled in, and then I saw the light out of the corner of my eye. It bounced along the rock face below me and to my left.

"She couldn't climb that," Terry said. I almost wished the light would find me just to prove him wrong, and I used my anger to heave myself up onto the next ledge. My feet were stable enough to swivel my head, and I watched the light scan the rock face on the other side of the cove. It looked like an easier climb, and I had a panicked moment wondering if I'd gone the wrong way.

The dinghy's engine sputtered back to life and then grew quieter as they moved away. I stayed in place, panting. If I climbed back down, I'd be trapped in the cove all night. If Lucien and Terry returned, I'd be discovered. Above me, Luke's house was wide open—a welcome shelter against the rain. I could hide inside until daylight.

I had to keep climbing.

I took my time, feeling every inch of the rock's surface, testing holds before I put my full weight onto them. I wasn't sure how much time had passed, but it felt like it took an hour to climb another ten feet. The more time I clung to the wall, the more rest I needed when I reached a ledge. Once I found decent footholds, I lay against the stone, catching my breath and reserving my energy.

There were no more engine sounds. All I heard was the rain and the scratching my fingers and toes made against the stone. Climbing became a rhythmic movement. I stabilized with my left hand, gripped high with my right, and slid my feet one at a time, pushing with my toes and pulling with my fingers. I discovered tiny muscles in my toes and became keenly aware of them as they stretched and cramped.

When I reached the boulder, I knew I was at the halfway point. The ropes were close. Behind the boulder was a long ledge—longer than I was tall and about three feet wide. I wanted to collapse, to rest my aching limbs, but the rain kept me moving.

I was resting on my hands and knees when something blew past my face. I recoiled and swatted, thinking it was another bat. I lost my balance, almost sliding off the ledge, but I righted myself and scooted farther, safe behind the large boulder, and the next time it blew past, I reached out and caught it. The rope!

I had to stop myself from crying out. I yanked on it, testing its strength, and it held. I pulled myself along the ledge and tied the rope around my waist, knotting it in a clumsy square knot.

With the security of a lifeline, I climbed past the boulder, traversing the rock face until I could see the rock cutter's wooden framework above. As I neared it, I untied the rope around my waist and retied it tighter. Then, I grabbed the next rope and walked up the rock face, hauling my weight with the last of my strength.

I collapsed onto the lower stone step, too exhausted to move out of the rain. Large raindrops hit my face with a splat. I closed my eyes against them and panted, and the storm finally took pity and stopped.

I lay for a while, flat on my back against the wet stone, and watched the sky change. The clouds thinned, and a sliver of moonlight bathed the rocks in silver. I silently thanked the storm for its discretion, for staying dark when I needed to hide, but secretly I wondered if it had wanted me to drown.

Then I heard another engine—this time a car. I thought about running into Luke's house but quickly realized I'd be cornered. If I stayed on the step, and they walked far enough out on the patio, they'd see me sprawled across the stone. I had to either escape into the trees, run barefoot in the darkness, or climb back down to the boulder.

I remembered the cactus I'd seen all over the island, and my decision was made. I was still tied to the rope, so I tested the knot and rolled over to sit up. I misjudged the distance and slipped down the sheer rock face, sliding on my rear end like a ride at a water park. I let out a loud gasp that was cut short when the rope caught, tugging painfully around my midsection. But it held, and I regained my footing and scurried into the shadow of the boulder as I heard footsteps approaching.

There were no voices, just the scuffling of feet on the concrete patio. I listened, afraid to move, afraid even to breathe. There was only silence for a moment, and then the scuffing moved away.

When I'd stared down the cliff face in the sunlight, it had seemed an impossible climb. No one would believe that I was here. I almost laughed. The safest I'd felt in hours was hanging from a rock wall in the dark of night. I hugged the boulder.

The ledge behind the boulder was level enough to lie on. As long as I stayed tied to the rope, I could stay hidden and wait them out. Once I knew they were gone, I could climb back up and shelter in the house until morning. I wedged myself into a crag between the boulder and the wall and tried not to think about the creatures that lived there.

Time passed slowly, and soon my thoughts moved from imagining what lived inside the cracks and returned to Sandy. Who was Dominik? And what was Sandy's connection to him? I thought about Terry's words describing Gilda's foolproof plan. Plan to do what? If they weren't stealing the money, what were they doing? I'd processed wires for a company called DG, Inc—did DG stand for Dominik and Gilda? They were in business together—with Terry. But not stealing money. If my company was denying that the wires were fraudulent, that meant they were aware of them.

They were laundering money.

The sky filled with a grumbling thunder—the storm's version of, "Duh, Anne."

Everything clicked into place. Money laundering was about moving dirty cash through legitimate business. Places like casinos, where cash was common. I'd seen both Lucien and Terry at the casino. Lucien also disappeared for over an hour while he left me playing slot machines. That was how they got the cash into the system—the casino. Then, they wired funds through companies like the one where I worked, legitimate companies. The wires—transfers I'd made, cleaned the money. I was involved. Unwittingly, but I'd processed the wires for them.

And the money in the banks, the cash that Sandy wanted me to find, was dirty cash. No, wait. That felt wrong. Terry had been surprised that it was in cash.

It was still dirty money. Maybe not stolen, but still illegal. I needed to tell the police.

I shivered as a breeze made its way behind the boulder. They needed me to get to the money, but once they had it, they weren't going to let me walk away. I knew too much. Terry had shared just enough for me to work it out, and I doubted he did it by accident. I understood why he'd been so careless. They were going to kill me just for knowing.

I squeezed farther into the crevice, no longer concerned about spiders or lizards, and rested my head on my arm to wait for the dawn.

Chapter 20

I woke with a start. Waves crashed below, and the boulder loomed overhead. My limbs were stiff and scratched, and I crawled from my hiding place, testing my muscles and stretching as much as I dared on the ledge. I inched toward the wooden framework, and when the sea appeared below, I suffered a wave of vertigo.

The darkness had been an ally. Staring down the cliff was dizzying. I couldn't have made the climb in the light knowing what lay below: jagged rocks.

The rain had kept most of the scratches clean, but my feet were crusted with blood, as were my shoulders. My shirt was torn in several places. My fingernails were broken and dirty.

I needed help. I thought of Luke and choked back a sob. I heard a car door slam and voices—the workmen beginning their day. I tested the rope. My arms were rubbery and untrustworthy, but I grabbed a rope in each hand, wrapping them around my wrists and pulled myself into a standing position.

I'd walked up the wall in the darkness, but the view below made my knees wobble. I wanted to hug the wall again, but I was stuck, standing, unable to move up or down, hoping my feet didn't slip out from underneath me.

"Anne," I coached myself. "You have to do this."

I bent my knees and reached up with my right arm, hauling myself six inches and then pulled with my left, altering my hands, resetting my grip on the rope each time, and walking up the wall in an awkward squat.

I reached the step and collapsed. My reward was the sun on my face. I lay still, catching my breath, and then untied the rope. Slowly, I stood, stretched to my full height, and climbed the ten wooden steps. I walked along the patio, circumnavigating the pool, and stepped into the house. A man in the kitchen stared at me, his mouth wide in horror at my appearance.

"Is Luke here?" I asked in a cheery voice that surprised me. I almost laughed.

He nodded and pointed down the hallway. I followed it into the master bedroom, and there he was, in his work pants and boots, his tank top already stained with sweat. He wore a tool belt loosely around his hips and a baseball cap backward. It was cliché to be so attracted to him at that moment, me the damsel in distress, him the tough hero. But I wasn't in distress. I'd saved myself, and he was simply a good-looking man wearing a tool belt.

My eyes teared up as he moved toward me, and I fell into his arms and let him carry me one more time to his pickup truck.

#

He drove me to his condo and drew a bath. I stayed in the water for a while, soaking my sore muscles, scrubbing the dirt underneath my fingernails and washing the blood away. When I was clean, he tended to my scratches with his impressive first aid kit.

"You require more first aid than anyone I've ever met," he said.

I dressed in a pair of his drawstring shorts that hung loosely on my hips and a T-shirt that was too big and smelled of fabric softener.

He made banana pancakes, and I ate while he packed supplies. I hadn't told him anything yet, but he made a plan, and I was relieved to let someone else make decisions.

"We'll go to my boat," he explained.

I didn't want to get on another boat, but I also didn't want to be on the island.

He drove to my car before I remembered the keys were in the locker at the marina. I told him the locker number, and he grabbed tools from the back of his truck and slipped into the marina. He came back with the backpack and everything I'd stowed in the locker and told me I owed the marina a new lock. We drove both cars to his friend's condo, parked my car in the garage, and I changed and packed my things. Again.

His boat was in a different marina on the other side of the island, but I was still wary as I climbed aboard. It was a fishing boat, smaller than *The Second Chance*, but it had a cabin below with a little galley and a bunk where we stowed our bags. He unpacked groceries into a small fridge, untied the dock lines, and we set off.

I sat next to him as he drove. He didn't ask any questions, but he kept glancing at me with a furrowed brow, and I knew he wanted to hear the story. I wasn't numb—my shoulders hurt every time the boat smacked a wave, and I felt cool sea mist against my face. But my mind was blank.

I stared at the water, still darkened from the storm. The clouds had retreated, and the sun warmed my back. We approached another island, and Luke slowed the boat and motored into a cove. He asked me to hold the wheel steady while he dropped the anchor, and then he beckoned me below.

"What happened?" he asked before I'd even sat down.

I told him everything. It took most of the day. I talked as he made us peanut butter sandwiches; I talked with my mouth full. I took breaks when I cried or when he got phone calls about work. I explained the clues from Sandy, the betrayal by Lucien, and how I'd spent the night on his wall.

"It hasn't been the greatest vacation ever," I said.

He chuckled. "You're a badass, climbing that wall."

"You climbed it."

"I did it in the daytime, and it wasn't raining."

"It was easier at night. I couldn't see down."

"What now?" he asked.

I shrugged. "I make a new plan."

"I know you're a pig-head, but will you let me help you?"

I could tell he was teasing me. He cocked his head to one side when he teased. "I'm not pig-headed," I argued back, good-naturedly. "I'm self-reliant."

"Whatever. Will you?"

I nodded. "Our stakeout was probably the best day I've had since I got here. As much as I hate to admit it, I need your help."

He grinned. "Are we planning another stakeout?"

"I need to find the rest of the money. I can't hand it over until I make a plan to run and hide, but I need to know where it is first."

"Do you know what the next clue means?"

"I didn't even read it. It's in that backpack with two hundred grand and the next key."

"I read it," he said. "I didn't mean to. I opened the backpack to put your stuff inside and saw the key. I was curious. I read the tag. Do you know what it means?"

I opened the backpack and pulled out the key. The tag read *The Other Sister.*

"No idea," I said. "But it usually takes me time to figure out the clues."

"I know what it means," he said. "Saint Martin and Anguilla are sister islands. This is Anguilla Island, the other sister. When I saw the clue, that's when I decided to bring you here."

"It's not enough of a clue, though. How will I know which bank it is?"

"Anguilla isn't like Saint Martin—it's smaller, and doesn't have as many businesses, so I doubt there are many banks. I want to tag along—not to take care of you, just to keep you company, and I'll buy you dinner. There's an amazing place for lobster here."

I was already nervous about leaving Saint Martin. The detective inspector had repeated his instruction not to leave several times, but Anguilla was the next clue. If I was going to find all fifteen million, I had to find the bank here to get to the next clue.

I stared into the backpack.

"I need to take the money I find back with us to Saint Martin."

"Agreed."

I unloaded the cash from the backpack and stowed it in my suitcase, hiding it underneath my clothes.

"Okay, let's get this over with," I said.

We took a water taxi to the dock and caught a taxi into town. We wandered through the shops, blending in with the tourists. Luke bought a new shirt, a short sleeve button-down with hundreds of tiny yellow sea horses.

"Like it?" he asked, twirling as he finished buttoning it.

I giggled. "I'm not sure I can take you seriously in that."

"Seahorses are awesome. Did you know the daddies are the ones that give birth? You have to respect that."

"Is that true, or did you just make that up?"

"Really," he answered. "It's a fact." But I still giggled.

When I caressed a lime-green, tie-died sarong, he bought that also.

I called all three banks, and only one had safety deposit boxes. The process was the same; I showed my ID and was taken into a room where I stuffed two million in cash into the backpack. It barely fit.

Wearing the heavy backpack felt like I was carrying a neon sign that read, *Get Cash Here.* I didn't want to sit in a restaurant with the backpack, but Luke had already anticipated that. He ordered food to go, and we took a water taxi back to the boat. He served lobster and plantain chips with a chilled bottle of Prosecco.

"Are we celebrating something?" I asked.

He did that tilted thing with his head and said, "I've never had that much money on the boat before."

"Don't get used to it."

"Easy come, easy go," he laughed.

After dinner, Luke fished off the back of the boat. He didn't catch anything, but he seemed to enjoy the mechanics of casting and reeling. He said it helped him think.

"What are you thinking about?" I asked.

"Just processing. That was quite a story."

I lounged, enjoying the rocking motion of the gentle waves. When I was quiet for a while, Luke nudged my foot with his. "Not thinking about jumping overboard, are you?"

I smiled. "Funny. Nah, I swam enough yesterday."

He joked easily—not making light of what I'd been through, but lifting it, letting the breeze carry it away.

"Have you ever been to prison?" I asked him.

He laughed. "That bothered you, didn't it? Not knowing something like that about your friend."

"Was I really her friend if I didn't know? If she didn't trust me enough to tell me something that important."

"Maybe she was getting there. She just needed a little more time. You said you only knew her a year."

"She ran out of time," I said and let the impact settle before I continued, "Wait, you didn't answer the question."

He laughed again. "Nope, I've never been to prison."

"Is there anything significant that happened in your life that you feel like I should know? Something you'd tell a good friend?"

"I was married once," he said.

I sat up, "Really? How long ago?"

"Ancient history. We got married too young. We hadn't finished growing up, and when we did, we were different people."

"How old are you?" I asked.

"Thirty-eight next month. You?"

He looked good for thirty-eight. "I'm thirty-one," I told him.

"You ever been married?" I shook my head. "Ever close?"

"No," I answered. "Not really."

"You ever been to prison?" he asked.

I smiled and shook my head. "I hope I can still say that when this is all over."

"I hope so too," he said.

We sat on the deck and watched the sunset. The storm had left clouds behind, gathered low on the horizon, and as the sun dropped behind the cloud bank, they turned to periwinkle cotton candy. We finished the bottle of wine and watched as the sky deepened into a violet, a slow-motion spectacle.

We endured the darkness in a comfortable silence until the moon arrived, and then I went below and climbed into the bunk.

#

The next morning, Luke took a water taxi to pick up breakfast, and we ate messy burritos, dripping hot sauce onto the white deck.

"Let's pull anchor and head back. Can you drive?"

"Uh uh," I mumbled, still chewing. "I don't know how."

He gave me a lesson on how to put the boat in gear and how to steer. I drove while he hauled a chain onto the front of the boat and stowed the anchor in a hatch, and I drove all the way back to Saint Martin. Driving a boat out in the open sea was even better than a car. There were no streetlights. I had the wind in my hair and the sun on my face, and I wanted to drive past the island and keep going.

"How long would it take to get home from here?" I shouted over the roar of the engine.

"To Miami? Couple weeks maybe," he answered.

"So, not a quick trip."

"Not really, no. That kind of trip takes planning. Gotta plan for weather, provision food and fuel, plan your stops. You don't just take off."

He took the wheel as we neared the harbor, and I leaned back into the seat and thought about the next clue. I had another bank to visit.

The Cookie Man.

It was an easy one. The Cookie Man made the best cookies at the farmer's market. We could eat them every weekend, but they were indulgent and oversized, so Sandy and I reserved our purchases for the days when we had something to celebrate. At times, the criteria for celebration were tenuous. Once, Sandy celebrated the landing of an especially turbulent international flight with a double chocolate macadamia. Another time, when I saw my favorite—ginger and white chocolate chip, I fabricated a promotion at work. I'd never come clean about that lie, but it was worth it because he rarely had my favorite. When we celebrated my thirty-first birthday, Sandy tracked down the Cookie Man and ordered a half dozen, and I ate a cookie every day until they were gone. That was a great week, having something to look forward to when I got home each night.

It wasn't just the cookies. We enjoyed the Man. He was attractive in an approachable way: soft, worn T-shirts, salt and pepper hair, and a friendly smile. He was easy to chat with, and we listened intently as he described the health benefits of adding flaxseed meal to his peanut butter crunch cookies. We didn't care about the extra fiber. We just liked to listen to him talk.

He seemed like a guy with a wife that played tennis and two kids that got good grades and smiled a lot. I imagined he had a Labrador and a pet turtle. Sandy imagined things about him too, and sometimes we spent the rest of our market time talking about his perfect life behind his white picket fence.

I think we both knew that the Cookie Man's reality was not as bright and shiny as we imagined. He probably worked a mid-level job in marketing, and the cookie stand was a sideline to help pay for one of his kid's braces and the other's traveling soccer club. His wife was probably resentful that she spent too much time baking cookies, and she only played tennis to keep the weight off because she ate their profits. But the reality didn't really matter. The Cookie Man made great cookies.

Where was the clue? I used my phone to search for bakeries or patisseries on the French side, but none of the names sparked a memory. It couldn't have been anything about the Man himself because everything we knew about his life was imagined.

Thinking about the Cookie Man made me crave ginger and white chocolate chip cookies. I'd tried to make my own batch once, chopping crystalized ginger into tiny bits and adding it to white chocolate chip cookie dough, but they didn't come out like his. In his version, the spice of the ginger complemented the creaminess of the white chocolate, but in mine, they seemed disjointed. I asked him about it once, and he told me he added a secret ingredient that made the difference, but he didn't share his secret.

I ran a search for ginger cookies and Saint Martin Island, and one of the results was a sushi place called Ginger. A bank was a block away. It wasn't an obvious connection, but it was close enough to follow up.

"We're here," Luke interrupted my thoughts. "Do you know how to tie off a boat?"

"No," I said.

"Well, get ready to step off and hold it for me."

He pulled into the slip and revved the motor in reverse. I stepped off the boat and held on.

"What's the plan with the backpack then?"

"Put it in the next bank or one of the others. I can't walk around with it."

"Yeah, it's making me twitchy."

I grabbed the backpack and my floppy hat, and we drove to the bank. It was down the street from the casino where I'd been with Lucien, and the proximity made me nervous. I pulled my hat down low.

Luke promised to wait out front for me, and I entered the bank and went through the familiar process until I was in the little room with the box.

There was no cash inside. There was a key with another clue and a scrap of paper with a series of numbers. I stared at the paper, reading the numbers over and over. It was a bank account. Sandy knew I regularly deal with account numbers at work. She'd known I'd recognize it. Also, I was in a bank.

I unloaded the cash from the backpack into the box, closed and locked the box, and left the room.

"Excuse me," I interrupted the man that had helped me into the box. "Can you look up this account number?"

He took the piece of paper I held out and began typing. "May I see your identification again, please?" I held up my driver's license. "What would you like to know?" he asked.

"What's the balance?"

He nodded and began typing again. I heard the whirring sound of a printer somewhere behind him, and he reached back and grabbed a single piece of paper. Toward the middle of the page, he wrote a number and handed it back to me. "That's the balance in US dollars. Can I assist you with anything else?"

I looked at the paper and then back at him. "No, thanks."

Then I walked out of the bank and jumped into Luke's pickup truck.

"Did the money fit?"

"Yeah, it fit," I said. "Barely. There wasn't any cash in the box."

"What was in the box?"

I handed him the paper. "Another key, of course, and an account number. Sandy put an account in my name. That's the balance."

He stared at the page, unable to comprehend the number of zeros.

"Whoa," he breathed. "That's a lot of money."

"It's what they're looking for," I said. "Fifteen million."

Chapter 21

He drove back to the boat. Every few miles, he whistled softly. And each time, I nodded.

"I feel like that bank balance is a game changer. You could run," he said.

I could. "I'd have to constantly uproot myself. I'd always be looking over my shoulder. Plus, I like my little house. My life is quiet and boring, but at some point, I want to go back to it."

"So, what then? Are you going to hand it over?"

"There's gotta be some way to use it as leverage, right? I'm no super-spy, but isn't there a way to set them up before I hand over the money?"

"But you don't have any idea where the money came from. Your friend obviously stole it from them, but I'm not sure how you'd set them up. You don't know they did anything wrong."

"They killed two people!"

"Well, okay. But I doubt they would trade the money for a confession. In my opinion, if they agree to leave you alone after you give them the money, isn't that the best option? I'm biased, though. I want the option that keeps you safe and keeps you here."

"I'm pretty sure handing over the money just means they don't have a reason to keep me alive any longer."

We boarded the boat, and he asked me to throw him the dock lines and push off. "Where are we going?" I asked.

"Just out of the harbor. I feel like you need time to think, so I'm taking you to the place where I go to think. Did you get a new clue?"

"Yeah, it's an easy one. *What I hate most in the world.*"

"You know what it means?" he asked.

"I know what it means, and I know where the bank is. I guess I've visited almost every bank on the island now. In Philipstown, there's a group of three banks within a couple of blocks. I've visited two so far. This is the third."

"How do you know?"

"Because Sandy hated spiders. She was terrified of them. If she saw a spider, she'd shriek and climb on furniture and wait for me to calmly take it outside. I like spiders. I wasn't going to go around killing them just because of her irrational fear. Anyway, on one of my trips downtown, I saw the Spider Club. It's just across from the third bank. That's the next location."

"Should I turn around? Do you want to go now?"

I shook my head. "No, there's no hurry, especially now that I have the money they want. You're right that I need to figure out how to approach them. You do realize I have more than what they're asking for, right? How much do I have now?" I counted to myself. "Six and a half in cash plus the fifteen in the bank."

But I hadn't come up with an explanation by the time Luke killed the engine.

"We're here," he announced.

I looked around, but there was nothing around us but water. "Where are we exactly?"

"Just below us is a rock formation. We're going to fish and hopefully catch something for dinner. Otherwise, we're eating peanut butter sandwiches again."

He handed me a rod and instructed, "Hit this button to drop the line. Keep your thumb here as the line drops or the line gets tangled."

I followed his directions, hitting the button and watching the lure at the end of the line drop into the water and descend, eventually disappearing into the depths below. We drifted across the rock formation I couldn't see, and then Luke told me to reel back in, and he started the engine and reset the boat where we'd started. He followed our progress on a screen and called out when he saw fish below.

He'd brought me here to think, but he talked constantly about fishing. At first, I feigned interest, but his enthusiasm was infectious, and before long, I was asking questions.

"Why do we keep reeling?"

"The fish think it's food, so they chase it and hopefully eat it. If that happens, you'll feel a tug and then start reeling fast."

"Why do you get that flashy, sparkly bait, but mine just looks like a little green fish?"

"Fishing is about trial and error. You would hate to eat the same thing every day, and it's the same with fish. You try different bait to see what the fish are in the mood for. Sometimes they're hungry enough to eat anything, and sometimes they won't eat anything at all. C'mon back in, and I'll reset."

I reeled as fast as I could, but the line felt heavier and then tugged against me. It felt like something on the other end wanted to reel me in. My reel began screeching and spinning wildly.

"You're hooked up!" Luke shouted. "Hold on tight, but just let it run."

"Run? You mean swim, right?" I asked.

"When it stops, I want you to reel fast, really fast, then lean back, pulling the rod, and reel fast as you lower the rod again."

He mimed the motion, rocking like a weeble-wobble toy. It was hard work, and my arm tired quickly, but then the fish ran again, and all my hard work was undone as the line was stripped from my reel. As soon as the reel stopped singing, I was fighting again, using my legs to stabilize myself, tugging a section of line from the water and reeling it in as I bent forward.

Luke cheered me on, but my muscles were still sore, so I asked him if he wanted to take over. "This is your fight, Anne," he answered.

I rolled my eyes and kept fighting. The fish ran, and when it tired, I reeled. At one point, a fish jumped from the water, startling me. I shouted, "There's another one!" But Luke laughed and told me it was the one I was fighting. "But it's so far away," I complained.

"Reel it in, then," he said.

The fight went on for over an hour. Luke moved around me with excited encouragement. He fed me bites of a peanut butter sandwich and held a cup as I sipped water. My legs ached. My arm burned, but I kept reeling with a fervor I thought I'd left on his rock wall. My stubbornness extended to sport fishing.

"You're almost there, Anne. Keep reeling, and don't stop for anything." Luke said. He held a long pole with a huge hook. I was too exhausted to ask him what it was for. "Good, just a little bit more," he coaxed, and then he reached the pole into the water and brought it back up with a fish on the end of it. A huge fish.

"You can stop reeling now," he said, and I collapsed onto the seat.

The fish was striped, black and white, with a thin line running down its back that turned cobalt in the sunlight. It had an elongated mouth like an alligator, full of sharp teeth.

"You caught a wahoo on the drift! That's so rare. I've never done it. We'll call that beginner's luck. Come hold it, and I'll get a photo."

I didn't even want to stand up, but he insisted. He showed me how to hold it, and he took a picture of me and my wahoo.

"It's a great size, definitely a keeper. We can head back soon."

"But you haven't caught anything," I said.

"I don't need to. Watching you fight that thing was one of the greatest things I've ever seen. And you caught dinner!"

"We're going to eat that?"

He laughed and opened a hatch in the deck of the boat and carefully tucked my fish inside. I watched him scoop ice, nestling the fish into a frozen bed. Then he offered me a celebratory beer. "I'm all out of wine," he said.

"No thanks. I don't like beer," I said. "I need water. I'm exhausted and thirsty."

I drank two bottles of water while he worked on the reels and stowed his gear. The boat drifted, and Luke seemed unconcerned about it. I relived my fish story, and even though he'd been there the entire time, Luke listened and laughed along, chiming in to mime my terrible form at reeling and the disgusted look I wore when I saw the fish bleeding on the deck.

After a while, the conversation returned to the fifteen million.

"Any ideas yet?" he asked.

"I'm going to text Lucien," I said. "I'll set up a meeting with him and then call the detective inspector. The simplest plan is the best. And I know enough now to share with the police. At least, I think so."

"I hope you're right."

I went below and reached into my bag for my phone. I'd tucked it into my suitcase with the cash. It was dead, and as I searched my bag for the charger, I found the letter from Sandy—the long letter she'd written when she was drunk. I'd gotten angry and tossed it aside, and then I'd gotten stuck on the boat with Terry. I'd forgotten about it.

I climbed into the bunk and picked up where I had left off.

But it's time for me to be honest with you. Lying wasn't easy, but it was essential at first. I had no plan. Running into you like that at the farmer's market was hasty and clumsy, but it worked. You were friendly, and I wasn't prepared for that. I'd watched you from a distance, and you didn't seem that friendly to other people, and that made me feel special.

Of course, I'd thought about you often enough, wondering what your life was like. I even wrote letters to you from prison (right, I need to explain that too,) but I never sent them.

I stopped reading and wondered aloud, "What the hell is she talking about? Why would she write to me from prison?"

"You okay down there?" Luke called out.

"I'm not sure," I answered. "I'm reading the rest of Sandy's letter, and it's really strange."

He appeared in the hatch opening, blocking the sunlight.

"It's sweltering down there," he said. "Come up here and read it aloud."

I climbed up and started over from the beginning. When I finished the part I'd already read, he interrupted, "See, she was going to tell you about prison."

"Why would she write to me from prison when I didn't even know her?"

"Keep going," he urged.

I was curious about you, and then when I actually liked you, it became harder to tell you. A month became three, and then it seemed like too much time had passed to be able to just blurt it out. Your life seemed okay, and I didn't want to ruin it again. Plus, I wanted to wait until my plan was complete. I'd planned my own restitution, and I was so close to being done.

I stopped reading again. "What is she talking about?" I asked Luke.

"Don't stop reading!" he cried.

I had to do this for you. Because you deserve a better life than the one you got. Because what you were supposed to have, the happy family, was all taken away from you. By me. I'm the one that ruined your life thirteen years ago. I killed your family.

I clutched my stomach as a wave of nausea hit me.

I never told anyone. I never got caught. But the guilt ate me up. I drank, and when that didn't help, I tried something stronger. I started dealing to feed my habit. I got caught. I deserved prison. But it wasn't enough. You had parents one day and none the next. You had a brother and a sister before. The Christmas you and I spent together was the best one I've ever had. You gave that to me despite the fact that you haven't had a good Christmas for thirteen years.

You gave me so much. You gave me a shoulder to cry on. You held my hair back when I threw up. You took care of me when I was sick. You're the best and strongest woman I've ever known, and the past year has been the greatest of my life. I never deserved any of it. I don't deserve your friendship.

I hope that you can forgive me. I know it's asking a lot. Like I said, there's no amount of money that can make up for what I've done, but I want you to know I tried so hard. If it had been in my power, I would have replaced everything that I took from you. I would have gladly given my life to bring back your family. I'm sorry. I love you, Anne.

I clutched the pages as the old wound opened, and I wept like I had on that night thirteen years ago. Luke held me tight, and we stayed there, sitting on the deck, bobbing in the choppy waves.

#

When I finally returned to myself, I wondered how far we'd drifted.

I sniffed and asked him, "Is the boat okay?"

"I'm sure the boat is fine," he answered. "Are *you* okay?"

I nodded, still teary. "I keep that part of me closed off. It's like a cork in a champagne bottle. When it comes off, there's an explosion." I sniffed a few more times. "I wasn't expecting that."

"You and me both. Just so you know, the entire thing was a surprise for me."

I smiled softly—anything more wasn't possible yet, but he'd done it again, lightening my grief with his easy humor.

"This floor is really uncomfortable," I said.

"Agreed, but I'll sit here as long as you need me to. Also, I may not be able to get up because my legs have gone to sleep."

"I'm sore, and my arm hurts. I really want a long, hot shower. Can we stay at your place tonight? Your condo, I mean. Not the house. It has a great view, but I already spent the night there, and don't take this the wrong way, but I hated it."

I looked up at him as he smiled and answered, "Maybe you could try sleeping inside next time?" I blinked and sent more tears streaming down my cheeks, but I didn't want to cry any longer. "Yes," he continued. "A shower sounds like a good idea. You smell like a fish."

I laughed then. More tears came, but residual ones, easy to blink away, and when my eyes cleared, he was still staring at me.

"You're amazing," he said. And he kissed me.

Chapter 22

Once we were docked in the marina, Luke pulled out a cutting board, a bucket, and set of sharp knives.

"We have to clean your fish. Have you ever cleaned a fish before?"

I helped by holding the hose, rinsing the inside of the fish, and I even ran my hand along the inside, feeling the firm flesh. He cut large chunks and handed them to me to seal in plastic bags. The muscles in his forearms flexed as he worked, and even though I knew they'd just been inside the cavity of a fish, I had to resist the urge to reach over and stroke his arms. He didn't seem to notice, and as I set the plastic bags in the cooler, I held my hands against the ice for a moment.

At the condo, we showered. Cleaning the fish had kept my thoughts from Sandy for a while, but as soon as the water hit me, I began sobbing again. Her letter had uncovered an old wound, deep sorrow that hadn't really healed—just scarred over by time.

How had she kept such a secret from me? Now I understood why she'd never told me about prison. If I'd known, I would have asked her what put her there. And she couldn't tell me that. She was right to keep it a secret. If she'd told me from the start, I wouldn't have been her friend.

I sank to the tiled floor and wrapped my arms around my legs, letting the hot water hit my back. I wasn't merely mourning my family. I was also mourning my friendship. All along, she'd been lying to me. About who she was and about her connection to me. Is that why she'd changed her name? So I wouldn't discover who she was? Our entire friendship had been a farce.

Except it never felt that way. It had felt real. Despite the fact that we never shared anything about our past, we did share our present. I shared everything that happened with her on a daily basis, and she did the same. Much of it was trivial, but it was *real*. She was my best friend. And I loved her. My tears were confused and complicated. I hated her for lying to me. And I missed her.

When I finally emerged from the shower, Luke was busy in the kitchen. He wore his apron and danced to loud music on the radio. I took the glass of wine he handed me, went to the balcony, and collapsed into a chair.

Luke joined me outside. He warmed up the grill and squeezed lime on my wahoo steaks. We ate on the balcony. He served green beans and wild rice on the side, and my wahoo was the best thing I've ever tasted.

When the sun set, he asked if I'd like to walk on the beach again, and I agreed. Before we reached the surf, he reached out and took my hand.

We walked quietly for a while before he said, "I took you to my favorite fishing spot for a quiet moment to think, and nothing about it was quiet. You were going to text him, remember? I take it you never did that."

"No," I answered. "My phone was dead."

"Are you sure about your plan? You don't have actual proof that what they were doing was illegal."

"Do you have a different idea?" I asked.

"Not really. My only thought is to keep you safe, and just handing over the money doesn't give you any guarantees."

"Can we sleep on it? I'm too frazzled to decide anything tonight."

"Of course," he said. "I'll make you pancakes in the morning. Brain food."

I smiled. "I can't keep eating like this, Luke. I'm going to weigh a thousand pounds. How do you stay so fit?"

"I run," he answered, and with a wide grin, he took off running, splashing through the surf. I smiled. I couldn't help smiling when I was with him. And then I chased him, running through the sloppy sand, messing up my last clean pair of shorts. He slowed and let me almost catch up before he took off again, and he kept running, staying just out of my reach until we tired and slowed.

"You're pretty fast on those short legs," he said. He caught me around the waist, and we supported each other as we trudged through the dry sand all the way back to his condo.

I had to shower again. When I walked out of the bathroom, wrapped in a towel, he stared from his bedroom doorway. I'd ignored the chemistry between us for the past two days, and he'd respected it, keeping his distance, but standing there in the hallway, with my wet hair dripping down my back, I couldn't ignore the way he looked at me. I moved toward him, and he closed the distance in one long stride.

He was so familiar; his movements considered and thoughtful. He was gentle and patient, waiting for me, watching my reactions, listening to my soft moans. Afterward, I drifted into a dreamy sleep. In the morning, there were more banana pancakes, and he remembered not to add syrup.

#

"I have to visit my job site for a while today," Luke said.

"You should. I appreciate you spending time with me, but you have work to do. I'll be alright on my own. Can you take me to my car?"

Before we left, I unplugged my phone from the charger and turned it on. On the way to the garage where we'd left my car, I texted Lucien.

I have the fifteen million.

Once I'd sent the text, being alone in my rental car made me apprehensive. I decided to visit the next bank— the one next to the Spider Club. I went inside and went through the vetting process once more, and then sat in front of the box, not opening it immediately because I was filled with more trepidation than I'd had at the first bank.

Everything had shifted. My feelings for Sandy had been a roller coaster of highs and lows since I'd arrived on the island. I'd started the trip angry at being ditched at the airport, and then I'd grieved her death. I'd endured confusion about her involvement with the missing funds and curiosity about her past when I met with her mother. The clues, the eternal, infuriating clues, were an involuntary stroll through some of the greatest and worst memories we'd shared. And then, her bombshell.

Had she doled out the clues that way on purpose? Reminding me of our friendship, our shared moments before telling me that she'd been the one that ruined my life. If so, it was a genius plan because I was conflicted. I wanted to hate her. I wanted to cut her out of my life like a cancer, but I couldn't because she was already taken from me, and I missed her. She was the person in my life that I would have shared my news with. She would have curled up in the corner of my sectional couch, pulling a pillow over her lap and folding her arms, and she would have listened to my story. I knew her well enough to know what her reaction would have been.

"So what, Anne," she would have begun. "Yes, your life was changed. Lots of people have terrible lives. Terrible things happen all the time. Get over it. Move on."

And she knew me well enough to know how I would react—how I did react. I felt betrayed and angry. I hated her for what she'd done.

But perhaps her influence over me during the past year was more substantial than I thought because part of me also loved her. I loved that she was sorry enough to care what had become of me. That she tried to find a way to make things right.

My phone buzzed with Lucien's answer, and the noise brought me back to the present. I looked at the phone.

Can we meet? he texted.

I didn't want to meet with him. The last time I'd seen him, he'd tied me up and chased me into the sea during a storm. I needed to leave the claustrophobic space inside the bank, so I opened the box. Inside was another million and a half. I did the math. Combined, I had eight million in cash and fifteen in the account. I had enough to run away and stay hidden.

The only other thing in the box was an envelope with another letter. It was only a page, but I couldn't stomach another of Sandy's notes, especially not in public—not if it was going to make me cry again. I pocketed the letter and left the bank. No new key? Did that mean I was done? I had mixed feelings—I wanted to be done with the searching, but I didn't have all the answers.

I walked back to my car. Not having another clue was like someone had taken away my compass. The one constant I'd had in this mess was Sandy's trail of clues. Was the point of her game really as simple as a pile of cash earned illegally as an apology for killing my family?

I didn't want to meet with Lucien. I never wanted to see him again. I sat in the car without turning it on, aimless and indecisive.

I texted him back. *I don't want to meet you. Send me an account number, and I will wire the funds. And then we're done.*

I opened her letter.

Anne,

I got greedy. Everything was going according to plan. I saved almost enough—well, it will never be enough, but I'd almost reached my goal. An opportunity presented itself, a chance to make so much money. I blackmailed some bad people, and things aren't going to plan, so I need to pivot. I have no idea what's going to happen, but if things go sideways, you need to be able to access the money and run. Only you. It's going to take some time to move everything, but it's almost over. I can't wait until I can tell you everything. We're going to tour the Caribbean! We're both going to get our happily ever after.

Love, Sandy

I turned on the car and drove. During my travels back and forth on the island, I'd learned the routes well enough. I drove to the top of the hill where I'd stood with Lucien at the very beginning. I parked on the side of the road and walked along the path. At the point, I sat on a rock and stared out to sea.

I pulled the keyring out of my pocket and twirled it around my finger. A part of me wanted to throw it into the sea. The nine keys represented Sandy's blood money—ill-gotten gains to buy my forgiveness. Why did she think money would change anything for me? Losing my family had isolated me, and having that much money meant I wouldn't need a job. It would serve only to further isolate me.

I wasn't isolated now. I had Luke. I'd been so wrong about him. I'd interpreted his easy humor as uncaring and cavalier, but he was the opposite. He wasn't a fly-by-night surfer. I wasn't even sure he surfed. He worked hard, and he had family. He'd built a life for himself here on the island, and I could become a part of that. Unless I was just fooling myself again, and he was in on it too. Was I making the right choice by trusting him? I certainly couldn't rely on my instincts after Lucien's betrayal.

I continued twirling the keyring in brazen circles, playing a version of Russian roulette. One slip, and the keys would fly over the cliff's edge. The money would be lost forever. The keys rotated smoothly along the ring: they were so similar, their weight balanced, and they made a comforting whooshing sound as they moved.

The wooden charm was the only anomaly in the movement. I stopped twirling and looked closer at the charm. It was a small rectangle, the same length as the keys, the same width, perfectly designed to fit within the keys. I traced the letters of my name with my finger. They were stained a darker brown to stand out against the chestnut of the wood. My finger found a tiny crack within the wood, and I pulled it to reveal the shiny metal of a USB stick.

I remembered Sandy's words from her first letter. *You have everything you need.*

The sound of a car door startled me. I heard voices approaching.

"Anne!" a voice shouted.

Suddenly, I didn't want to throw the key ring over the cliff, but I also didn't want it on me. I panicked and hurled the entire keyring into the bushes.

"I thought I might find you here," Lucien called out.

I looked right and left for an escape route, but there was only one path, and Lucien blocked it. The point was a beautiful vista of the island, but it was a dead end.

Lucien stopped about twenty feet from me, and Terry appeared from behind him. Lucien was wide enough to hide another person. His size, once attractive, was now menacing.

"Don't run away, Anne," Lucien said. "We just want to talk. We need your help."

"I told you I found all the money. I can wire it to you today."

"That's good news, but we have a new problem," Terry called out.

Lucien held up an arm, motioning him to stay quiet. It made me angry, his assumption that he was better equipped to communicate with me. He was the last person I wanted to deal with. Even though Terry had hit me, I preferred his honesty to Lucien's manipulative lies.

"Please don't run away, Anne," Lucien repeated.

"Look at where we are! Where would I go?" I shouted.

"You were trapped before, and you escaped," he said.

But I knew I was trapped this time.

"What do you want?" I asked.

"Come with us," Lucien said. "Dominik wants to talk to you,"

I took a step toward them, and they both backed up, Lucien because he seemed nervous that I might actually go over the cliff's edge and Terry because Lucien took up most of the path. I followed them back to the road.

"Give me your keys," Lucien said.

I hesitated, thinking about my options. If I ran, they'd follow. Lucien was in great shape. There was no way I could outrun him. I knew they needed me, and I hoped that was enough to keep me safe. I threw my car keys to Lucien and turned to Terry. "Can I ride with you?"

He sneered. "Of course. I'd prefer it that way. Guess your charm wore off, Lucien," he called out.

I got into the passenger seat of a black sedan, and Terry sped away. He drove too quickly around the corners, as if he was trying to outrun Lucien. I recognized our route and knew where Terry was headed. As we passed the driveway to Luke's house, I stared out the window.

"Don't worry about lover-boy," Terry said.

"Don't call him that," I spat. "I never want to see Lucien again."

He laughed. "I wasn't talking about Lucien," he answered, and I shuddered in the hot car.

CHAPTER 23

He pulled into a long driveway, similar to the one that led to the gray house, but the house at the end of this drive was a smaller, one-story, white villa with a red-tiled roof. The gray house was next door. I could see the dark roof towering farther out the peninsula. This was the same house they'd brought me the night of the storm.

I stepped out of the car. I wanted to run again, to swim around the point and climb the stone wall, but Terry's chilling words held me in place. I was once again on his leash. I followed him into the house.

Luke was inside. All of the air left my body in one long breath.

He'd fought them. His lip was bloody, and a bruise was forming around his left eye. He was tied to a chair, the same kind Lucien had tied me to, but this time they'd used duct tape—not the cord from the blinds. They'd learned that lesson. He looked up at me, and I mouthed, "I'm sorry," but he just smirked and winked.

Lucien arrived, and Dominik appeared from another room.

"What do you want?" I asked. "I told you I had the money."

"Would you like to sit down? Can I get you a drink?" Dominik asked.

I shook my head. "No. Tell me what you want so I can give it to you, and then Luke and I can go."

"I'm afraid it's more complicated than that," Dominik said. He dragged a chair close to Luke and sat down next to him, draping an arm around Luke's shoulder. It was an awkward movement—Luke was much taller, and Dominik pulled away and brushed off his hands. I remembered that feeling that Luke was dirty. Now all I wanted was to free him.

"Before Gildy disappeared—" Dominik began.

"You mean before you killed her," I interrupted.

Dominik held both hands up in mock surprise. "I didn't kill her, but I understand why you suspect me. I mean, here you are, seeing how we've treated your special friend. It makes sense that we'd hurt Gildy too, but I swear we gave this big guy a chance to come along nicely, and he chose the hard way. So, all of this," he gestured to Luke's bleeding face, "this is on him."

I sighed loudly and said, "Just tell me what you want."

"Gildy had a gift for managing the money. I admit after she showed such an aptitude, I was lax on my controls. It's how she was able to steal without me noticing. There was a constant flow of funds through the accounts, and she manipulated the account balances. I see it now, and while I'm unhappy about it, I do admire her brilliance."

I understood what Sandy saw in him. He had a haughty confidence, and Sandy would have been drawn to someone like him—not attracted to him, she would have seen him as a mark. His confidence was something for her to manipulate. And she'd accomplished it. His anxiety showed in the way he balled his fist when he spoke. His words were calm and composed, but his body language told the real story. I wondered if he was capable of beating someone to death. He had soft hands, but they were angry.

"What does any of this have to do with me?" I asked.

"Some of the funds are stuck in accounts that we can't access. It took me a while to unravel the mess, and it turns out Gilda used an alias on a series of accounts. We tried to get into them online, but now we're locked out. That's where you come in."

"I don't understand."

He reached inside his vest and pulled out a passport book. He opened it to the photograph page and flashed it to me like I was a customs officer. The picture inside was me.

"I don't understand," I said. "The name on this passport is Senna Linow. Not me."

He laughed. "Agreed. But for today, you are Senna Linow. Senna needs to go to the bank and issue wire transfers."

"I can't do that. I'm a terrible liar."

Dominik nodded to Terry, a subtle enough nod that I reacted too slowly. I lurched as Terry's right arm swung in an arc toward Luke's face, but Lucien's reflexes were faster, and he caught me as Terry's fist connected with Luke's head with a crunch that I assumed was the sound of Luke's nose breaking. A fresh flow of blood erupted from his nose and ran unimpeded onto the front of his shirt.

I fought against Lucien's grip—because I wanted to go to Luke and because Lucien's touch was repulsive. I pushed too hard, so when he let go, I stumbled and fell to the floor. Terry laughed, and my hatred launched me from the floor. I shoved him and watched his face change in slow motion from levity to surprise as he fell. His fall took forever. His arms swam, searching for a handhold, but there was only air. He landed against the sliding glass door, but instead of the glass breaking his fall, his fall broke the glass. He landed on the concrete outside in a pile of glass shards.

Lucien moved to help Terry, but the corners of his mouth turned up with a smile he couldn't suppress. I went to Luke and wiped the blood from his face with my hand.

"I'm sorry," I whispered. "I'm so sorry I got you into this."

"It's okay," he answered. "To be honest, that guy's punch is pretty weak. Looks worse than it is." He smiled at me, a gruesome smile with blood running into his mouth, staining his teeth red, but it was so like him to smile in that moment, with his nose broken, and his hands tied behind his back.

I stood up and faced Dominik. "I'll do it. I'll go to the bank. I'll do whatever you want. Just don't hurt him anymore."

Dominik nodded once. "Great. Go wash your hands and fix your face. Terry, you're going to have to stay here. You're in no shape to go out. Lucien, you're with me."

Lucien was still brushing glass from Terry's clothes. Terry lifted his T-shirt, and there were tiny cuts all across his back, but they looked superficial.

"I'm all cut up, Dom. I need a hospital."

"No time, Terry. You need to stay here and babysit lover-boy. Lucien, get her into the car."

I found a bathroom, washed my hands, and splashed cold water on my face. "Who is Senna Linow?" I asked the mirror. "Another one of Sandy's aliases?" It was a strange name, and why did the passport have my picture on it? Another question Sandy would never be able to answer.

I glanced at Luke when I returned. "I'll be okay, Anne," he said.

I gave him a brave smile and walked out of the house with Lucien.

#

Dominik retrieved my purse from my car. He took away my phone, but he let me fix my face while he drove. I applied tinted moisturizer over the bruise on my cheek and brushed my hair. I rubbed the bloody smudge on my shorts. Luke's blood.

He primed me during the car ride.

"There are two accounts. Both are in the name of Senna Linow. Transfer the balance of both to this account." He handed me a piece of paper with the details.

Dominik drove to the Cookie Man bank—the one near the casino, and I hoped the teller didn't recognize me. Once he'd seen the fifteen-million-dollar account balance, he'd studied my face. Someone with a bank balance like that was worth remembering. How would I explain that I was Anne Wilson two days ago and Senna Linow today?

Inside the bank, I breathed a little easier when I saw the only teller was a woman. But there were other issues. What if she asked me security questions to verify the account? If Sandy had set up security codes, I wouldn't know any of the answers.

"Hello," I greeted the teller. "I need to send some wire transfers. Can you help me with that?"

She nodded and asked a series of questions. What was the account number? What was my name? I'd practiced saying Senna Linow on the way over, and it came out easily enough. Something about it felt familiar. I showed her the fake passport, and she accepted it without question and accessed the account.

"Can you provide the security code?"

My throat went dry, and I coughed.

"Can I get you some water?" she asked politely.

I cleared my throat and nodded. "Yes, please."

She walked away, and I tried to remember Sandy mentioning a secret code. Had she anticipated this? She'd given me everything else.

When the woman returned, she handed me a small cup of water. I took a sip and cleared my throat.

"The security code is four-zero-zero-two."

She nodded and continued typing, and I tried to hide my relief. My guess was based on another Sandy memory. The last time I saw her. We'd been eating dinner, and she'd said, "Can you remember something? My security code is four-zero-zero-two. Just in case you ever need it?"

Her words had seemed out of place. I'd raised my eyebrows, and she'd asked me to repeat the number. And then she'd changed the subject, and I'd forgotten it until now.

She'd locked Dominik out of the accounts, but she made sure I could access everything. She'd planned for her death—buried her clues and codes within my memories. She had given me everything I needed. I thought about the USB drive and wondered what was on it.

"What is the amount of the wire, please?" The woman interrupted my thoughts. I handed her the paper with the details, and she turned back to her monitor to input the account details.

Lucien entered the bank as she was completing the first transfer. He stood in the line, waiting for another teller to help him, but he watched me, making sure I was following Dominik's instructions. That's how he fit into the group: he was the watchdog, the muscle. I ignored him.

I had time to think while the teller entered the details. Sending the funds made me culpable in their money laundering scheme. I was operating under duress, but no one was holding a gun to my head. I thought of ways to foil Dominik's plan. I could wire the funds into the account in my own name. I could transpose two digits so the wire wouldn't go through. But any of those options put Luke in danger, so when she asked me for the wire details for the next account, I gave her the information.

I completed the transactions and carried the printed confirmations outside. Inside the car, Dominik reviewed the paperwork. Lucien was still in the bank, but Dominik started the car to turn on the air conditioning.

"Well done," Dominik said.

I glared at him and said, "Now that I've cleaned your dirty cash, you'll let Luke go?"

As soon as the words came out, I wanted to take them back. Until that moment, Dominik thought I was a naive bystander. Now he knew what I knew. I waited for him to respond. His face registered surprise and then relaxed into something else. He smiled softly.

"We underestimated you from the start. I shouldn't have. I underestimated Gilda, too, and she stole fifteen million from right under my nose. But you, you're something else. I figured you'd drowned the other night, but two days later, you show up, barely a scratch on you. You knew nothing about any of this when you arrived here, and you figured it all out."

He tapped the points of all his fingers together. He seemed like he was considering something—my future, probably. I sat quietly, waiting for him to finish.

"You know too much now. The way I see it, you have two choices. You could join us, take Gildy's place, or…"

I waited for the other option, but Lucien opened the car door and slid into the backseat next to me.

"Let's go find out how Terry is doing," Dominik said.

He pulled the car onto the street and headed back to the villa. Lucien must have felt the tension in the car because he gave me an inquisitive look, but he didn't say anything.

I stared out the window, watching the familiar scenery, wondering what Dominik's other option would be. I assumed the worst—I'd endure the same fate as Sandy. It seemed poetic; Sandy and I both ending up dead at the end. But I still had some leverage. I had the money.

We climbed the hill where I'd fallen, where I'd met Luke for the first time, and when we drove past Luke's driveway, I hoped that Terry hadn't touched Luke while we'd been gone. I hoped Terry was suffering from a million tiny cuts.

As Dominik pulled off the road, I caught a glimpse of the catamaran. Another boat was anchored nearby— *The Second Chance* was still there.

Then we pulled into the driveway, and I was confused as Dominik sped up instead of slowing down.

Through the windshield, I saw Luke—untied, standing in the driveway with a phone at his ear. He was covered in blood—not just from his nosebleed. His arms and pants were soaked in blood. He shouted, but his words were drowned out by the sound of the engine as Dominik revved it and aimed the car directly at Luke.

I screamed and clawed the air in the backseat when my seatbelt held me in place. I hit the button to release the strap and reached over the seat, hitting Dominik, trying to grab the steering wheel. Lucien unbuckled himself and pulled me back, but I fought him. I landed only useless slaps in the small space, but I wedged my body between the front seats and used my legs to pin Lucien against the back seat. Luke stayed in place like he didn't understand that Dominik was trying to run him over. We were almost upon him when I reached the wheel and wrenched it up and left, away from Luke.

We hit the front corner of Terry's black sedan at full speed. I cradled my head in my arms and flew into the front seat, slamming against the dashboard and landing in a heap on the floor of the passenger side.

I couldn't breathe. I struggled for air, but it felt like something was pressing against me, preventing my lungs from filling. Just when I wondered how much longer I could go without air, the invisible vise released me, and I gasped.

Dominik was still in the front seat. His head had slammed into his window, creating a head-shaped bloodstain, and he wasn't moving. I pulled myself up from the floor and peered over the seat to find Lucien laying still. He was face down on the seat, and his leg was bent behind him at an odd angle.

Luke opened the door and helped me from the car. His face was bleeding again, but he seemed unhurt.

"Are you okay?" I cried.

"Yeah, I think so. Are you okay?" he asked me.

"Where did all of that blood come from?"

"Terry. I tried to help him. Tried to stop the bleeding, but it was too late. He's gone."

"Gone?" I asked. "You mean he's dead?"

"Yeah," Luke answered.

"I killed him?"

"No. No, Anne. It was an accident. You didn't mean to."

"Why are you out here?" I asked. "Did he untie you?"

"I could tell he was in bad shape. He started sweating and complaining that he was really thirsty. He finally listened and untied me, but then he wouldn't let me touch him until it was too late. One of the glass shards must have severed an artery. I tried to save him. But…"

"Where is he?"

Luke led me inside. Terry lay in the middle of the living room. He was pale, and his pants were a mess, but he looked like he could open his eyes and sit up. And I wanted him to. I didn't want to be someone that had killed another person.

Luke waved several flies away, but more arrived and landed on Terry's pant leg. I rushed outside, slipping on the broken glass. The railing caught me, and I leaned over and threw up.

When the retching subsided, I walked back inside.

"I killed him," I said.

"It was an accident. I called an ambulance, and the police are on the way," Luke said. He approached and tried to put his arm around me, but I pushed him away.

"Luke, you don't understand. The police already suspect me, and now…there's no way they're going to believe my story. But it's okay. The boat's out there. We can run."

"Anne, that doesn't make any sense. Stop and listen to yourself. You haven't run away from any of this. Why run now?"

"I feel like that's all I've done. Run away from everything. My whole life has been running and hiding. Why change now?"

"Anne—"

"Stop saying my name!" I was shouting now. "I hate it when people do that. Stop trying to control me."

Luke's answer was cut off as Dominik appeared next to us, and I heard sirens in the background.

"We need to get out of here," Dominik said.

"Don't go," Luke said, but he was quieter now.

"I killed him, Luke. And I just wired money for these guys. I'm neck-deep in this now. I don't have a choice. I have to run."

He gave a quick nod and stepped away.

Dominik reached out for my hand, but I slapped it away and ran. Out of the house and down the path to the beach. Together, we pushed the dinghy into the water, and Dominik waited for me to jump inside before he followed me and started the motor. He steered us toward *The Second Chance*. And away from Luke.

Chapter 24

Dominik tied the dinghy to the back of the boat while I started the engine and put it in gear. I remembered everything Luke taught me.

"Where are we going?" I shouted.

I assumed we needed to head away from the harbor, so I turned the boat left, what I assumed was north. I accelerated too quickly, and I heard Dominik yell, "Wait until I get inside, at least." But I didn't care if he fell in or not. I only knew I needed to put as much distance between us and the scene in the driveway.

Dominik made his way forward and sat next to me.

"You're a crazy driver," he said. "Where are you headed?"

"This way," I pointed straight ahead. "I have no idea where I'm going."

"We can either risk crossing to St Bart's, or we can double back and ditch the boat and hide out on the island until we figure something else out. I have contacts that can get us off the island when things cool off. And if the police radio ahead, we'll be caught as soon as we try to get close to any of the other islands. How much fuel do we have?"

I looked at the gauge. It was half full, but I had no idea what that meant.

"I think we need to stay in Saint Martin," I said. I didn't know anything about St. Bart's, but I knew Saint Martin. And the money was here.

"Agreed. Turn on the navigation system, and let's figure out where we can ditch the boat. I think it was smart to head out, but you've gone too far now. We can't tell where we are any longer."

"Okay." I did as I was told. "That's Anguilla ahead, right?"

"Yeah, you keep going, and you'll run right into it. But we're going to head west. He selected a place on the map and plotted our course. "I think putting in here will give us a little cover, and then we'll round the point in the dinghy and go ashore here. We won't be able to walk on the road, but we can stay close by. Nobody uses that road. The only thing up here is a dump."

"How far do we have to walk?"

"It's probably an hour."

We drove in silence for a while. I needed to get rid of him. I needed time alone, somewhere safe to think.

"I'm going below for a few minutes," Dominik said. "I need to gather a few things. We'll need supplies. Can you keep this steady?"

Part of me wanted to do the opposite, but I realized I needed him to get back to the island.

It didn't take long to pull the boat into the tiny cove he'd found. I slowed down, and he went out on the front of the boat to release the anchor. I scanned the controls, trying to find the button that Terry had used, but I'd reached the limit of my boating knowledge, and I had to step aside and let Dominik take over.

"I wish we'd taken my boat," he grumbled. "But it's too slow."

"That catamaran? That's your boat?" I asked and laughed—a hysterical sound. I'd daydreamed about sailing away with Lucien on Dominik's boat.

But then we heard the anchor chain begin to move, and he was busy navigating, so he didn't answer.

"Ready?" he asked me once the anchor was set. And I climbed back into the dinghy and returned once again to Saint Martin. I was an escaped prisoner, returning to my cell after a botched escape.

We crossed a narrow beach and trudged up a hill through long grass. The blades of grass made my legs itch, and I walked in a crouch, scratching. I tried to stay in Dominik's path, where his footsteps had flattened the grass.

Soon, the grass thinned but became brush, and I walked around it when I could and through it when there wasn't another option. The brush reminded me of the keys. I needed a plan to get back to the middle of the island, to climb the vista point and search for the keyring. The USB stick was my only hope. It had to contain proof of my innocence—something substantial enough to negotiate my freedom.

#

We climbed a hill and another one that lay behind it before we found a road and hiked alongside. Dominik was silent, and I stayed quiet, trying to keep up with him. There was no shade, no escape from the afternoon sun, and I began to fall behind.

"You need a break," Dominik announced. "Me too. It'll take them a while to find the boat, and once they do, they'll be looking in the wrong direction. We can rest for a minute."

He led us farther away from the road and found a section of taller brush that provided shade. He took off his backpack and handed me a water bottle and a granola bar.

"Where are we going?" I asked.

"There's a motel that takes cash and doesn't ask questions. We'll hole up there tonight. Tomorrow, we'll get you to the bank and you can wire the funds."

"And then you're done with me?"

He shook his head. "You still think I hurt Gilda."

"Who did?"

"Terry," he answered. "I could never hurt Gilda. She was like a sister. Even as angry as I was with her, I could never lay a hand on her. I could always make more money, but I could never replace Gilda. Terry had a temper. He'd banked his future on the money, and Gilda took it away. I think he was in deep at the casino."

"Why are you telling me all of this?"

"I don't think it matters anymore. Without Gilda and Terry, I can't continue. I need someone like you." He was quiet, drinking for a moment, and then, "You have the skills. And you're smart. You could make a lot of money."

I didn't answer, and he continued in a quiet, sad voice. "It was late that night, and Terry was drunk. Gilda started in on him, threatening that he was going to prison for killing that guy back in Florida."

"Mr. Sampson?"

"Yes," he answered. "He lost control. Went too far. She said all kinds of other stuff that night. Some of it didn't make any sense, but it set him off." He paused, and when he continued, his voice was far away with the memory. "I was angry with her. I could have stopped him, but by the time Lucien got there…"

We shared a moment of silence. I grieved Sandy. He grieved Gilda.

"Why did you leave Lucien behind?"

"He was useful but easily replaced. Guys like Lucien are easy to come by. Loyalty can be bought. But Gilda's skill set—that's the real value."

He looked at me with one raised eyebrow, asking me without saying it.

"No," I answered.

He laughed then. "You're out of options. I'll give you Gilda's share. That's generous. It's a good offer. Help me move money—just for a few weeks, and then I'll help you escape."

"I have other options. I can become Senna Linow, whoever that is." I could feel the imprint of the passport in my back pocket.

He laughed. "You figured everything else out, but not that?"

"I don't get it. What's funny?"

"You. Senna Linow is an anagram for Anne Wilson. Took me a few days to work that one out. Genius. If Lucien hadn't found you, I wouldn't have figured it out. When I found the passport on the boat, I put it together."

"I thought she used Sandy as her alias."

"Yeah, she did. I'd never heard of Senna before. It was a new one. But she was full of surprises at the end. Like the boat. She didn't share that with me. Terry followed her there the day before—"

"How long did you know her?"

"Four years. I met her here on the island. She was something. She practically threw herself at me, but she's not my type. Lucien stood a better chance."

"Oh," I said.

"She followed me around for months, pestering me about my plans until I finally told her. And then she delivered the greatest plan." He sighed. "C'mon, we need to keep moving."

#

We were back in the itchy grass, traipsing along the side of the road.

"So, what was Gilda's plan?" I asked. "How did she do it?"

"Like I said, Gilda stalked me until I finally let her in. Wasn't intentional. I had too much to drink one night and talked too much. She already knew the broad strokes, so she put it all together after that. She'd hung around long enough to know who some of my clients were. She knew the connection to the casinos here in Saint Martin. She knew enough to be dangerous. So I let her all the way in. And she delivered."

"You said that already. But what does that mean?"

"She had this crazy idea to take everything to a huge scale. She wanted to use American corporations to wash the funds. Big companies—the kind nobody would ever suspect. When she brought me the idea, I thought it was crazy, but she convinced me to try it."

I stopped to scratch my legs again.

"You can walk on the road," Dominik said. "We're far away enough now."

"She moved money through companies in the States," I prodded him.

"Yeah, she brought me this shady CEO, and we tested her plan. Her creativity was astounding. She set up so many companies, there was a point where I lost track of how many she owned. But after a while, the details didn't matter. We made more money in a month than I used to clear in a year. She got Terry a job in the accounting department to run things from inside, and we'd cycle through funds until someone got suspicious, and then Gilda found a new company, made contact with management, and we moved on."

He was quiet for a while, and I wondered why she'd decided to use my company. If Sandy had to make a connection with the CEO at the company I worked, had she targeted him, or had it just been a coincidence?

"We were happy," Dominik mused. "I bought my house, and when the property next door went on the market, she bought it so we could be neighbors."

"She owned the gray house?"

"Yeah, but she never stayed there. That place is a dump. It's falling apart. The plumbing barely works, and the walls are moldy. But she loved that pool. She spent money to repair it, and she stayed with me or in the little house out back. She talked about tearing down the gray house, rebuilding." His voice trailed off.

We walked on the road like two tourists returning from a day at the beach. Dominik didn't seem to mind approaching the motel in daylight.

"And where did you come from?" he asked.

"What do you mean?"

"Until a few days ago, I didn't know you existed. Lucien told me you knew Gilda, that you were friends. How did Gildy have a friend that I didn't know about?"

I shrugged. "I didn't know you existed either. I guess she kept her life compartmentalized."

"I thought I knew everything about her," he mused.

"Yeah, in the past few days, I've learned a lot about her I didn't know. Did you know she was in prison?"

He laughed. "Yeah, of course. She bragged about it all the time. She thought it made her seem tough."

"And you know why she went to prison?"

"Yeah, armed robbery."

Armed robbery?

"We're almost there. We'll get a room, and then I'll go find something to eat. Are you hungry?"

I was. Hungry, thirsty, and tired.

The motel wasn't the kind of place with a star rating. It needed a new roof and a paint job. A few of the rooms had discarded furniture out front. But I didn't complain when Dominik emerged from the office with a room key. He let me inside and left, and I avoided the sagging bed and walked into the bathroom to wash my itching legs.

"What now, Anne?" I asked the mirror.

I had no intention of helping Dominik; I'd be better on my own. Except, I had barely any cash left. I pulled everything out of my pockets and threw it on the bathroom counter. I had about twenty dollars and Senna's passport. No phone, no keys.

I splashed cold water on my face and used a dingy washcloth to scrub away the dried sweat, but my reflection conjured images of Terry—how pale his shin had been, and my stomach roiled. I sat on the edge of the bathtub and hung my head between my legs.

I missed Luke. I wanted to feel his hands on me, his breath in my ear, the scratch of his stubbled chin against my neck. I wanted him with a longing I didn't recognize.

And I realized I'd made the wrong choice.

CHAPTER 25

I stuffed the money and passport back into my pocket and opened the door, peering outside to make sure Dominik wasn't nearby before slipping outside and closing the door behind me. I hurried to the end of the motel and peered around the corner. He was headed right at me, so I ducked back around the corner before he noticed me and ran to the far end of the motel.

The motel sat on a road in a part of the island I'd never traveled before. I knew the direction we came from was a dead end, and that's where we'd left the boat, so the cops would be looking in that direction. I needed to go the other way—past Dominik's motel room.

I waited for him to go inside, and then I sprinted across the front and rounded the corner, and I kept running. My sandals slapped the pavement, and I blocked the sound and imagined my feet splashing in the surf, chasing Luke. People stared as I flew by, but all I saw was Luke's smile as I ran.

I didn't stop when a barking dog pulled on its leash, wanting to chase me or wanting to run alongside me. And I didn't stop when the aroma of garlic from an Italian restaurant made my stomach growl. I ignored the honking cars, their drivers swerving to avoid me.

When I finally slowed, I was in a residential area, and I climbed a hill until I reached the next intersection. And then I knew where I was—still on the north end of the island, but at a mid-point. I'd crossed half the island on foot in one day.

I slowed to a walk, finally thinking about where I was headed. To Luke, but where? His condo was on the southern end of the island. I couldn't walk that far before nightfall. But his marina was close. I could get to his boat and climb aboard. It was a safe place to spend the night.

Having a plan spurned me on, and I ran again. But what then? Luke wasn't going to run away with me. I'd have to turn myself in. And if I was going to the police, I needed the flash drive at the top of the hill. That was my leverage. I knew it. Sandy had left me something—a way out of this mess. She'd told me: *You have everything you need.*

My legs tired, and I slowed as a blue car passed slowly and honked. The man in the back seat turned, and I saw his profile—the way his hair stuck up in front. Dominik.

I turned away from the road and ran down a hill and into the trees. When the slope leveled off, I entered someone's backyard—a patio with a pool. Beyond the yard, the hillside was a cliff that dropped into a valley with a bay—the northern end of the island. Luke's marina was southwest, so I turned and ran across several more backyards. There were no fences, only scrub brush and open space in between.

I hopped the smaller brush and ran around anything larger. On the far side of another road, at the top of another hill, I spotted a group of trees and sprinted toward them. My lungs burned; I needed a break.

Once inside the grove of trees, I stopped, panting, my hands on my knees. From within the cover, I had a vantage point of both directions. At the bottom of the hill lay an airport. From there, I could hail a taxi and then disappear into the marina. I sank to the ground, the shady dirt cool under my legs.

I needed to stop running and face what I'd done. I'd killed Terry. The image of his pale face resurfaced, and I fought new nausea, wondering if Sandy had felt the same way. She'd killed four people—my entire family was wiped out in one accident. I wondered if she'd been hurt in the accident. Or had her only pain been to stay alive with the knowledge of what she'd done? She'd spent years in prison with nothing to do but think about that night. Would that happen to me? Years in prison with only my guilt.

She hadn't wanted to kill my family any more than I'd wanted to kill Terry. And more than at any other time I'd spent on the island, I wanted to see her one more time, to tell her that I wasn't mad anymore. I wanted to explain that I understood how she felt. I didn't need millions of dollars in restitution. All I really wanted was my friend back.

I watched the sunset from underneath the canopy of the trees, and then I stepped back out to the road and began to walk. The road was quiet in the darkness. The moon hadn't risen, but the pavement glowed in the starlight. Occasionally, a car passed, and I stepped as far away from the roadway as I dared in the darkness.

When I could see the airport lights, I knew I was almost there. But lights from an oncoming car blinded me, and I stumbled off the road and slipped, and then I was tumbling, head over heels, crashing through the brush, the brittle shrubbery not substantial enough to break my fall until I hit the trunk of a small tree. And then because I'd hit my head, or because I was too tired to care any longer, I remained still and thought of Luke as everything went black.

I woke to the blinding whiteness of the hospital.

"Hey," Luke called out softly.

"Am I dead?" I asked.

"Not for lack of trying. You have a concussion, but otherwise, you're okay."

"Who are you?" I asked, but I was so happy to see him; I smiled too soon to maintain the ruse.

He raised a hand over his heart. "Whoa, you had me for a split-second. Good to know your sense of humor is intact."

"Is everything else intact? What happened?"

"It's like you have a death wish, riding bikes and strolling along mountain roads. A passing car stopped when they saw you go down the hill, and they went after you. You rolled fifty yards. No idea how you didn't break anything. You're like a cat with nine lives, and you seem to keep landing on your feet—or your head."

"And Dominik?"

He shook his head. "Haven't found him yet. They searched all night, but Moreau was hoping you'd wake up soon and tell him where to look."

"Not sure I can help. The last time I saw him, he was in the back of a car. He could be anywhere now. Is he mad at me? The Detective Inspector, I mean."

"No, he seemed genuinely worried about you. He sat here with you most of the night."

"He was probably just afraid I would run away."

Luke chuckled. "Can you blame him? He'll be back soon. Are you hungry?"

"Starving."

"They brought you a tray earlier. It's cold now, but I'll get it. If nothing looks good, I'll go get you something better."

He set a tray in front of me and uncovered a plate of cold, runny scrambled eggs and toast.

"Luke, I'm sorry. Running was stupid. I was scared. I shouldn't have yelled at you."

"It's okay. You don't owe me an apology. You've been through so much." He pushed away the tray and sat on the edge of the bed. I leaned into him, letting his arms encircle me. He smelled like clean laundry. "Will you please stop running off?" he spoke into my ear. "I'm really getting tired of patching you up."

I closed my eyes and lay my head against his shoulder. "Okay. I promise not to run anymore. Because I'll probably be in jail."

"Then I'll know where you are. Eat something." I knew he was grinning.

He moved away and returned the tray. I sat back in the bed and nibbled cold toast.

#

The detective inspector arrived only a few minutes later. He wore a wrinkled suit without a tie. He strode into the room and sat next to me. He settled into the chair and crossed his legs before opening his notebook.

"Miss Wilson, Mr. Beaudelaire," he began.

After everything we'd been through, I hadn't bothered to ask Luke's last name. Luke Beaudelaire. It suited him.

"Seems you have gotten into a bit more trouble since you've been here in Saint Martin."

I nodded. "Not on purpose, and to be fair, you told me not to leave."

He smiled, a little smile, but I took it as a good sign. "True. If I knew what you'd get up to, I might have reconsidered. Please tell me in your own words what happened. Can you start with the events since fleeing the scene of a crime yesterday? I'm most interested in the whereabouts of Dominik Cerna."

"We ditched the boat on the northeast side of the island and took the dinghy along the coast. You'll find the dinghy in a cove. From there, we walked along the road for about an hour. I'm not exactly sure where we were, but there's nothing there. We didn't pass any houses or hotels. Just lots of grass along the road."

He nodded, and I continued, "He found a motel—I don't know the name of the place. It didn't have a sign. It was the first thing we saw when we approached from the road. It was pretty run down. When he went to get food, I ran off." I turned to Luke. "I don't know what I was thinking, running away like that. I've never…hurt anyone before, and I didn't react well."

"And then what," the detective inspector prodded.

"I left the motel. He chased me. I ran. I found a place to hide in some trees and then walked along the road once it got dark. And then…"

He knew more about what happened after that point, so I stopped. He picked up his phone and typed with his thumbs for a minute.

"Where did you last see him?"

"In the back of a car. It was blue, I think. I saw him, and I took off running. I didn't look back. At that point, I was in a neighborhood. But I'm sure he's gone now."

"Did he mention where he was going?"

"He talked about hiding out here on the island until things cool off. He said he had contacts that could help him get off the island. But he didn't say anything specific. Nothing helpful. Sorry."

Another nod. "And before that?"

"It all starts with the wire transfers I told you about. Dominik and Terry laundered money by moving funds through the banks here on the island. Sandy, sorry, Gilda Jorgensen was the one who handled the money transfers. I think Gilda double-crossed them and took the money, and that's why Terry killed her. Dominik confirmed that Terry killed her. He said he was there at the time, and Lucien too but I think Lucien showed up later.

"Dominik kidnapped Luke to get me to send the final wire transfers—which I did illegally, by the way. I posed as someone named Senna Linow at the bank and transferred the money."

He nodded, so I kept going.

"And I shoved Terry through the sliding glass door, and that's how he died."

Luke interrupted, "I'm going to get you something better to eat, okay? I'll be back in a little bit." He nodded to the detective inspector and left.

"Do you think you can walk?" the detective inspector asked me.

"Yeah, I guess so," I answered. I pulled down the blanket and swung my legs over the side of the bed. I was still dressed in my clothes, but I was missing shoes. He held up a pair of gray socks—the kind with non-slip bumps along the soles. He carefully slid them on my feet, one foot at a time. It was an intimate gesture—one he'd performed before.

"You have kids?" I asked, and he nodded. It made sense. He looked like someone's dad.

"Thanks," I told him as he led me from the room. "Where are we going?"

But he didn't answer.

Chapter 26

He led me down a corridor and into another room. I backed away when I saw Lucien in the bed, but the detective inspector beckoned me inside.

"Miss Wilson, may I introduce you to Inspector Smith of the Manchester Police Force? He is currently acting in a capacity for the National Central Bureau."

"You're a cop?" I asked.

"I'll give you two a moment to catch up," the detective inspector said. "Please try not to get into any further trouble. I'd appreciate your cooperation in the next few days to answer questions. We will not be holding you responsible for the death of Terry Stoller. I have statements from both Inspector Smith and Mr. Beaudelaire that confirm Terry Stoller's death was an accident."

"Thank you," I told him. He gave me a quick nod and left the room.

"You're a cop," I repeated. "Why didn't you say something?"

"Hard to stay undercover when you share the secret. At first, I didn't know if you were a part of this. I didn't think so, but I couldn't be sure."

"Are you sure now?" I asked.

"Yes," he said. "I'm sure. And I never lied to you. I just…didn't tell the truth either."

"Yeah, you were good at holding back," I agreed. I entered the room but remained standing. "What happened to your leg?"

"Broken tibia and tore my knee to shreds. Surgery is scheduled in a few days, and after a few weeks of therapy, and I'll be right as rain."

I hovered in the doorway.

"Anne," he said, and his voice no longer made me cringe. "I'm sorry. About not telling you about me and Gilda. And for letting my personal feelings get in the way of doing my job. I walked away a few times, but I should have done a better job of it."

"Are you saying it was my fault for not letting you walk away?"

I was being unfair. It was my fault, and I knew it. He'd shown restraint, but I'd pushed.

He dropped his head. "There's no excuse for the way I treated you, Anne."

My heart melted. "It was my fault as much as it was yours."

"Thank you. I couldn't bear to think I'd hurt you." He reached out for my hand, and I moved closer and gave it to him. "On the shelf by the window is your phone. Detective Inspector Moreau told me what happened. He's hoping that you'll help bring in Dominik. Moreau will do a better job of protecting you than I did."

"Is that what you were doing? Protecting me?"

"Poorly." He smiled. "I'm usually better at my job. You didn't require much protection. You surprised me at every turn. I wish we'd met under different circumstances."

Something in him had changed; I felt like I was finally seeing him, and he wasn't the carefree, mysterious man I'd thought. He seemed sad. I recognized the same look I saw in the mirror every day.

"You'll hear from Dominik," he said. "Soon, probably. He needs the money. He's in trouble with a client for holding back funds. The money you sent yesterday? Gilda was supposed to issue the funds the day before she died, but it never happened. Instead, she moved them into a new account. The client wants Dominik to run a new scheme as compensation for the delay, but Dom can't do it without Gildy. He might ask for your help. Don't feel obligated, though. I told Moreau what you've been through. Nobody would blame you if you left the island."

"Dominik already asked for my help, and I turned him down. Did Gilda know about you? Being a cop, I mean."

He shook his head. "She knew everything about me that mattered."

"Were you in love with her?"

"No. I just needed to get close to her. I'd learned enough to know she held all the answers. Dominik was my connection to the clients, but if I was going to get evidence, that had to come from Gilda."

He paused, and I waited. It didn't matter any longer, but I still wanted to know.

"Gilda was damaged. I knew it, and I knew better than to get involved with her, but I couldn't find a way in without starting a relationship with her. That plan backfired when I developed feelings for her. She was like a wounded bird. It was impossible not to feel something."

I tried to imagine Sandy that way—as something broken that needed to be cared for, but I couldn't. My

Sandy had been strong. I wondered which one of us had known the real Sandy. Had she seen Lucien as a mark and acted that way to draw him in? Or had she put on a show for my benefit, knowing I'd admire someone I saw as stronger than me? Or both? Maybe neither of us really knew her.

He looked away. "What you did to Terry…thanks for that. I almost killed him myself that night."

"Dominik told me you showed up just afterward."

He nodded. "I was too late."

"And me? You thought I was involved?"

"They almost pulled me out after Gilda died, but then you showed up. I had no idea you existed. She never mentioned you before. Running into you at the market was an accident, but then Gildy texted and asked me to keep you busy. I followed you, trying to figure out who you were. I couldn't tell whether you were involved, but then you got that email."

"Right."

"Before then, I thought Terry was just being paranoid, that Gilda would never doublecross Dominik. She actually cared about him. Thinking about it now, all the things she said, she must have made it all up. She was planning a bigger score—bigger than anything she'd done before. She didn't share the details, but she and Dominik were excited about it. I could tell. But once you showed up, I figured out she'd been lying. To all of us. She was really planning to leave. With you.

"I'm not sure what upset me more: losing her or finding out I never meant anything to her. Her email to you proved how far she was willing to take it. She *became* her alias. That was proof she'd taken the money. I needed to know who you were and how you fit in. I wanted to track the money, but a huge part of me wanted to know what you meant to her, that she could leave me behind to run away with you. I was angry. Jealous. But then I got to know you. And I understood."

"There's nothing special about me."

"You have something…a quiet confidence. You've lost so much, and you're not angry or bitter or even sad. You accepted your loss and moved on with your life. That takes strength—more strength than most people have. That ability to continue on when you've lost everything and not spend the rest of your life complaining about it. You don't use your family's death as an excuse not to live."

The room grew claustrophobic as his words stirred my emotions. The memory of that night was still too raw, so recently exposed by Sandy's letter.

He was wrong. I *was* afraid to live. But he didn't know that part—no one did because I never talked about it. It was a secret I'd never shared with anyone. I'd closed that part of my life, hidden it away from everyone and myself.

I excused myself and wandered back along the corridor, relieved that Moreau wasn't waiting for me. I needed a moment alone to pack the memory away again, to store it deep within me. But tendrils reached out, threatening to escape, pointing out my hypocrisy. I had my own secret. And it was worse than Sandy's.

#

Luke returned with breakfast as I buckled my sandals.

"What's happening?" he asked. "I thought we agreed you weren't going to run away any longer."

"I need a ride."

"Where?"

I took the coffee cup he handed me. "I guess I should ask if you even want to help me. After everything I've put you through?" I reached up and stroked his face with the back of my hand. He had deep purple circles under his eyes and a cut across the bridge of his nose.

"Just so we're clear, I'd take a regular beating to be with you." He kissed me gingerly at first, but then he pulled me into him.

"Thanks, Luke," I whispered.

"Sit. Explain. And you're not going anywhere until you eat something."

I climbed back onto the hospital bed, and he handed me a warm paper bag. He pushed the table back over the bed and sat back in the chair. I bit into the burrito and realized I hadn't eaten a meal in over twenty-four hours.

I chewed slowly, considering my words.

"I need a ride. And you told me not to go off on my own any longer. So, I have to go do something that might be stupid. Can you help?"

"Sounds fun," he answered.

"You remember the keyring? The one you pulled from the locker in the marina?"

He nodded.

"On that keyring is a wooden charm. Except it's not—it's a USB drive. And I think it's where Sandy kept the evidence. I'm not sure why, but I think she was planning to turn Dominik and Terry in. She stole the money to run away. So I think that USB drive contains proof of what they were doing."

"Where is it?" he asked.

"I threw it into the bushes. We have to find it."

"We should tell Moreau."

I shook my head. "No, I want to know what's on it first."

We left the hospital, and I directed him up the hill.

"So, you left the keys up here the whole time?" he asked.

"Only since yesterday morning. I had to get rid of them. I couldn't risk Lucien finding them. I was standing about here. And I tossed them that way." I pointed to my right.

Luke followed the direction I pointed. "How hard did you throw? Did you hear them land?"

"I don't remember, and it was a gentle toss. Not far."

He pushed his way into the brush. "Careful, there's cactus in here."

"I'm not as worried about cacti as I am about snakes."

He laughed. "We don't have snakes here. Well, nothing poisonous."

"Good news."

"The thing to watch out for here is frogs. The small ones are very poisonous. But there won't be any frogs up here."

I followed him into the brush. "Should stand out, right? Shiny metal keys?"

"There are rocks here, so if it slipped down into a crack between rocks, we might not find it without a metal detector."

"Do you have one of those?"

"Not on me," he grinned. "But yeah, I can rent one if we need it. I'm worried about you being out here. You're not safe until Dominik is caught."

"I still have the money, so he's going to resurface soon. Part of me wants to give him the money just so he'll leave. But Moreau probably wouldn't be okay with that."

"Lucien, either. He worked hard to bust Dominik, so he probably won't be okay with you just letting him leave."

"No," I said. "I don't think Lucien was after Dominik or Gilda. I think he wanted their clients. And hopefully, that's what's on the drive. Proof of something more than just the money. But that's just a guess. Anyway, we won't know for sure until we find it."

"Got it!"

He held the keyring overhead and jangled the keys.

"All nine of them are there?"

"Yes. And the USB drive. Now what?"

"Now we need my laptop."

#

We returned to Luke's condo, and I booted my laptop and plugged in the thumb drive.

My phone buzzed with a text. *I need the money.* Dominik.

Where should I send it? I replied.

Meet me at the bank. Four pm. Text me the address.

I dialed Moreau's number and left a message with someone, and he arrived only twenty minutes later. By then, Luke and I had seen enough to hand over the USB drive. Gilda had kept details of drug smuggling and human trafficking. We read a few files, and then Luke snapped the cover shut and removed the USB stick.

"I'd rather remain ignorant," he said.

I'd agreed and handed Moreau the wooden charm as soon as he walked in the door. He handed it off immediately to a uniformed officer who left with it. I breathed easier once it was gone.

But the keys I kept hidden.

"I'm not letting you meet with Dominik alone," he said.

"I have to. I think he trusts me. He trusted me enough to share details."

Moreau nodded. "Yes, but that knowledge makes you a threat."

"I'm not exactly a fan of Dominik, but I think enough people have died. So, you can be there, in the background, but I need to talk to him first."

"You don't owe him anything," Luke added.

"I know," I answered quietly. "I'm not doing it for him. I've made so many mistakes. This is the one thing I can do to help. You need him. right?" I asked Moreau. "What Sandy compiled on that USB drive is only one piece. Dominik was involved with the people that did those *things*."

"Yes, having him as a material witness would be helpful," Moreau agreed. "But not at the risk of your safety. I'll be out of sight, but I'll be there."

"Okay," I answered.

#

Dominik was already at the bank when I arrived, pacing the sidewalk like a caged lion.

"Why did you run away?" he asked. "All I want is the money."

"Did you know Gilda was building a file on your customers? She was going to send you and Terry to prison." He said nothing. "And Lucien's a cop." His eyebrows lifted, but he remained silent. "Yeah, he fooled me too."

His reaction was calmer than I'd expected. "And the police are waiting in the wings right now?" he asked.

I nodded. "You have a choice. The police want your clients. You could make a deal, stay out of prison, go into hiding."

"And if I don't?"

"The police have the file. If you want to run, I'll send you the money. Just tell me where to send it and go."

He looked right and left, considering his options for escape. "What would you do?"

I chuckled softly. "I wouldn't run. I'd face it, fight it, and give myself a chance for a life."

He stood there, tapping his toe, and I knew he needed time—not to make the decision; the decision had already been made for him. He needed time to accept it. He took the time, and I waited for him. It didn't take him as long as I thought.

"Okay."

"Can I have my boat keys, please?"

He pulled the keys from his pocket and offered them to me. "You seem different today," he said.

"All of this is over now," I answered. "I get the happy ending that Sandy promised me."

"Gilda didn't keep her promises to me," he mused.

"No," I said. "But Sandy did."

After everything that had happened, walking with Dominik across the street to Detective Inspector Moreau felt anti-climactic. We strolled along the sidewalk, shoulder to shoulder, and I should have felt something more, a sense of accomplishment, victorious that it was all over. Terry was gone, Dominik was taken into custody, and Lucien turned out to be one of the good guys. But I just felt empty. I missed Sandy.

I caught Dominik's arm and asked, "Where did you put her stuff? From the boat?"

"No idea. Terry threw it all away." We'd almost reach Moreau, and Dominik stopped and turned. "I'm not sure that stuff was even hers. Terry said he found peanut butter, and Gildy was deathly allergic to peanuts."

A uniformed officer handcuffed Dominik and helped him into the back of a police car.

"Well done," Moreau reached his hand toward me in an offered handshake.

"Question," I asked. "Gilda Jorgensen was in prison years ago. Do you know why?"

"Yes. She served eight years for armed robbery. Why?"

"If someone went to prison for dealing drugs, what would the charge be?"

"Distribution. Possession in some cases. Why do you ask?"

I shook my head because I couldn't answer.

Luke approached and said something, but all I heard was the echo of Moreau's answer. *Armed robbery.*

CHAPTER 27

My heart raced. A burning hope grew within me, but I worried voicing my thoughts might break the spell.

"Sandy's favorite cookie was peanut butter crunch," I told Luke. "Sandy isn't Gilda," I whispered.

Luke watched me quietly. His eyes narrowed as the words took root and widened as the idea bloomed. He looked at me, forming a *What?* that never left his lips, and then his gaze shifted into the distance as he searched the surrounding buildings for confirmation.

I stayed silent and watched the shock cross his face and turn into something else. And I waited for him to argue with me—or agree with me.

"How?" he asked, and I waited for his next question—the important question. "But where is she?"

Sandy wasn't Gilda. She was alive. But where? Had she run away? Leaving me to deal with the mess?

"She's here," I answered. "All this time, I've been trying to match everyone's else's description of Gilda to what I know about Sandy. They felt like two different people because they *are* different. Sandy didn't leave me. She wouldn't do that. She's here on the island. Her money is here. And her boat."

"But, if she's here, why hasn't she called you? Where is she? This sounds crazy."

He was right. It *was* crazy. She wouldn't have been quiet, watching me flounder as I followed her stupid clues, and she wouldn't have left without saying goodbye. She wanted us to leave together.

He tapped his foot while he waited for my answer, "Where is she?" he repeated.

"Trapped."

"All this time? Where?"

Where was she? There was only one option. I'd traversed the island so many times. I'd followed her trail, stayed in the guest house, and been on her boat. But there was one place I hadn't explored.

"She's in the gray house."

"How do you know?"

"It was Gilda's house. Sandy was there. She left me a note when I arrived, and then I never saw her. She texted me when I arrived and the next morning, but I never heard from her again. Gilda had Sandy's phone on her when she died. Sandy must have been with Gilda right before Gilda was killed."

"But what if—"

"Don't," I raised my hand against his thought. Sandy wasn't dead. She was here. Alive, trapped. And she'd been trapped for so long. I couldn't wait any longer. "We need to go get her. Now!"

"Wait. We need Moreau." I shook my head, and he grabbed my shoulders. "Anne, you've done everything your way since you got here. You've been in the hospital twice in two weeks. We're doing this my way."

"Two weeks!" I shouted. "She's been locked up somewhere for two *weeks*, Luke. She can't wait any longer."

"You're right. We'll hurry. But we're getting Moreau. C'mon."

#

Moreau believed me. He ushered Luke and I into the back of a police car and climbed in the front seat. A uniformed officer drove, and we sped across the island.

"I'm not sure it makes sense yet. We met her mother," Luke said.

"We met Gilda's mother. I've never met Sandy's mother before. I never met any of Sandy's family."

"Why did you think they were the same person?" he asked.

It was the same question I'd been asking myself. I'd assumed it was Sandy because Moreau had her phone, and he'd shown me a picture of her tattoo.

"They must have gotten the same tattoo. She talked about doing that sometimes—getting tattoos together."

We were quiet as Moreau took a phone call. When he ended the call, he turned around and said, "Immigration just confirmed that Sandy Brown arrived twenty days ago. I should have checked sooner. I assumed that all the movements by Sandy Brown were the alias of Gilda Jorgensen. I assumed the cell phone belonged to Gilda, and she used it as Sandy Brown." He paused and then, "I was wrong."

"Me too," I said. "But I knew Sandy. I knew she was here. That she was real. I should have known better."

Even in the bright sunlight, the crumbling facade of the gray house made me shiver. Drooping shutters gave the house a lopsided frown. Perhaps the house felt guilty for holding such a secret. I stood in the cobbled drive, staring up at the house, afraid of what I'd find but anxious for the truth.

More police cars arrived, and the front door was broken in a splintered crash. Uniforms filed inside, and I followed. Moreau shot me a disapproving look, but he let me pass. Maybe he thought he owed me after I helped bring in Dominik, or maybe he didn't think we'd find Sandy.

A putrefied smell slammed me backward into Luke. I recognized the scent. On a hike with my dad when I was twelve years old, we'd passed the carcass of a large animal, a panther, according to my father. I'd run away, gasping for air free of decay.

The gray house was filled with the same scent: death.

I didn't run away. I covered my mouth and nose with my hand and ventured inside. The entryway was circular, with two staircases that curved to meet at the top. I walked between them and through a wide space broken only by gaudy, white, Corinthian columns. I yanked a heavy curtain and coughed as a cloud of dust erupted into the room. Behind the curtain, French doors opened onto the patio, and I unlocked them and swung the doors wide open to gulp the fresh air.

My eyes watered as I climbed the stairs, and I retched at the top but breathed through my mouth, squashing the nausea.

They found Sandy upstairs.

She'd spilled onto the carpeted floor when an officer opened a closet door. And that's where she lay when I rounded the corner and saw her.

"Is she—"

But I couldn't finish the question. I landed on the floor next to her and carefully lifted her head into my lap.

"Sandy," I whispered. "Sandy, please be alive."

"She has no pulse," an officer said.

But then Luke was behind me, forcing me aside. He leaned over her, his body almost touching hers, and his voice was calm as he told the officer, "Call an ambulance, please."

The officer moved away to make the call, and Luke turned Sandy's body onto the side.

"Sandy, stay with me, okay? Just hang in there a few more minutes." And then he called out, "I need water. Does anyone have water?"

A flurry of activity erupted around me as officers hurried to find water. Moreau arrived and crouched next to me. He took my hand and squeezed it.

"You found her," he said.

"I was too late, though," I answered. Tears streamed down my cheeks, and I crawled back to Sandy and stroked her hair. "Sandy," I leaned to her and whispered. "Please wake up."

But her eyes remained shut, her arms limp at her sides.

The water arrived, and Luke wet her lips.

"C'mon, Sandy. I need you to wake up and drink."

She remained still. Luke lifted one of her arms and dropped it, catching it with his other hand and placing it across her chest.

"She's alive, but barely."

We heard heavy footsteps in the hallway, and Luke stood and pulled me out of the way. A team of paramedics arrived. I buried my face in Luke's chest.

"I should have known. I should have figured it out sooner. Why did it take me so long?"

"It's okay, Anne. She's alive. She'll pull through."

"You don't know that. She's been locked in here for weeks. With nothing to eat, nothing to drink. Stuck there in the dark. Alone."

"C'mon. We can't do anything for her now. Let's get you out of this place. Get some fresh air."

He pulled me toward the stairs, and I descended alongside him. The smell had faded, either because the fresh air had cleared it or because my brain, overcome with worry, no longer registered the scent. Outside, I sat on the wooden steps and wiped my nose with my hand. Sandy was carried past me, embraced within a bright yellow plastic gurney, and the ambulance pulled away, siren blaring, lights flashing.

"I need to go with her," I said.

"We will. Soon," Luke answered. "I'll find Moreau and ask for a ride."

I stared at the palm trees lining the drive. They swayed in the wind, oblivious to my pain. How many times had I walked by her? How many times had I climbed into Lucien's convertible with a smile? How many days had she spent in that closet calling out for me? Had she heard us? At what point had she given up hope that I'd come for her? Had her descent into unconsciousness been a welcome relief from her agony?

New sobs threatened to choke me as I remembered knocking on the door when I'd arrived. Had she been here then? Had she heard me? Had she called out?

Luke held me tight. I didn't voice my thoughts, but he heard them. "You found her. You did, Anne. Nobody else was even looking for her. You found her. And she'll be okay."

I nodded. "I want to be with her."

"Soon. Moreau is organizing it. She's going to be okay. You saved her, Anne."

But I didn't believe him because I'd held her limp body. I knew the life had already drained from her.

Moreau appeared and motioned us to follow him.

"I'll drive you back to the hospital," he said.

For a few miles, the only sound inside the car was the click-clicking of his turn signal.

#

I couldn't see her yet. She'd been taken into the ICU, and they were still examining her. But a nurse told me she was alive, and I nodded and clung to Luke.

"How long can someone live without food?" I asked.

"A while. Months maybe. Depends on the circumstances. Water is the real issue. She must have had water. You can't live very long without water."

"Who put her there?" I asked.

He shrugged.

"Must have been Gilda. And then Terry killed Gilda. Had to be Gilda. Nobody else knew Sandy was there."

"Why did Gilda lock her up?"

"I don't know."

I paced the room, rethinking everything I knew. I started at the beginning and worked my way forward. Gilda ran the money laundering scheme—not Sandy. But the money was in Sandy's name. Was Sandy working with Gilda? If so, why had Gilda locked Sandy away?

I knew Sandy had been here for weeks. Sandy hid the money. Sandy left the clues. Had Gilda found out? And that's why Sandy was locked away?

Luke watched me with a careful stare.

"We know Terry killed Gilda," I said. "He was angry that Gilda stole the money, but what if wasn't her? Maybe Sandy took it, and when Gilda figured it out, she locked Sandy up."

"Then Terry killed Gilda for no reason."

"I was the only one that knew Sandy was here. Everybody thought I was talking about Gilda because Gilda used Sandy as an alias. Nobody else knew about the real Sandy."

Luke rubbed his forehead. "I still don't understand the part about the tattoo. That was the reason you believe it was Sandy."

"It *was* her. Moreau showed me a picture of her tattoo. It was Sandy's tattoo. But there's an easy way to confirm that. I need to talk to Lucien. Can you stay here? Call me if there's news."

I didn't wait for him to agree. I hurried along the corridor and into the elevator.

Lucien sat up when he saw my face. "What's happening?"

"Did Gilda have a tattoo?"

"Yeah. On her shoulder blade."

"What was it? The tattoo?"

"A bird. A dove. It was how I identified her when the police called me."

It wasn't Sandy's tattoo I'd seen. It was Gilda's. They *did* have the same tattoo.

"When was she in prison?" I asked. "Do you know? And where?"

"I can find out. Why? What's going on, Anne? Have you been crying?"

"Sandy, my friend Sandy, isn't Gilda. Gilda used her as an alias, but Sandy Brown was—is a real person. Sandy was—is my friend. And she's downstairs in the ICU."

"So, all this time—"

"I never knew Gilda, Lucien!" I shouted. "That's why everyone seemed to know a different person than I did.

Because she *was* a different person. Gilda and Sandy knew each other." And then I realized one important thing, "She never told me about Gilda or prison because she couldn't talk about it. Not without telling me everything."

"What? Why?"

"Never mind. There are so many secrets. And the only reason I didn't figure it out sooner was because of what Sandy kept from me."

"I'm not following," he said.

I smiled softly. "I know. It doesn't matter. Thanks, Lucien. I'll come back and explain later. I need to go check on Sandy. *My* Sandy." I turned back from the doorway. "I'm sorry that Gilda's dead, Lucien."

#

I returned to the waiting room, and another hour passed before a doctor arrived with news.

"She's not out of the woods yet, but all signs are positive. You can see her now, but she's still unconscious. She might be out for a few days."

I left Luke in the waiting room and followed the doctor to Sandy's bedside. I took her hand.

"Hey, Sandy. I'm not sure if you can hear me, but they say you're going to be okay. I'm sorry it took me so long to find you. I was angry and confused. And I had to follow your stupid clues. But you're going to be okay. And when you are, we need to have a long talk. You need to be honest with me, and I need to be honest with you. There are things I haven't told you. But first, get better. Because you're my best friend, and I need you."

After a while, I returned to the waiting room.

"Luke, I need to be here. Go home. Thanks for being here, but I'm going to be alright. I just want to sit by her. I want to be here when she wakes up."

He nodded. "I'm going to visit the job site, but I'll be back to check on you. I'll bring you food. Stay with her." He kissed the top of my head. "She's going to be okay."

I nodded and hugged him.

"I love you, Anne."

I smiled on the way back to Sandy's room and kept smiling for hours until I finally fell asleep in the chair next to Sandy's bed.

<h1 style="text-align:center">CHAPTER 28</h1>

Eight hours after Sandy arrived at the hospital, her heart monitor began to beep with an alarm. The sound startled me, and a nurse hurried into the room.

"Is she okay?" I asked.

"She's waking up," she answered.

Sandy opened her eyes and whispered, "Anne."

"Yeah, I'm here," I said, squeezing her hand. "Don't try to talk yet."

"I'm sorry," she whispered.

"It's okay. I forgive you. For everything. Don't think about any of that right now. Just get better."

The nurse brought a cup of water with a straw, and I held it while Sandy sipped. She swallowed loudly as if her throat hurt, but her voice improved.

"You read the letter."

I nodded. "Yeah."

"But you found me anyway."

"I was mad for a while. Well, not that long, really. But there's more to the story. There are things you don't know."

"Tell me."

"When you're better."

"No. Now. I had a lot of time to think, and I promised myself that if I ever saw you again, I'd tell you everything. It was my one regret—well, other than the accident. But lying to you was worse."

"I understood. If you had told me when we met, I would have pushed you away."

She smiled. "You tried to push me away anyway."

"That's what I do."

"Because you don't want to lose anyone else. Because you lost so much that day. You deserve to never lose anyone else your whole life."

"But that's no way to live," I said. "You're right. I didn't want to be close enough to anyone to feel anything ever again, but I was wrong. And there was another reason I pushed everyone away."

"Tell me," she said.

"It's a long story."

"I'm not going anywhere."

I set down her cup and sank into the chair. And remembered that day.

"I was supposed to be with them on that vacation, but there was a party I didn't want to miss. I begged my parents to stay, and they let me. They left for the weekend with James and Mia, my brother and sister."

"That's why you weren't in the car with them," she said.

I nodded. "They left Friday morning. I went to school that day, and that night was the party—the one I wanted to attend so badly. I remember that night so clearly—a lame high school party, and I'd missed out on vacation with James and Mia to watch my friends get drunk and hook up."

Sandy cleared her throat, and I reached for the cup and held it while she sipped again. "Keep going," she said.

"That night, someone spread the news that my parents were out of town. I never invited anyone: in fact, I discouraged it, but you know how something like that takes on a life of its own, and I did what every seventeen-year-old does. I went along with it. The party started out quiet enough. Someone brought a keg, and we hung out in my backyard, drinking a few beers. But more people arrived—people I didn't know, older kids. You get the idea. It got out of control. I tried to shut it down and kick people out, but they just ignored me, and more people arrived. The neighbors called the cops, and then they called my parents."

I paused to offer her another drink, but she waved it away.

I exhaled and continued. "My parents were at the beach all day. They'd eaten a late dinner, put James and Mia to bed, and they'd just fallen asleep when my neighbor called. Then my parents called me. I told them I was trying to get everyone to leave, but I didn't know how. My dad was calm and understanding, but my mom went ballistic. She was so angry."

I stared at my hands, hearing my mother's last words to me, spoken with so much anger and so much disappointment.

"I thought you were better than this, Anne." The last thing she'd ever said to me.

I couldn't tell Sandy that part. I'd only ever told one person, and that had been a mistake.

Sandy was quiet while I took several deep breaths. Thirteen years had passed, but the memory of those words brought fresh pain. When I looked back up at Sandy, my eyes were rimmed with tears, but I kept going.

"I told them I'd handle it, but they woke the little kids and packed everything into the car. To drive home."

Sandy continued the story for me. "Except they didn't make it. Because of me." I nodded, and she continued, sharing her side, "I'd been at a party that night. I shouldn't have been driving. I knew it. But I'd gotten into a fight with my boyfriend, and I was mad."

I interrupted her. "But the part you didn't know— you couldn't have known, is that the accident wasn't your fault. Not yours alone. I put them in that car that night."

She reached for me, but I shook my head.

"No, let me finish. There's more. And I want you to know all of it."

I held the cup so she could take another sip of water.

"I couldn't handle the pain. I wasn't strong enough. I'd lost everyone in one night. I couldn't face what I'd done, so I took the easy way out. I found a bottle of sleeping pills in my mother's medicine cabinet, and I swallowed them. But it didn't work. My aunt found me and put me on a seventy-two-hour hold which turned into three months of intense psychiatric treatment."

Sandy stared, unblinking. "I didn't know," she whispered.

"How could you? I've never told anyone this. When I read your letter, I was so mad. I was angry about what you'd done, but I got over that part quickly. The thing that really hurt was that you never shared any of it. You never told me about prison."

She opened her mouth to speak, but I cut her off.

"No, wait. The thing is, I can't be angry with you because I never shared anything either. I was never as mad at you as I was mad at myself. I was never honest with you either."

Tears streamed down Sandy's face.

"No," I said. "Please don't cry. You can't afford to lose the water."

She smiled. "I wished I'd told you," she said.

"Me too," I answered.

"How did you find me?"

"It's a long story."

"Seriously, Anne. I can't leave. Captive audience."

So I told her. I started at the airport and told her everything that happened while she'd been trapped in a closet. Luke brought breakfast, and I ate while he helped me finish the story.

"I missed a lot," Sandy said.

"Yeah, it was a busy couple of weeks."

"All I did was lay around. The whole time you've been running around the island like a crazy person, I was there."

"How did you stay alive?" Luke asked.

"It rained," she answered. "I'd given up by then. I'd shouted until I was hoarse. I beat on the door and kicked it until my strength was all used up. I slept and woke up, but it was so dark I lost track of time. I was laying on one side of the closet when I heard dripping. The roof leaked. It wasn't much, but it revived me, and gave me hope that I could last long enough for you to find me. But days went by, and I faded in and out before it rained again."

We were all quiet while the nurse entered the room. She checked Sandy's monitors and left again.

"You followed the clues?" Sandy asked.

I nodded. "Yes, all of them."

"And you still have all of it?"

I nodded again. "Where did it come from, Sandy?"

Luke stood. "I'm not sure I want to hear this part," he said. "I'm going to work. I'll come check on you in a bit."

#

"Now you can quit your job," she said. "And we can go on vacation."

"Where did the cash come from, Sandy?"

"Did you tell the police about the cash?"

"No," I answered. "It's all there. Right where you left it. More or less. No—wait. Terry took seven hundred and fifty thousand. And I spent six thousand on a villa."

"Good for you!" she squealed. "I didn't know you had it in you. There's hope for you yet."

"Where did it come from, Sandy?"

She smiled. "Blackmail."

"What?"

"Shush. I'll tell you. I promise I'll tell you everything, but you must promise me one thing. If you can't handle the truth, if you feel obliged to tell the police the truth, and I'll understand if you do, but if you do, please allow me time to get away. My plan all along was for you to come with me. I want you to come with me. But you're a better person than me, Anne. And if you can't come, then you have to give me time to run."

I sank into the chair and considered the implications.

"Please come with me. I know I don't deserve to ask you for anything. Ever. But you are my person. I need you. You saved my life by pulling me out of that closet, but you already saved my life years ago. Back then, you weren't the only person that wanted to give up. I did too, and the only thing that kept me going all those years was the desire to find a way to make your life better. To find a way to make up for what I'd done."

"And blackmail was your answer?"

"Promise," she urged.

"Okay, yes. I promise." I held out the boat keys, and she took them with a smile.

"Thanks. And you'll come with me? No—don't answer yet. Think about it."

"Explain the money, Sandy. Who did you blackmail?"

"You remember that chair you had in your backyard? That ugly patio chair that ripped, and I almost fell through?"

"I remember."

"I was at Beall's a few weeks later, and I saw a patio set, the kind with cushions. I decided to buy it, and the salesperson asked if I wanted to apply for a store credit card and save twenty percent."

She paused, and I wondered how patio furniture had anything to do with blackmail.

"I always say no to that question. They ask every time. But the set was like a grand, so I could save two hundred dollars. I said yes. But I was denied. I shouldn't have been denied. I had good credit, so I decided to leave the store and figure out what had gone wrong with my credit score. I left the furniture, and I never even thought about it for weeks after that. Because that was the day I realized Gilda was pretending to be me. She'd taken my identity. She'd ruined my credit. I decided to follow her."

I interrupted her. She was taking too long. "And that's how you ended up here."

"Not at first. She took out a credit card in my name, so I was able to access it and trace her purchases. I tracked her for a week or so while I waited for my credit history to show up. She had tons of bank accounts in my name. Most of them were here on the island. So, I booked a flight."

Another nurse arrived to change the bag on her IV, and Sandy and I had a staring contest until the nurse left the room.

"She made it so easy for me—by putting everything in my name. I could walk into any bank and just take the money. And that's what gave me the idea. I needed to put the money where she couldn't get to it. If she could be me, then I could be you. So, I went back home and spent another week becoming you. I had someone forge your passport. I rifled through your house to get access to everything I needed, and then I went back."

"You searched my house?"

She nodded. "When I got back here to the island, I lucked out. I'd been watching her, and I knew she had a boyfriend. One day, she went into the pool with him, and I copied everything from her laptop. Juicy stuff."

"You didn't blackmail Gilda. You blackmailed the people who needed their money cleaned." She nodded. "Are you insane? I saw what was on that drive. Those were seriously bad people. How did you think that was a good idea?"

She shrugged. "It worked. At first, I reached out to one of Gilda's contacts in the States. A bent CEO that took ten percent of everything he washed through his company. It was so easy. I texted him and told him I would tell his Board of Directors unless he paid me fifty thousand. And he did. In cash. And from there, I just kept going. All I had to do was ask for money, and they gave it to me. There were making so much money I think nobody really cared about the small amounts. I never asked anyone more than once, but there were so many to choose from. It was so easy."

"That doesn't mean it was the right thing to do."

"I know. I knew it was wrong. But I justified it. Gilda used me to set everything up. She owed me."

"But she found out."

"Someone talked, and she got suspicious. I had so much money by then that I didn't need any more. But I got greedy. And I was mad at her. I knew if she got caught, she could pin the whole thing on me."

"She found you."

"Yeah. I stayed hidden on the boat for a few days, but she found it. That last day, I barely had time to leave the clue with Wilda and schedule the email to auto-send in case something went wrong. When I got back to the boat, she was there. Waiting. It was okay at first. I told her about the blackmail, and she seemed almost impressed by it. She said she liked the idea of playing both sides—she wanted to know more. She said she wanted to partner with me.

"She invited me to stay at the guest house, and we went there together. I left you a note, and she put a key under the mat, and then we left the island for the night. She had to meet a contact, and she wanted my help. For a few hours, it was like it used to be when we were in prison together. We were friends again."

Sandy's voice went flat as she continued. "You have to understand that prison wasn't like real life, Anne. Gilda held some kind of power over me in there. She never threatened me directly. I just knew I had to do everything she wanted me to do, or bad things would happen. So, I did what she asked. And that day, it was like we were right back there. She was masterful. We flew to Guadeloupe, and we met with one of her CEO contacts. She introduced us and told him he needed to get me a job in his company. He agreed. And for several hours, I really believed that she was happy to have me as a new partner. We partied that night and returned to Saint Martin in the morning.

"When she drove me to the gray house and took me inside, I realized my mistake. She'd just been stalling, trying to figure out who you were and how you fit in. And I told her everything she needed to know.

"I texted you right before she took away my phone. Then she started in with the questions. She wanted to know where the money was. She told me the funds I took belonged to very bad people that wanted it back. And she got really angry."

"Why did she put you in a closet?"

"She got a call. She was really upset, screaming at me about someone named Terry. She looked scared, and she shoved me into that closet and locked it. And I never saw her again."

"Jesus, Sandy."

"Yeah, I know. But it's going to be okay. We'll take the cash and leave. It's going to be okay."

I didn't answer. Just stared.

"Don't answer right now. Just think about it."

Chapter 29

"You're quiet," Luke said over dinner. "What's up?"

I hesitated. Sandy had asked me to keep her secret, and if I did, if I ran away with her, it would become my secret also.

"I need another car. You can't keep driving me around."

"This is about more than a car, isn't it?"

"Yeah," I answered. "I have a decision to make, and I need some time to think about it."

"You're leaving again?"

"You knew I had to. One way or the other. My life is in Florida, and I have to return to it…or start a new one with Sandy."

"You have a third option."

My fork was midway to my mouth, and I froze, waiting for him to continue, hoping he said it, and hoping he didn't. I wasn't ready to choose between them.

"Stay. Move in with me. Make a life here. Don't decide right now. Think about it."

I smiled. "That's exactly what Sandy said." I sighed. "You're going to hate this, but—"

"You're leaving, aren't you?"

"I need to be alone. To think."

He stood and opened a drawer, and I heard the jangling of keys. "Moreau returned your car while you were gone today. It's parked out front."

"You aren't going to stop me?" I asked.

"Never. You're right. You need to figure out what you want, and I respect that you need space to do that. Just so there's no ambiguity about how I feel, I want you to know that I'm in love with you. I want you to stay."

He leaned down and kissed me.

His kiss melted my anxiety. Everything slipped away, and the only thing that existed was Luke. He heard me moan and kneeled next to me and buried his face in my lap.

"Don't go," he murmured.

The bedroom was too far—the couch seemed a mile away. He pulled me onto the floor next to him, and we ended up half on the rug under the kitchen table and half on the tile floor. The silverware rattled on the table above as we bumped the table legs. Afterward, I looked at the semi-circle of discarded clothing around us.

"That's why I have to go," I breathed.

I packed my suitcase and left. It was the most difficult thing I'd done in two weeks, but I drove away from him.

For the first time since I'd arrived on the island, I checked into a hotel. I chose the place Gilda's mom had stayed, and after I dropped my bag in my room, I went to the bar and ordered a rum punch.

#

Three days passed slowly. Each morning, I delivered breakfast to Sandy and Lucien before visiting the police station to answer questions. There were so many questions, and they were repeated over and over. In the afternoons, I returned to the hotel and sat among the vacationers on the beach. I read my book and stared at the ocean. Sometimes I waded into the water and swam. I drank rum punches. And I slept a lot.

When the police allowed me onto *The Second Chance,* I checked out of the hotel and moved my things onto the boat. I liked the hotel. I enjoyed room service and housekeeping. I enjoyed being one of the tourists, but when I was there, I avoided thinking, and I still had decisions to make.

I knew I wasn't going home. I had nothing to go back to except bad memories. If I returned, I'd fall into the same routine: work, swim, eat, sleep, repeat.

Sandy and the boat offered a way out. I knew I had a lot to learn, but just as I'd learned how to clear my gutters and repair the shutters on my house, I could learn to tie dock lines, pull anchor, and launch the dinghy.

Luke texted each night.

Did you have a good day?

And I answered, *Almost,* every time.

He wanted to say more. I pictured him holding his phone, willing it to give him the answer he wanted, but I was glad he'd given me the space I needed to choose.

The boat was comfortable. I spent the first day cleaning, throwing away everything that belonged to Terry, including the bedding. Everything else I scrubbed as if I could erase his time on the boat by wiping out every fingerprint, every footstep.

When the boat was clean, I visited Wilda. We hugged. She cut and styled my hair, and then I walked across the street. The saleswoman remembered me, and together we built a new wardrobe.

I returned to the boat laden with shopping bags and unpacked everything into my closet. Then I returned to the shops and purchased new linens, new dishes, and new cookware. In only a few days, I built a new home.

On the third night, I texted Luke. *Dinner tonight?*

#

I arrived at the construction site at six-thirty. The sun was just beginning its showy descent, and Luke's house competed with the sunset with an impressive display of candlelight. During the week I'd been away, he'd made a lot of progress. He'd installed a front door, and he had a kitchen with cabinets and appliances.

"Nothing works yet," he said. "But it's getting there."

There was no furniture, so we sat on the patio with our legs dangling over the edge, and I peered down at the stone wall and silently thanked the boulder for providing refuge from the storm.

We ate pizza from the box and drank Cabernet out of plastic cups while he talked about tile patterns for the kitchen and paint colors for the bedrooms. When we finished eating, the moon was just peeking over the horizon, and Luke blew out the candles. I'd watched the moon rise on so many nights since arriving in Saint Martin, but this time, it was full, and the light surprised me.

"How are you?" he asked tentatively.

"I'm good," I said. "Really good, actually. I slept a lot this week."

He nodded.

"So, there's something I have to tell you," I said. "And it's going to take me a while, so I hope you'll be patient with me."

"Okay," he said.

I told him my story. About how my family had died and my part in it. I told him about my reaction.

"My aunt arrived to handle the funeral arrangements, and she planned to pack up my life and take it back with her to Tallahassee. She barely found me in time. I was unconscious and unfeeling. I woke up in a small room where I spent the next two weeks, alone with my grief. The solitude was impossible to bear, and I reacted with violence. I was restrained and medicated. The medication dulled the pain, but it dulled everything else, and the effect lasted over a decade.

"I spent three months locked away. I missed my family's funeral. I missed my eighteenth birthday and my high school graduation. They gave me a diploma, of course. They couldn't withhold a diploma from a sad, broken, suicidal girl. After three months, I emerged an adult, cured, according to their definition.

"I learned one very important lesson in those three months: don't show emotion. Control your feelings, and you can get out. Keep control, and you can stay out. And I followed that lesson. I got a job and maintained control, and I stayed out of that place. And I stayed numb for twelve years until I met Sandy."

My truth was painful and sad, but the telling lifted a weight I'd carried alone for thirteen years. He listened quietly, and I watched him endure my pain, and in the places where I expected pity, there was none. His face shone with silvery light, and he felt sorrow and empathy and mostly love.

"I don't want to be alone anymore, Luke. And I don't want to hide from my past. I wanted to tell you because if you really want to be with me, you should know what kind of person I am. You should know that what happened all those years ago wasn't just Sandy's fault. I share some of the blame. Since then, I've held back from close relationships, afraid to endure any more heartbreak. When Sandy barged into my life uninvited, she accomplished the one thing she thought was impossible: she taught me how to open up and let love back in. She wanted to bring my family back, and she did, in a way. She *became* my family."

I paused. And he held his breath.

"She wants me to come with her. I had to choose between you. And it was a hard choice. She can't stay here, so I can't have both of you. She did something wrong, and I can't tell you about it because that's her secret. I can only tell you that she can't stay."

"I don't really care what she did," he said. "I know she got involved in something, and it wasn't her fault. I know enough. I don't have to know the rest. I know what matters: I know who you are. You're strong and kind. I don't care about the rest of it."

"I spent the last two days setting up Sandy's boat so that it's all ready for her when she gets out of the hospital. I told her today. That I'll keep her secret, that I'm not going home. And I'm staying here with you."

His smile in the moonlight was more dazzling than it had ever been.

"I want you to live here with me in this house unless it's too hard. I don't know if your memories of what happened here would make it difficult. If so, I'll sell it, and we'll build another one."

"This house saved my life. And so did you."

"Several times," he grinned. "And I'll go on saving it for as many times as I need to. Okay?"

"Okay," I answered. "I love you."

And after he kissed me, I let him carry me one more time to his pickup truck.